# Maelstrom of White

by

# Angela Hossack

The first book in the Superintendent Lorrie Sullivan Series

Dedicated to all those who love me and who had faith.

Other books by the author
The Superintendent Lorrie Sullivan series:
*A Murder of Clowns*
*A Flock of Innocents*
*A Bouquet of Brides*
*A Rhapsody of Rage*
*A Brace of Fiends*
*A Bloodbath of Bones*
The Detectives Friar and Tuck series:
*Case Number One - The Missing*
*Case Number two – The Forsaken*
*Tomorrow – an apocalyptic dystopian thriller*
The Beyond the Bloodline trilogy:
*The Empty Throne*
*The Rise of the Witch*
*Kulku*

# DAY ONE: MORNING

Mary Hastings was the first to die. It wasn't a good death. No death could ever be considered good, but, in the scheme of things, Mary's demise was a doozey.

To say that Mary was excited was an understatement. This was her first time flying. She was eighty-five years old, and she had never been on an aeroplane before. Although she couldn't help but be a little nervous, she was overwhelmed with pleasure at the thought of the journey and seeing her granddaughter for the first time in eighteen years. Whenever she thought of Annette, her only grandchild, her mind conjured up a picture of a chubby two-year old toddler. Now, that baby had a baby of her own, and Mary was off to the christening in Barcelona. She was going to spend a week with her family and, for a few days at least, she wouldn't be lonely.

Although Mary presented herself as a woman who could cope on her own, she was, nevertheless, a woman who desperately needed family. Over the years, there had been too few occasions where she was able to spend time with her daughter, and she had only ever had one opportunity to meet her granddaughter. To have her daughter, granddaughter and great granddaughter all waiting expectantly at the airport for her, was a dream come true, but excitement was the very least of Mary's emotions.

Her experience on the plane didn't exactly get off to a good start. It was just her luck to get allocated the middle seat between a large, fat man and a purple-haired, tattooed girl. Mary was a rather large lady herself and the leg and arm room left a lot to be desired. Neither of her fellow passengers made any allowances for her age nor her size, and both of them claimed the armrests from the get-go. That left Mary nowhere to place her elbows. She was hot, uncomfortable, and frightened to fidget in case she disturbed them. She didn't know what the etiquette was for those unfortunate enough to be allocated the middle seat, so she chose to sit rigid and still, eyes straight ahead, all the while trying not to breathe too anxiously.

She put the increased beating of her heart and the sudden butterflies rampaging in her stomach down to the nervousness of the first-time flyer.

They were fifteen minutes out of Heathrow, and all of the passengers were still in the throes of settling into the flight. The cabin crew completed the in-flight safety demonstration. Mary had wanted desperately to follow the flapping of the arms and the pointing of the hands, but her ears were still popping, and a feeling of claustrophobia was slowly stealing over her. She hadn't a clue what the hand and arm signals meant. She hadn't been able to hear their instructions, and if the plane crashed, she realised she wouldn't know what to do.

She filled her mind with pictures of what the few days with her family would entail. She wondered if they would feel the strength of her love for them, but she also told herself not to be too demanding of that love. She would try not to overwhelm them – after all, she was a virtual stranger to her granddaughter. Eighteen years was a long time to be simply a voice on the other end of the telephone.

The fat man shifted in his seat and accidently elbowed Mary in the chest. He didn't apologise, and Mary turned to look at him. He was sweating and she felt a sudden sympathy. Perhaps he was a first-time flyer too?

She was taken unawares by an unexpected tightness in her chest. It was a completely different sensation, and less akin to the anxiety she was just beginning to get used to. Mary's body was beginning to tell her that something was wrong. She looked up and then turned her head to look once more at the fat man at her side. She wanted to get his attention, tell him she didn't feel well, but he was so very obviously wrapped up in his own discomfort.

From the start of her symptoms and until the moment of her death, the time elapsed was just short of four minutes.

The tightness in her chest was quickly followed by a scratchy feeling at the back of her throat. She tried to compensate by sucking a mint, but it didn't help. A short minute later her nose felt stuffy and then her tongue and lips started to tingle painfully. Previously, she had put her symptoms down to feeling stifled, nervous and excited, as well as breathing in other people's air. She'd heard stories about germs circulating and people catching all sorts of diseases on aeroplanes, and that worried her, because her granddaughter had just had a baby and there was no way she wanted to catch something and spread it to the new-born.

If Mary had been familiar with an aeroplane cabin, she might have raised her hand and pressed the call button for one of the crew. She might have insisted the tattooed girl move so she could get out to stretch her legs and may even have walked to the toilet. But, Mary suffered in silence. She didn't want to cause anyone any bother. She thought her symptoms would pass once she got used to the rhythm of the plane and the stale air.

She didn't begin to panic until she felt her tongue begin to swell. Panic is a great leveller of people. It doesn't care if it causes the person to make a fool of themselves. It is a 'no holds barred' emotion that causes a fight or flight reaction, and even the most timid, and the most well-mannered of people, don't give a damn how they come across to others. All that matters is escape – escape from whatever is confining them, from whatever it is that is frightening or hurting them.

She didn't begin to attempt to get out of her seat until the size of her tongue began to block her airway.

The fat man flinched and then jolted back when Mary's elbow made sharp contact with his gut. It looked to him, as if the old woman was having a seizure and he did what Mary didn't know how to do – he pressed the call button and summoned the steward.

For a brief second, the fat man and the tattooed girl made eye contact and there was a shared impatience in their look. Neither could be bothered with the hassle of sharing space with an old woman too sick to be flying. With any luck, the cabin crew would move her further up the plane and they'd be able to stretch out and enjoy the rest of the flight in peace.

Mary couldn't breathe. No air could squeeze past her bloated tongue and her mind and body went into survival mode. Her panic intensified and her mind screamed at her to escape the confines of the seat. If only she could get out of the damned chair, then she would be able to breathe. Her body betrayed her. Her fingers wouldn't do what her brain instructed. She fumbled and scrabbled at the seatbelt buckle but to no avail. It remained firmly clasped.

Her mouth wouldn't open wide enough to drag in air. She couldn't even scream and, God, how she desperately wanted to scream. As she became more and more oxygen depleted, her panic rapidly grew, and she began to flail. She threw her arms out and lamped the fat man on the side of the head with a fist before rearing round to her left and head-butting his startled face. She pulled at her hair. She drew blood as she clawed at her throat. Her heels drummed on the floor as she began to convulse and, by the time the steward arrived, the fat man was nursing a bloody nose.

The tattooed girl, whilst attempting to subdue the violence of Mary's seizure, was rewarded for her efforts with hair torn from her scalp and a broken tooth. The steward hadn't a clue what to do, and Mary died – still strapped to her seat - two minutes later. Her last conscious thought was the sad realisation that she would never get to see her family again.

There was a hush. There was a sudden stillness throughout the plane. A woman had died, and no one dared move.

Then - a scream from further down the aisle. Passengers stood and craned to see what was happening.

The scream was quickly followed by another and then another, and soon, no one could differentiate the screams of the dying with the screams of the terrified onlookers.

The steward who was hunkered down beside Mary's row of seats, was jostled and thrown to the floor as passengers exited their seats and began to move towards the front of the plane.

The steward covered her head with her hands to protect it from the feet stomping past and she found herself having a weird thought. She suddenly thought – goodness, panic actually has a smell. She hadn't realised that fear and freaking out could have an acrid, sweaty stench.

She drew her knees to her chin and tucked her head further to her chest as, all around her, all Hell broke loose.

The pilot fought a losing battle to restore calm. His voice was barely heard over the noisy mayhem. Fearing that the plane was in danger, he decided to abandon the flight.

The Airbus A320-200 returned to Heathrow.

When it landed, a total of eight passengers were dead and multiple others had been injured.

# DAY ONE: AFTERNOON

'Sod off, Colin. I can't believe you dragged me away from work just so you could have a moan about Ollie.'

Colin Sullivan looked at his wife and scowled. She was beautiful, that was for sure, but, God, he hated her. If moaning about her precious son got a rise out of her and messed up her day, then he was okay with that.

She did that thing with her eyes that annoyed the living Hell out of him. It was disrespectful. It was infuriating and it enflamed his fragile equanimity.

He stepped closer to her and bent forward at the shoulders so his face was mere inches from hers. He knew that, although not intimidated, she hated him invading what she called her personal space. That was simply one more thing he did to rile her.

Lorrie wrinkled her nose. He still smelled of the previous evening's garlic chicken.

'I'm not having him in the warehouse again,' he said. 'I'm sacking him as of right now.'

'Well, good for you.' She took a step back from him. 'I never wanted him anywhere near your poxy warehouse, or anywhere else in that little empire of yours.' She took a deep breath. 'Anyway... You've got a short memory, Colin. Who was it who insisted he spend time with you? Who insisted that he worked to help pay back all the mon-

8

ey we gave him for books. university fees, food and clothes and even the fucking air he dares to breath in your fucking house?'

She knew her words and her tone would seriously piss him off and that he would make her pay, but she was past caring. 'Sometimes, Colin, you really are an arsehole.'

Lorrie watched as her husband's eyes darkened and observed the tell-tale signs of one of his famous temper tantrums building. She decided not to wait around for the show and stalked from the lounge and made her way quickly through to the kitchen.

They had a beautiful kitchen. In fact, their whole house was a beautiful example of what a successful couple could acquire. It should have been a home to be proud of, but Lorrie hated every brick of it with an adulterated passion.

She had to get out of the house. She feared that, if she stayed even a moment longer, she would say something to her husband that would take everything just that step too far.

With one last look behind her to ensure he hadn't followed her through from the lounge, she picked up her coat from the hook on the back of the door, snatched up her bag and her car keys and thought about how much of a bad idea it would be to go back through the lounge to the front door, instead of heading out the back way. Going out the front would mean facing off with her husband again. She was sure that, as God made little apples, he would waylay her with more complaints about Ollie and, frankly, she wasn't it the mood.

She stepped towards the kitchen door leading to the garden. She would go out that way and avoid any further confrontation. She would take the path around the side of the house to the front and to Hell with saying goodbye to her prick of a husband.

She opened the door and gasped as the icy wind caught in her throat. Jesus, it was cold. She pulled on her gloves and pulled the collar of her coat up to cover her ears.

She was halted in her tracks by her mobile ringing and simultaneously vibrating in her pocket. She fished it out and accepted the call.

She said, 'Superintendent Sullivan.' There was more than a hint of impatience in her tone.

'Yes, yes, DI Grant, I know what time it is, and I know I'm AWOL. Stop being a dick and tell me what you want.' Lorrie knew that she was taking her bad temper out on her DI, and she felt a pang of regret. Simon was a good lad and she wished she had the ability to completely divorce the raw emotions elicited by an encounter with Colin from her relationship with others.

Superintendent Lorrie – short for Lorraine – Sullivan listened to her DI's words on the other end of the phone, and her demeanour visibly altered. She was no longer impatient. She was no longer preoccupied with her husband's behaviour. As she continued to listen, Lorrie's face went through a range of expressions – mainly disbelief that she was being bothered with it – and her features finally settled into acceptance of the fact that it was a serious matter.

DI Simon Grant was one of the best. She had chosen him personally, poaching him from MIT – the Murder Investigation Team – some years before. They worked well together, and she had made a point of bringing him with her to this new gig. He wasn't one for melodramatics. He never made a drama out of a crisis and, better still, he didn't take offence when she turned her sarcastic tongue on him. She knew that if he was rattled then she should be rattled, so she accepted his assessment of the situation and listened to him without further interruption.

When he finished speaking, she asked, 'Do you know why they want us on it and not MIT?' Her squad was new within the Met's Serious Crimes and Operations Division, and the majority of murders weren't within her remit. Her squad – the National Major Crimes Unit – focussed on murders that had tentacles that spread across the

UK. These unexplained deaths – which might not even be suspicious - hardly merited her attention.

She asked, 'How do we even know a crime has been committed, never mind murder?'

On the other end of the phone, DI Simon Grant replied, 'No one confides in me, Guv. All I know is that we have the shout. I can tell you, though, that the Commander's knickers are well and truly in a twist. He's been looking for you. I didn't know what to tell him.'

'The Commander doesn't wear knickers. 'Y' fronts aren't knickers.'

'No, Guv.' Simon couldn't keep the smile from his voice.

'Okay,' Lorrie said. 'I'll be twenty minutes. No one gets off that plane until I get there. I want everyone on the ground suited and booted and get hold of some airport buses... Enough to hold all the passengers. I want everyone accounted for, so don't lose anyone, Simon.'

Disconnecting the call, Lorrie decided she would go out the front way after all. Time was of the essence.

Colin met her at the kitchen door and followed her through the lounge before stopping her in the hallway with a look that spoke volumes. The look said – you're walking out on our conversation... really?

Lorrie's stride did not falter as she pushed passed him. 'Grow up, Colin,' was her only reply to his look of incredulity. As she pulled open the door, she added a parting shot over her shoulder, 'Don't wait up.'

Despite a wintry sun battling with the icy wind and attempting to warm the afternoon air, there was ice on the driveway and Lorrie slipped and slithered her way to her car, silently cursing a husband who couldn't even be bothered to put down a bit of grit.

COLIN WAS BASICALLY a wanker. He was successful – owning his own business – handsome in a pretty boy kind of way, and cock-sure of his own importance, and yet he was an utter waste of space. Lorrie thanked God that Ollie wasn't his son. She doubly thanked the Lord that he'd never impregnated her. A child with Colin the wanker would have been the death knell on her sanity.

Oh, Colin had wanted a child. He wanted to ensure that his genes weren't lost to humanity, but Lorrie had other plans. Her career came first.

She was thirty-nine years old, and it had taken her twenty years to get to where she was. The fact that she always looked younger than her years – with her small frame, slim build and, in particular her passive grey eyes – made her journey to Detective Superintendent all the more problematic. It was easy to underestimate her. It was easy to categorise her as innocent and naïve. Right from the very beginning, her male colleagues thought she needed to be sheltered, protected or – when their more primal instincts kicked in – they thought that she needed to be shagged. She made enemies amongst her male colleagues because they couldn't equate the tiny, beautiful woman – who had a very obvious air of vulnerability – with the savvy, ballsy police officer who could swear right along with the best of them. They couldn't reconcile what their eyes told them with the reality of who she was. The outcome for Lorrie was not pretty. They ostracised and demeaned her in equal measure.

Where her job was concerned, Lorrie had never wanted to be sheltered or protected, and apart from the one, doomed relationship – which resulted in a broken heart and an unplanned pregnancy – she had refused all the cack-handed advances of those of her male colleagues who had chanced their luck. But Lorrie did have an air of vulnerability about her. She may have put on a hard, brave face, and she may have been assertive and super confident in her job, but that wasn't her whole character. Although she took no prisoners when it came to establishing a no-nonsense approach to her leadership role, in her private life she was less sure of herself, less assertive and much less confident. Outside of the job, she let her guard down and was prone to naivety. It was this private Lorrie – this less than streetwise woman – who had fallen prey to Colin. Fifteen years of marriage later, and she was finally beginning to see what an utter fool she'd been.

She had put her life and her job on hold for the first four years of her child's life, and oral contraception after her marriage to Colin meant she could take the opportunities, the promotions and climb the greasy pole with impunity. At first, she felt guilty about denying her husband a child of his own, but Colin soon wiped the guilt from her mind and her heart. Psychological and emotional torture was his speciality, and it was about time she left him. She'd been saying that to herself on and off for years and, if she was being honest with herself, she doubted she ever would. Leaving was simply too much hassle and being a senior female officer in the not so modern police force, meant having a successful husband was helpful when it came to the politics of the still male dominated institution. Anyway, she could handle Colin.

Luckily, for Lorrie, The Assistant Commissioner, Annie Gordon, had seen past the superficial outer layer of Lorrie's persona and had taken her under her wing to support and mentor her. Annie didn't see Lorrie as being the sum total of her looks. Rather, she saw her strength and her character and her absolute single-mindedness when it came to superior police work. She had seen in Lorrie, a woman who could circumnavigate the politics, work her way around the misogyny, and who could knuckle down in a pragmatic way to simply get the job done.

Lorrie's phone sent out its melodic ringtone once more. Juggling her bag in one hand and attempting to press her key fob with the other meant that, before she could answer, it went to voicemail, causing her to curse under her breath.

Frustrated, she threw her bag to the icy ground and unlocked the car door. She bent and retrieved the bag, removed her phone, and then flung the large designer handbag onto the passenger seat.

Seated in the car, she turned on the engine and ramped the hot air up to maximum. She then listened to the message. It was forensic pathologist, Ricky Burton, informing her that he and his evidence recovery team were on site at terminal three and just about to board the plane. He wanted permission to get the passengers unloaded so he could get them out of the way and get on with the job of beginning to suss out what in Hell's name had happened to cause the sudden death – of however many people – on a bog-standard, low-flight airbus on its way to the sun.

Lorrie respected Ricky Burton, but no one would ever guess the extent of her respect by her manner towards him. She treated him rather disdainfully and her nickname for him was now his de-facto non de plume. Ricky Boy – as he was now widely known – was a self-employed Home Office registered pathologist who was the Met's main 'go to' guy. He ran a huge laboratory in central London, employed eight pathologists and had unprecedented access to the forensic facilities at new Scotland Yard, Lambeth and Newlands Park. He was often the supervising and lead pathologist in many murders and his evidence at many Old Bailey trials left no one in any doubt that he was a bloody genius.

She decided against calling Ricky back, instead, she reached DI Grant. 'Ricky Boy is straining at the leash,' she said. 'Put the reins on him and keep him and his team off that plane until I get there. We have no real idea of how many are dead and God knows what's floating in the air. I'm taking no chances.' She sighed. Ricky, bless his fat little arse, had a tendency to shoot off the starting post like a caricature of Usain Bolt. 'Handcuff him if necessary. He's too gung-ho for his own good.'

On the other end of the phone, standing in the freezing cold and shivering uncontrollably, Simon Grant closed his eyes and took a deep breath.

'There are nearly two hundred of them on board, Guv,' he said. 'We've been on the radio to the pilot, and he says quite a few of the passengers are injured. It's mayhem, and the whole lot of them are still panicking. There's been a bit of damage and there are more than a few bones broken. A few heads cracked as well by all accounts. Perhaps we could get the injured off?'

'Didn't you hear me, Grant?' Lorrie interjected impatiently.

'Yes, Guv,' Simon sighed. His boss really could be a bitch at times. 'I guess we'll wait until you get here.'

'And keep Ricky Boy at bay?'

'Understood.'

'Good. I'm on my way. I'll see you in twenty.'

COLIN WATCHED HIS WIFE leave the house and slither down the driveway to the car and wondered – for the millionth time since he'd met her – why she made him act like such a prick. What was it about her that turned him into the type of man who could quite happily flay his own wife alive?

He wasn't a bad man. He wasn't a bad husband. Bad Husbands beat ten buckets of shit out of their wives on a daily basis, or frequently screwed around on them. He'd never raised a finger to her and any women he'd screwed behind her back – and there weren't really that many of them - were wholly inconsequential. So, he was at a loss as to why she was such a bitch to him and why she had the knack of bringing out the worst in him.

He was genuinely perplexed and annoyed. For years he'd had Lorrie's complete and utter obedience. Oh, he'd realised that her subservience and her desire to keep the peace was for Ollie's sake. Nothing had to rock the boat and upset her golden boy, but he'd accepted her reasons with good grace, after all, he had what he wanted, and it didn't matter to him how he got it. His wife's compliance and unfettered submission to his every wish had, over the years, kept the more obvious psychopathic traits of his personality somewhat in check. However – since her recent promotion and her new job role – he was finding it almost impossible to deal with her belligerent insubordination without his anger and frustration giving vent to some rather distasteful behaviour.

As he had watched her drive off, he'd inhaled deeply and imagined all the ways he could eviscerate her. He had then counted to ten before donning his coat and following her out of the house. He was sick of the way his ideal marriage was disintegrating. The fact that he could quite cheerfully annihilate her was enough to give him pause. He wanted to remain married to her. He wanted things to return to normal. He would choose that over killing her. For the time being, anyway.

Someone needed to change in order for their marriage to work and, if Colin was sure of one thing, that person certainly wasn't going to be him. No – Lorrie had to change. She had to be made to see the error of her ways and he was just the man to ensure that happened.

IT TOOK HER FORTY MINUTES to reach the airport from her house. Traffic was shit, and the weather didn't help. Despite the gritters being out, the roads were like glass, and Lorrie was amazed at just how few people knew how to drive in winter.

Her credentials got her through security quickly and she was soon shivering on the tarmac next to the aeroplane. Its doors were shut tight, but two sets of steps – those giant ones on wheels – had been placed at the exits at the front and rear of the large, grey bird. Someone, in their wisdom, decided against linking the aeroplane to the terminal with the long tunnel – the passenger boarding bridge – and under the circumstances, Lorrie thought that had been a wise decision. The scene, and the disembarkation of the passengers, could be much better managed using the stairs.

Four paramedic ambulances, a fire engine and three long buses sat idling side by side, their exhausts belching out smoke and fumes into the frigid air. Men in full hazmat suits stood waiting patiently for the word to climb aboard.

Simon approached. He was accompanied by a short, ginger-haired man dressed from top to toe in white overalls. You could be forgiven for thinking he was a Teletubby.

'They're ready to go on board, Guv.' DI Grant gestured across to the hazmat clad mixture of forensic officers.

Lorrie turned to the Teletubby. 'You're not exactly dressed for the occasion, Doctor Burton. I don't imagine that flimsy get up will protect you from what killed those poor buggers on board.'

'As usual, Superintendent Sullivan, you tend to lean towards overkill. Fact is that, as far as we can tell, only eight out of two hundred succumbed to whatever got them. Everyone has been on board for over two hours now and I would hazard a guess that whatever it is, isn't airborne. I'll be safe enough with my usual precautions.'

Lorrie ignored him and turned her attention back to Simon. 'Get the Hazmats on board and tell them to make sure everyone is seated and strapped into their seats. Get any readings done ASAP and tell them to use best judgement on whether we take the injured off and into the ambulances.'

Doctor Burton scowled up at her. 'You trying to do my job, Superintendent?'

'Oh, just chill, Ricky. You know I love you and don't want you dead just yet.'

'I feel I should be insulted by your total lack of respect for my superior intelligence, but you said you loved me, so I'll let it pass.'

Lorrie smiled then turned to watch as DI Grant co-ordinated and orchestrated in his own quiet way. If it had been her, Lorrie would've been shouting and giving orders like a drill sergeant. She liked the way her DI worked.

Within seconds, radios were crackling all over the place as instructions were transmitted and orders relayed.

The door at the front of the plane opened from the inside and one of the cabin crew poked her head out. Her distress was only too evident. Her features were ravaged, and those on the ground could clearly see how much strength it took for her not to clamber down the steps to safety. She was buffeted from behind by the sounds of the terrified passengers and by bodies attempting to push past her. She held her ground. No one overtook her. No one escaped.

Voices were raised in a high crescendo of fear and panic. There was wailing, screaming and general cursing. Unintelligible words, but the pleas for help were unmissable to those on the ground.

'My God, listen to that,' Lorrie said slowly, thoughtfully. 'Poor buggers.'

DI Grant signalled and the Hazmats climbed the steps slowly – their suits hampering the elegance of their ascent – and, as they disappeared inside, there was an increase in the sounds coming from the plane. The sight of the men all togged up in suits that suggested extreme danger of contamination, was enough to send the passengers into an increased frenzy.

'Get another six on board from the rear,' Lorrie called over to Simon. 'And arm them with Tasers.' She had a feeling that the Tasers weren't an overreaction but hoped they wouldn't be used.

The wait was excruciating. An hour passed before word came down that twenty-two injured passengers were getting ready to disembark. The news was that Doctor Burton had been right – no sign of biohazard on board. Lorrie hoped they weren't wrong.

Ricky refrained from an 'I told you so' look – not that Lorrie would have given a toss – and made to walk towards the stairs.

'Hang fire, doctor,' Lorrie said, placing a hand on his arm. 'Let's clear the way for you first. Let's get the injured into the ambulances and all the other live ones off and into the buses.'

Ricky's face was inscrutable. 'You know what, Superintendent? If the aeroplane is truly a crime scene, then all of the evidence will be well and truly fucked. Nothing will have been preserved. Two hundred pairs of feet will have trampled it.' He shook his head in frustration. 'I hope you're not expecting miracles. I can't give you miracles.'

'I'm not expecting miracles, Ricky Boy.'

'Just as well.'

Lorrie nodded. 'We can only play the hand we're dealt, doctor. Try not to sweat the small stuff.'

COLIN WENT TO WORK, and, for a time, all was right with the world. He was his own boss and everyone in his employ regularly ensured his ego was well stroked. Even Ollie – who was becoming more like his mother every day – most times towed the line and bowed to his God given right to rule his empire and not be questioned or made to explain himself. He'd intimated to Lorrie that he didn't want Ollie working for him, but that was far from the truth.

The more he got Ollie on his side and the more Ollie depended on him, then the more it annoyed his wife. Annoying his wife was one of the highlights of his day. Another reason he wanted Ollie working for him was that he savoured the fact that the clever little prick – the boy genius with the massive ego - was earning his crust doing manual labour and dancing to his stepfather's tune. Ollie was at his beck and call and that turned Colin on.

Colin was a self-made man. He'd left school without a single qualification and, truth be told, he never understood Lorrie's obsession with her son's education. Yes, the boy was smart. Yes, the boy had more going on in that brain of his than the average teenager, but where would it get him? It certainly wouldn't get him a flourishing business with reach across the whole country as well as Europe, and it certainly wouldn't get him the fuck-you money that his stepfather had.

If he had a son, he wouldn't molly-coddle him the way Lorrie molly-coddled Ollie. Every king needs an heir and the fact that Lorrie wouldn't give him one was the main reason he hated her more than he loved her. She was getting a bit long in the tooth now, and her bloody career took precedence over everything, including their marriage, and that meant Ollie was his heir by default. Colin didn't like that fact. There was no way that little know-it-all was going to get his hands on his business when he popped his clogs.

He walked into his office and was surprised to see Ollie.

'You looking for me?' he asked, surreptitiously looking over at his desk to see if Ollie had disturbed anything. 'You shouldn't be in here.'

'I just popped in to ask if you would give me a lift,' Ollie replied. 'It's too icy for my bike.'

'Sorry, mate,' Colin replied. He didn't quite believe his stepson and looked directly at him, trying to read what was going on behind the boy's eyes. He had a feeling he'd been snooping. 'I wish you'd let me know earlier. I've got a meeting in half an hour.'

'Oh, okay,' Ollie replied. 'I'll risk my bike on the roads.' He stepped out from behind Colin's desk.

And perhaps you'll break your fucking neck, Colin mused. 'Be careful,' he said, instead of voicing his thoughts. 'You know how your mother worries about you and that motorbike.'

Ollie smiled tightly and walked away. That had been close. He hadn't expected Colin to walk in on him and he'd been lucky that he hadn't arrived five minutes earlier. For an instant, as Colin had stood there and looked at him, he'd thought his stepfather had seen right through him. It had been a tricky moment. He would have to be more careful from now on. His stepfather was about as trustworthy as a snake and Ollie had always known that he had an awesome shit-detector. He was sure that Colin suspected something, but he was also sure that he had covered his tracks sufficiently to keep him off the scent.

His motorbike was where he had left it in the parking lot, and he put on his helmet and climbed on board. He had no qualms about riding on the icy roads. The danger thrilled him. Like all young men on fast bikes, he believed that he was invincible. His mother worried - he didn't need Colin to tell him that – however he was not destined to die under the wheels of a car or a lorry. His death, when it came, would be a much bigger statement than a road traffic accident.

He headed out towards London's inner ring road. He had places to be and things to do and the day was marching on too quickly. He wondered briefly what it would take for his mother to leave her husband and then, as the bike gathered momentum and he was flying towards the city, he closed his mind to everything but the next step of his plan.

# DAY ONE: EVENING

Commander Abraham Scully and Chief Superintendent Geoffrey Connor squeezed into Lorrie's small office and began the ritual of firing questions at her with increasing velocity. They wanted information and they wanted it fast. The press were already baying at the doors, and the Home Secretary was waiting on confirmation on whether a COBRA meeting was warranted.

Everything had spiralled out of control very quickly. Lorrie never ceased to be amazed at how quickly the press managed to get hold of a story, and she marvelled further at just how quickly her superiors began to disappear up their own backsides whenever a big case threatened to escalate and de-rail their careers.

Scully was a man with a huge chip on his shoulder. She almost believed that it was a real chip the size of a boulder, as he had the uncanny habit of leaning over to the side whenever he stood or walked. He had a large head and huge, mushy features that made him look almost comical – like a clown but without the make-up. She didn't like him one little bit and he hated her, so any meetings between them were always destined to disintegrate into a war of wills and words.

Geoffrey Connor – her immediate superior –was a different kettle of fish. Lorrie almost liked him. He was equally annoying and just as power mad as Scully, however he had a few redeeming features that kept him the good side of worthy. She did not, however, trust either of them as far as she could spit.

Lorrie batted back her standard responses, refusing to be brow beaten into saying anything other than, 'I don't know, sir. Too early to say, sir. I'm awaiting a report, sir.'

The two senior officers were frustrated with her responses, but they weren't stupid. They didn't really expect her to have any answers for them at such an early stage, nevertheless they wouldn't be doing their bit for crown and country if they didn't badger her for information. Lorrie's refusal to give them anything at all pissed off the Commander. He didn't believe she was a team player. Despite his better judgement, and the fact that he was being unfair in expecting her to be more informative, he couldn't help thinking that she was stonewalling them.

'You know you're on trial, don't you, Superintendent?'

Lorrie eyed the Commander and feigned ignorance. 'On trial, Commander Scully?'

'Don't get smart with me. This squad of yours may be the brainchild of the Assistant Commissioner, but don't think for one minute you'll be protected if you screw it all up.'

'I've only just picked it up, sir. Bit early to worry about me screwing anything up.'

'Counter Terrorism should've had it,' Scully scowled. 'Beats me why the Assistant Commissioner insisted it came to you.'

'SO15, sir? We're not even sure a crime was committed, never mind a terrorist act.'

Connor attempted to be the peacemaker. He might not really like Lorrie Sullivan but she was the apple of the Assistant Commissioner's eye and he had the sense to realise that it bode well to bear that fact in mind.

'It is a bit too soon to be worrying about all of this, sir,' he said to Scully. 'It might be something and nothing.'

'Bollocks, Connor. Eight dead on a fucking aeroplane with symptoms of poisoning...'

'We don't know that it's poison,' Lorrie put in.

'Perhaps not, Superintendent, but if it quacks like a duck then it is a fucking duck!'

'Yes, sir.' Lorrie lowered her chin and attempted to hide the flash of irritation on her face.

'You'll cock this up, Sullivan. I have no doubt about that, and then let's see how much the Assistant Commissioner has your back when that happens. This squad is a mistake. I always said so. I'll be proved right... You'll see.'

Lorrie's voice lowered almost to a murmur, and she shook her head. 'Yes, sir,' she said. 'Anything else, sir?'

Under his thick brow, Scully's eyes were like black pools of fouled water. 'Nothing else, Sullivan. Just get your finger out sharpish. Remember – all eyes are on you.'

When the Commander left Lorrie alone with Chief Superintendent Connor, she gave herself permission to let out a long sigh. 'Bloody hell,' she said. 'He gets worse.'

Connor took a step towards her. 'Do you have to make it so obvious?'

'Make what obvious?'

'That you think he's a prick.'

'He is a prick.' She closed her eyes and sighed once more. 'Sorry, sir.' She knew that Connor disliked her nearly as much as Commander Scully did but, at least, he made a pretence at being on her side.

'Look, Lorrie, you know how it is... You're a woman, you're not even forty years old and...'

'And, what, sir? What's the usual story all you men make up when a woman makes it to Superintendent?' Her question was rhetorical. 'Well, on this occasion I can't be accused of sleeping with the Assistant Commissioner to get this job as I'm straight and she's straight. I got this job on merit and the Commander can't stand that fact.'

'Careful, Lorrie,' he warned. 'You've a habit of not knowing your place.'

'Barefoot and pregnant at the kitchen sink?' she snapped back.

It was the Chief Superintendent's turn to sigh. 'This is ridiculous. You need to know how to play the game, Lorrie. You make too many enemies. Try not to be so bloody confrontational. You'll get a lot more with honey.'

Lorrie visibly bristled. 'You think I should bat my eyelashes and wiggle my bum, just so I don't make enemies?' She held his gaze. 'I won't apologise for getting this job and I won't suck up to the likes of Scully... Sir.'

'Fuck's sake, Sullivan. Draw your horns in. It's all very well being all high and mighty but it's a long way to fall and, the way you're going, no one will put a hand out to help you.'

There was some truth in his words. Lorrie was only too aware of the tightrope she had to walk across for the likes of him and Scully. It took all her savvy and all of her skills to ensure she was well enough armoured with good results and successfully closed cases so that they couldn't pull her off that tightrope. Yes, he was right – she ran the risk of a mighty fall, but she liked the giddy heights. She thrived on the excitement of the job and relished being in charge and she knew they couldn't stand the fact that one of her sex could run rings around them.

'Well, good luck with the case,' Connor said. His eyes were suddenly sharp with ominous calculation. 'I think you're going to need it.'

Lorrie ignored the naked cunning in his eyes. She had seen it all before. They all thought they were so clever, so much better than her, but they always paled in comparison against her wins.

He had one piece of information that she wanted, though, so she sucked it up, ignored his old-boy stance and asked, 'Tell me honestly, sir... This case... It should've gone to MIT in the first instance and then to Counter Terrorism if appropriate. Why did it come to me? It doesn't exactly fit the profile for one of my cases.'

Connor shrugged. 'You're asking the wrong person. Your benefactor made that happen. The Assistant Commissioner made the call and Scully is, quite rightly, livid. She went over his head and, I'm afraid, you're going to get a lot of flak from him over it. If you think his demeanour was pissy just now – wait until he really gets going.'

Lorrie realised she was grinding her teeth and she made a concerted effort to relax. The rumour that Annie Gordon – the Assistant Commissioner – had singled her out and promoted her above her capability, was beginning to wear a bit thin. Yes, she had the support of the AC. Yes, she was lucky enough to have been spotted and mentored by her, but that was as far as it went. Any promotion – and especially being given the lead on this new squad – was because she was the most qualified and by far the best person for the job. An old anger rose in her chest. Would they never even give her the benefit of the doubt?

Lorrie's desk phone rang giving a welcome interruption.

It was Simon. Lorrie listened for a moment before replacing the receiver and, turning once more to Connor, said, 'Apparently a courier dropped off a USB stick and a note at the front desk. The note is addressed to me and advises me to watch the video... Says it pertains to all the people who have died and are going to die. It's signed The Reaper.'

'The Reaper, eh? As in, the Grim Reaper?'

Lorrie shrugged.

'Sounds a bit iffy,' Connor said. 'Best get the techies to look it over first.'

Lorrie nodded her agreement. 'I'll get a fast-track forensic examination of the stick. We'll rule out viruses and then I'll take a look. Do you want to stick around, sir?'

Connor nodded. 'I wouldn't miss it.'

'Shall I get Scully back?'

This time Connor shook his head. 'Let's see what we've got, first.'

Everything in the major incident room was new – new computers, new chairs, new electronic screens, and even new staff. Her team was recently appointed, and no expense had been spared in equipping the large room. The six feet by four feet monitor with its super-duper controls and high-resolution screen took centre stage, and the image it portrayed stopped Lorrie and Connor in their tracks.

The Reaper – complete with death mask, hood and scythe – filled the screen. The image was paused and, once Lorrie had taken a steadying breath, she nodded and detective sergeant, Annie Baxter, aimed the remote at the screen and pressed 'play'.

The voice was electronically disguised. 'I hope, by now,' the Reaper began, 'you will know what I am capable of.... Or, more accurately – you will think you know what I am capable of. Actually, you really have no idea.' He paused to let his words sink in and then went on, 'I'm hoping my timing is correct and there have been a few corpses.' He giggled. 'I'd certainly look like a fool if there's been no dead bodies.'

Lorrie scrutinised the image on the screen and took in every detail of the costume. She tried to read the eyes behind the mask, but she couldn't even determine their colour. The techies will enhance everything, she assured herself. Before they were finished, she hoped they would know everything about this man, right down to what he looked like naked.

She focussed on his voice, but that was a waste of time, so she tried to listen for any nuances that the distortion failed to hide. That, too, was a waste of time.

The Reaper continued, 'I'm not completely sure how many dead people there are.' He shrugged and shook his head. 'Sadly, that's something I can't determine. I don't even know where they will be when they die, but I can hazard a guess.... Can only be a few places. Anyway...' The Reaper went on quickly, 'Serendipity plays a big part in the grand scheme. You see, I can set things up, set things in motion, but kismet plays a part.' He bent his grotesque head and giggled once more.

The bizarre distortion of that giggle set Lorrie's teeth on edge. She wondered if their computer whiz kids could remove enough of the electronic distortion to at least hear what that bloody giggle actually sounded like.

There was complete silence in the room.

The giggling came to an abrupt halt and Lorrie wondered how much of his demeanour was an act? The Reaper was, once again, all calm and business-like. 'I want to avail you of some important information,' he went on. 'I want to confirm to you what I am but, more importantly, what I am not. I am not a terrorist.' He let that be digested. 'I have no religious or political axe to grind. I have none of the other motivations for what I am about to unleash upon you. I don't give a shit about God or Allah or any other man-made deity. I don't love my country, nor any other country for that matter, so don't go down that road. You'll only make fools of yourselves.'

The weird electronic distortion of his voice made the Reaper sound like a cross between Darth Vader and Miss Piggy from the Muppets, but the comical tone of the voice did not detract from the seriousness of what they were all being told. This... creature... said he was not a terrorist. He laid claim to the deaths of people he obviously didn't know and intimated there were more deaths to come. That, in Lorrie's book, made him a terrorist - regardless of what he claimed.

You could hear a pin drop in the room. Everyone watched the monitor with the same expression on their face – a mixture of disbelief and awe – and each listened with intense concentration. No one moved a muscle for fear that any slight movement would make just enough noise that they would miss anything that the apparition on the screen said.

The Reaper continued, 'I tell you this because it is important. I don't want you to be under any illusion as to what I am. Oh, I realise...' He flapped a hand at the screen. 'I realize this get-up...' he twirled for the benefit of his audience... 'looks quite foolish. I realise you might not take me seriously wearing this Halloween costume, but I like it and, if nothing else, it makes the right statement. I am the Reaper. I collect souls and lead the dead to Hell.' He pointed his long scythe at the screen. 'But, what else am I?' He thought a moment. 'Simply put... I am a serial killer. Not the run-of- the- mill serial killer, mind you. No. No. No. Not for me the stalking and the raping and the ripping out of tongues. I have no interest in killing people based on some psychological profile. I simply want to kill and kill as many people as I can, and I want to do it in a clever way. I want to use my brain. I also don't want your limited resources used in the wrong way. I don't, for example, want counter terrorism brought in on the act because of a misguided belief that I am a terrorist. I will inflict terror – yes – but I'm not someone who is on their radar or someone their resources can identify. So, no COBRA meetings and no Counter Terrorism. It's all down to you, Superintendent Sullivan.'

'Jesus,' the Chief Superintendent muttered under his breath. Lorrie glanced briefly at him and mirrored his horror at what was being said.

The Reaper hadn't finished. He went on, 'I didn't wish to waste time so I ensured the first victim would grab your attention early on.

Perhaps there is more than one victim? Who knows? I hope I succeeded in rattling your cage, Superintendent Sullivan? Did I give you a captured audience, so to speak? The others may be harder to pin down - initially anyway - and, just so you know – London will be first, but keep an eye on the rest of the country.'

Although it wasn't visible behind the mask, no one was left in any doubt that the Reaper was smirking. 'One last thing,' he went on. 'I don't know exactly who my victims are. I don't know much about how the deaths will go down or exactly when. I'm hoping that the timing of this video actually coincides with the first stage of my plan.'

'Bastard,' Lorrie muttered under her breath.

Connor looked at her and shook his head. The killer was making it personal by mentioning Sullivan. How the Hell did he know the case would be assigned to her? Even he didn't know that much until Scully ungraciously informed him after the event. By rights, the case shouldn't have gone anywhere near Sullivan nor her National Serious Crimes squad.

The Reaper wasn't quite finished. 'Before I say my farewells, just one more thing... be warned that I will not stop. I'm going to enjoy it all far too much. Goodbye everyone.' He giggled and waved before the screen went black.

There was a shared letting out of breath across the whole room.

Lorrie looked across at Annie Baxter and said, 'Play it again.'

# DAY ONE: NIGHT

Midnight approached, but their day was not yet over. There was too much to do to allow anyone to go home, so, when death number nine and death number ten were reported to Lorrie a few minutes after midnight the whole team were still there in the major incident room doing their jobs.

Number nine and number ten were completely random deaths insofar as the two people didn't know each other, didn't live anywhere near each other, and neither had been on the fated aeroplane. They did, however, have two things in common – both had been at Heathrow airport briefly that evening, and both had died in a similar manner to those on the plane.

Lorrie scrutinised the details. Nine and ten had parked and then headed to arrivals to meet relatives. Their relatives had flown with two different airlines on two different planes. They had arrived from two different destinations and pitched up at two different arrival gates.

None of the travellers were met as arranged because, even before they'd cleared customs, their rides home were already dead.

Lorrie sent DI Grant and DS Lovell to the airport with strict instructions to trace every step the two victims had taken prior to collapsing and dying. She wanted them to ensure that the forensic team accompanying them picked up and bagged every piece of litter. She also instructed them to question everyone who'd been within ten feet of the victims.

It was a tall order. She knew they had their work cut out getting anything of significance from the busy airport, but she was confident that those two officers would rise to the task. DI Simon Grant was nothing if not tenacious and she was already beginning to like and respect DS Lovell.

Lorrie felt that bedlam threatened. Chaos seemed to hover just on the periphery of the case that had begun with eight deaths on an aeroplane. She didn't believe that the ten deaths to date were the end of it and, in her heart, she wondered if she would be up to the task of leading the investigation to a positive conclusion. Despite her bravado and despite her position with both Scully and Connor, Lorrie wasn't one hundred percent sure of her ability to cope with what she perceived as one humdinger of an assignment.

Lorrie and the rest of her team planned to work through the night. They had two hundred or so potential aeroplane witnesses to screen for interview. They had to interview the families of the two people who had most recently died. They had to attempt to glean something from the killer's video by watching it over and over and over again, searching for clues in the background, clues in his language, clues in his mannerisms. They had to try and make sense of the reports coming thick and fast from forensics and from Ricky Burton, the pathologist. In other words – they had a bruiser of a night ahead with no hope of rest and little hope of finding a single clue as to who the killer was and how to stop him.

DS Baxter and DS Powell had the unenviable task of visiting the next of kin of all the victims, primarily to give formal notification of the death of their loved ones, but to also attempt to gather information. What that information would be and how it would help was anyone's business, but nothing was to be left to chance.

By three o'clock in the morning, Lorrie was goggle-eyed from watching the video. She was troubled by something but couldn't put her finger on it. There was something she was either seeing or hearing that gave her an itch at the back of her brain and that itch caused her to continually replay the video. She gave up.

She inhaled her sixth cup of coffee and contemplated calling it a night.

SIMON GRANT AND SONIA Lovell had arrived back shortly after three o'clock, just as Lorrie had turned off the video. They were exhausted and worn down by the job of overseeing the death scenes at the airport and of questioning everyone who had even glanced in the victims' direction. Lorrie immediately sent them home.

She spent an hour going through their handwritten notes and, when Baxter and Powell rolled in, she sent them and every other member of the team home to bed. She spent another hour sifting through all the information to hand and finally threw in the towel at five o'clock.

She too, headed home.

# DAY TWO: MORNING

Lorrie arrived home at five thirty, exhausted, frustrated and more than a little anxious about what her reception was going to be from Colin. She was surprised to find Ollie making breakfast in the kitchen.

'What are you doing up this early?'

Ollie shrugged and placed two fried eggs on a slice of toast. 'Been working all night,' he said. 'Professor Napier allows me to use the lab at the university out of hours sometimes. He knows I'm a bit behind on my research.'

'I didn't know you were behind, Ollie. It's working with Colin that's the problem. You should knock it on the head and concentrate on what's important.'

'I like working there. It breaks the monotony.'

'A production line? A warehouse? A distribution centre?' Lorrie couldn't keep the incredulity from her voice. 'Really?'

'You're such a snob, mum. Perhaps if you didn't look down on Colin's little empire quite so much then he wouldn't be such an arse to you.'

'So, him being an arse is my fault?' Lorrie was hurt and it showed.

Ollie began to wolf down his food and replied through a mouthful of egg, 'I didn't mean that, but you must admit you take the piss out of his business.'

'I don't think I do that, Ollie. Anyway, I'm too tired for this shit. Is that fresh coffee in the pot?'

'You don't need coffee. Make some hot chocolate. You'll sleep better.'

She ignored his advice about the hot chocolate and poured herself a mug of coffee then flopped down into a chair at the table.

She was so tired she could barely see straight. She thought about what Ollie had said about Colin. Ollie's perception about what she thought of Colin's business was way off the mark. She gave Colin credit for his successes. He'd worked hard and there was no way she looked down on what he did for a living. Perhaps what Ollie was seeing was her disdain for her husband in general? The fact that Ollie saw fit to defend Colin was an eye-opener. He usually barely tolerated him and never spoke up for him.

'What's kept you out all night?' Ollie asked.

'Murder and mayhem... what else?'

'I heard something on the radio this morning about people dying on an aeroplane.' He tried to draw her out. 'Sounds a bit on the sci-fi side to me.'

'I'm not talking about it, Ollie.' She dismissed his interest with a narrowing of her eyes. 'Nose out, buddy.'

'Fair enough.' He finished his breakfast and placed his plate and cutlery in the dishwasher.

'I haven't seen much of you lately,' Lorrie commented. 'Share some of your life with me. You got a girlfriend yet?'

'Hardly,' Ollie snorted. 'When do I have time for a girlfriend?'

Lorrie was deeply saddened by her son's words. Ollie never seemed to relax. He never seemed to have any sort of a social life. He was eighteen years old – already three years at university having won a place at aged fifteen – and too smart for his own good. God knows where he got his brains from, Lorrie mused.

He was the spitting image of his father and, over the years - as he'd grown and matured - her heart had been broken time and time again as she'd witnessed him growing up, learning and maturing without the steady hand and guidance of his father.

She had loved his father. Truth be told, she never stopped loving him. She wondered, not for the first time, how this son of hers would have turned out if he'd had the benefit of two loving parents as opposed to a mother who worked all the hours God sent, and a stepfather who was a molecule short of a psychopath.

'Why don't you make some time for a bit of a social life?' she asked. 'Before you know it, you'll be forty and on your own.'

'Most mothers would be pleased that their son was concentrating on their studies rather than chasing girls and getting drunk with his delinquent friends.'

'I'm not most mothers.' For an instant, Lorrie thought she saw disappointment in her son's eyes. 'You do know how much I love you, don't you Ollie?'

'I suppose,' he replied slowly.

She had no idea what he meant. 'You suppose?'

He sighed. 'Yes, I know how much you love me.' Then, 'Why all the sudden attention? You feeling guilty, or something?'

'Yes.' She decided to be honest. 'I don't give you enough attention. I don't ask you often enough how you are or what you're getting up to. I feel guilty about a lot of things where you're concerned, Ollie.'

'Well, there's no need. We are what we are and there's no point crying about it.'

Oh, but she wanted to cry for this son of hers. She wanted to weep over the fact that, despite his intelligence and his obvious maturity, he was virtually all alone in the world. She worked all the time.

Her mind was always on the job, and she had raised her son in a house that had never been a home to either of them. The years of his childhood had passed her by, and she had hardly noticed when he failed to bring classmates home to play or when he never seemed to get an invitation to the birthday parties of the boys who should have been his friends. It was a wonder Ollie had turned out as well as he had.

'Colin doesn't want you in the warehouse anymore.' She hadn't planned on telling him, but she now saw it as an opportunity to free up some of his time and perhaps he would use that time to live a more normal life.

'He doesn't mean it,' Ollie retorted. 'You know what he's like. It gives him satisfaction to use me to wind you up and then watch you dive off the deep end. It's always been like that. I've learned not to take any notice.'

He had such insight for a young boy, and it grieved her to know just how astutely he summed up her relationship with his stepfather.

Things could have been so different. She could have been happily married to Ollie's father and their son would have had a normal up-bringing. She conveniently forgot that Ollie's father was already married when they had their affair.

There was no point in wishing for something that had never happened. When the Reaper case was over, she would try with her son. She would take more interest in what he was doing, try to influence him and direct him towards a more balanced life.

Lorrie drained her coffee mug and dragged herself to her feet. 'I'm going to bed for a couple of hours. You should get some sleep too.'

'I have plans,' he replied, 'and they don't include sleep.'

If Lorrie hadn't been so utterly exhausted, she may have enquired about her son's plans. It was, yet another, nail in the coffin of motherhood. She kissed him, walked on unsteady legs from the room, and climbed the stairs to bed.

Ollie watched her go and sat a while. His mother took the biscuit, she really did. All the questions and concerns about him were too little, too late, as far as he was concerned.

He'd been without a real mother all his life and, now – this phantom mother – had the audacity to be worried about him having no friends and no girl on his arm? It was a piss take, really. Where was her concern when he was growing up and she was spending every waking hour at work? He'd been the proverbial latch-key kid and when she'd married Colin, the arsehole, his loneliness had actually worsened. He could never depend on her to be there for him, and he'd learned to depend only on himself. That way he wouldn't be let down.

He could have accepted his life a lot better if he'd been sure his mother was working all the hours God sent, so as to put a roof over their heads and food on the table but, apart from when he was very little, that had never been the case. She worked day and night for her own ambition. She missed the parent's evenings and the sport's days and everything else that was important to him as a child because of her ambition to get as many promotions as she could, as soon as she could. He felt cold towards her and that hurt him more than he could say. What hurt him even more was that his mother didn't have a clue who he really was. She didn't know what made him tick and Ollie knew that one day – and one day very soon – she was going to be shocked to her very core when his real self was exposed to her.

LORRIE DIDN'T SHARE a bed with Colin. Lately, they had separate bedrooms. It had been her idea. She'd said it was because she didn't want to disturb him. She often received telephone calls through the night which resulted in frequent trips out to one crime scene or another. Those telephone calls made Colin angry. Everything to do with her job made Colin angry.

The separate bedrooms weren't about disturbing her husband. That was the excuse she came up with to get away from his mouth and his hands and his body. The truth of the matter was that she couldn't bear him anywhere near her. She'd suffered long enough and now, she couldn't remember the last time they'd had any sort of sexual contact, never mind actual intercourse.

Of course, he had made her pay. He wasn't very subtle when it came to punishing her for denying him her bed and her body, but she remained steadfast. It was difficult to keep up the pretence and now there was no longer any deception about her reasons for insisting on her own bedroom. Colin asked her and she told him.

Colin stood in the doorway of his own bedroom and watched his wife go into the room at the other end of the hallway and, not for the first time, he wished he had the gumption to follow her. He wanted to take her forcibly and slap her around a little. He'd lost count of the number of times she'd deliberately refused to even acknowledge him, never mind give him access to what was rightfully his. As her husband, he owned every bit of her and that included the bits between her legs.

It was all much worse now that she had the fancy job title. Superintendent Sullivan. Well, lah-de-fucking-dah. She thought she was too good for him. Well, didn't she know that her shit still stank to high heaven?

He always seemed to be simmering with anger and was constantly on the verge of a full nuclear meltdown. He did everything he could to get her to want him. Unfortunately, he didn't realise that what he was actually doing was tormenting her. What he mistook for arduous overtures, she saw as skin-crawling lechery. Colin thought that he loved her, but he also knew that he loathed her in equal measure. He wished with all his being that he had never met her.

When he had first clapped eyes on her, Lorrie MacDonald, as she was then, was a sight for sore eyes. He'd been a witness in a hit and run and Lorrie had interviewed him. He'd wanted to have her and to own her from the first moment he'd set eyes on her. He had made it his mission in life to get her.

He remembered the first time he'd taken her. She wasn't a virgin – in fact she had a bastard son – but she'd been shy, and he appreciated that she didn't take the initiative in any way. Right from the start, she was subservient and catered to his every need. For a time, they'd been happy. He was over the moon when she agreed to marry him, and he even looked forward to being a father to her son. Colin believed he was her world and then her fucking job began to interfere in their lives far too much. The job took her away from him. It kept her out all hours of the day and night and turned her into a stuck-up know-it-all who looked down her nose at him.

He had absolutely no failings as a husband. He didn't see how much his words and his mind games demoralised his wife. He didn't see how his attempts at fully controlling her every thought and every move alienated her. No, it was the job. Everything had to revolve around the fucking job.

He missed the early days. She was just a detective sergeant then and wasn't too sure of herself. She depended on him for support. She said she liked nothing better than to be at home with him and Ollie. So what if he said her friends were all parasites and madly jealous of her? So what if he refused to speak to her for weeks on end if she defied him and stayed out after work to drink with her cronies? So what if he lied to her and made her doubt herself? Didn't she realise just how much he sacrificed for her and her son? He had paid for the boy's education for fuck's sake. He had given that boy the means to carve out a brilliant future for himself. Didn't she realise that without him, her son wouldn't be at university but probably hanging out with a gang, smoking dope and robbing old-aged pensioners?

As Colin stood outside her bedroom door, thoughts of the past fuelled his anger. Then, there was tonight. She'd been out the whole night without so much as a phone call or a text. She knew the rules – she had to phone or text. He had the right to know where she was and what she was doing. She was well out of order not sticking to his instructions.

He had been drinking for hours and, although a little voice was nagging at him to leave her alone and get himself off to bed, he couldn't tear himself away from the door. He had things he needed to say to her, and, by God, he would make her listen. He was drawing a line in the sand. She would toe the line, or God help her.

He reached for the door handle and hesitated. Just then he heard Ollie downstairs opening and closing the front door and seconds later he heard his motorbike start up on the drive. Colin smiled and tested the door. It wasn't locked. How remiss of her. He pushed it open... There would be no witnesses. He could do what he wanted. The nagging little voice telling him to leave her alone was suddenly silent.

There was no one to hear Lorrie's cries when Colin hurt her and no one to see her tears when Colin finally left her room some twenty minutes later. She had endured the lashing of his tongue and all the vileness he spewed forth and she had then endured his drunken apologies and the wet, slobbery kisses that followed. What she did not endure – would not endure - was sex with him. She had pushed him off and, for the first time in their marriage, he had physically hurt her. Of the two of them, she didn't know who was more shocked.

Her tears were tears of shame. She was so ashamed of herself for putting up with him, for accepting his behaviour and his torment of her. No one would ever believe that the woman who was so strong and opinionated and aggressive in her working life could be such a weak and utterly powerless person in her private life. Anyone who knew her or who worked with her would say she was the last person they would have expected to put up with any form of abuse. But Lorrie knew – from her own experience and the experience of countless run-ins with domestic abuse victims over her working life – that you never could tell why a victim was a victim and why that victim remained in the abusive situation. Everyone had their reasons for accepting the abuse and for living with it.

She was ashamed and, illogically, it was that shame that had kept her with Colin. The thought of anyone finding out about how she had allowed herself to be treated for years was what had kept her mouth shut and what had kept her from divorcing him.

10AM AND DI GRANT AND DS Lovell were in a greasy spoon around the corner from the Imperial War Museum having breakfast. Lorrie had allowed them home just after 3am to sleep with instructions to meet with the pathologist at 10.30am to get first hand reports on the post mortems completed overnight.

Simon Grant wasn't a handsome man but what he lacked in good looks he made up for in intellect and charisma. Sonia Lovell was in love with him but had the good sense to keep that fact to herself. She knew he was out of bounds and not only because he was her superior, but because his heart was very much given elsewhere. He loved a woman who didn't love him back – a woman who he had married and who had divorced him; a woman he couldn't forget or give up on. So, Sonia loved him in silence and in private.

Sonia and Simon worked well together and anything other than a professional relationship was out of the question. She knew that and she'd learned to come to terms with it. There was no point beating a dead horse, after all.

'Did you manage much sleep?' Sonia yawned around the question.

'A couple of hours,' Simon replied. 'That bloody video kept play-ing over and over in my mind. I couldn't switch the fucking thing off.'

'Same here. I'm knackered.' She yawned once more.

'Get that coffee down you. We'll stop off and get some Red Bull later.'

She took a long swallow of the hot, bitter coffee. 'What do you make of him - the killer?' she asked.

Simon shrugged. 'Intelligent. He uses a lot of proper English, but a bit immature.'

'Young, do you think?'

'Can't be that young.'

'Oh?'

Simon offered an explanation. 'Stands to reason – someone be-low thirty-five, forty? Well, I think it takes experience and an older, wiser head to pull something like that off. It's sophisticated. The fact that we haven't got a clue as to who he is or what he's actually doing, or planning means he has the upper hand. I can't see a youngster get-ting the upper hand this early on.'

Sonia thought a moment. 'What is it all about, exactly? I mean...' She placed her coffee cup gently into the saucer and leaned forward. 'What's his game? I don't believe all that serial killer bullshit. This isn't the profile of a serial killer.'

'Terrorism?'

'He said not.'

'Since when do we believe what terrorists tell us?' Simon's lips thinned and he shook his head. 'I don't believe a fucking word that arsehole said. As far as I'm concerned, he's a terrorist all right.'

'I... I don't know,' Sonia returned. 'I think it would be unwise to write off anything he told us... Not the serial killer stuff – I don't rate that - but I don't get the feeling he believes he's a terrorist. Not in the traditional sense.'

Simon looked across the table at the woman who had worked side by side with him for three years and found himself agreeing with her. Sonia was clever. She saw things no one else saw and had a copper's instinct for bullshit. He knew she was secretly in love with him and, instead of it making him uncomfortable, he was flattered. Sonia was pretty, sexy in an understated way and was loyal to the bone. If things had been different...

'Let's go see what Ricky Boy has to say. With any luck he'll know exactly what went down and we can nip this in the bud.'

Sonia wiped her mouth and threw down her paper napkin. 'I'm not going to hold my breath. Something tells me we're going to be turning in circles for a while.'

'Let's hope that, for once in your life DS Lovell, you're wrong.'

DOCTOR RICKY BURTON had personally performed three of the post-mortems and his colleagues had, between them, performed the remaining seven. Blood, saliva and tissue samples were currently with toxicology, but Ricky was doubtful the initial screening would flag anything of significance which meant further, more specialised screening would have to be done and that would mean days, if not weeks, of waiting for results.

Stomach contents were inconclusive. Initial bloodwork, just that minute back from the lab, was inconclusive. The toxin did tell a little bit of a story, though. It told a story of its journey. It ravaged – that was the only word that Ricky felt legitimately described its destruction of tissue. It had entered the bloodstream through the mucous membranes in the mouths of the victims. It left a trail all the way through the circulatory system to the respiratory system, but it was elusive. Ricky had no clue what it was or how the victims had come into contact with it.

'So,' DI Grant said, 'basically, you can tell us jack shit?'

Ricky sighed and shook his head. 'I don't know what else I can tell you.'

'Go over it again,' Sonia said impatiently.

'Okay, but bear in mind that until toxicology throws us a bone, we can only go with the little we have. No point throwing your toys out of the pram, Simon. I can't see what isn't there to see.'

Simon acknowledged the sense of the doctor's words with a curt nod of his head.

Ricky said, 'Right... so... what I know for sure is that each of the ten victims ingested some sort of toxin, but it wasn't something they swallowed. It entered the body... I think...' He paused to confirm that both police officers acknowledged the certain amount of educated guesswork involved in his primary conclusions before going on. 'I think it got in from the lips, travelled to the tongue and then into the bloodstream via saliva and the mucous membrane of the cheeks. I believe this because this toxin... whatever the hell it is... left great big ugly footprints. The damage to tissue is horrendous. The breakdown at cellular level is something I've never seen and that's why I'm not optimistic that initial toxicology screening will name the bastard.'

'Any idea of how long before we get the results?' Sonia asked.

'A couple of days? Weeks?' Ricky replied on a shrug.

'Jesus.' Simon ran a weary hand through his hair and began pacing. 'Anything on the clothes? Anything on the plane?'

Ricky shook his head. 'I don't know. Forensics at Lambeth and Newlands Park are going through possessions as we speak, but we've got zilch so far.'

'Did they drink anything on the plane?' Sonia asked.

'There wasn't time for the drinks trollies to be wheeled out. They'd only been in the air a quarter of an hour,' Ricky replied.

'So... Lips, tongue, cheeks, bloodstream?'

Ricky nodded at Simon. 'That's the journey all right.'

'Causing everything to swell in the mouth and block the airway?'

'Correct.' Ricky nodded once more. 'Then, it attacked the lungs.'

'Witnesses say it was all over in a matter of minutes. There was nothing they could do to help. Do you have an opinion on timeline from exposure to death yet?'

'I'm not hazarding a guess at a timeline yet. Until we know more, I'm reserving my opinion.'

'But all the witnesses were pretty clear on how long it took them to start choking to ending up dead with their tongues virtually sitting on their chests.'

'That's as may be, Detective Inspector, but how long had they been exposed? Fact is, they could've been dying a lot longer than that three or four minutes.'

'Anything else? Anything at all?' Simon probed.

'Nothing at the moment.'

'Right. Okay.' Simon ceased pacing and gestured for Sonia to follow him out of the lab. They had to report to Lorrie. Simon only wished he had more news for her.

'Should we ring her?' Sonia asked. 'She won't be in until midafternoon, but she might want an update now.' The Superintendent was a bit of an enigma to DS Lovell, and she deferred to Simon's knowledge of their Guvnor's particular wants. 'Would she want us to disturb her at home or should we let her sleep?'

'She'd want the report, without a doubt, but let's give her another hour's shut-eye.'

AS IT WAS, GIVING LORRIE another hour's sleep proved unnecessary. When Simon and Sonia entered the major incident room she was already there.

Lorrie felt and looked like death warmed up. Her eyes stung, her body felt ten stones heavier than normal, and her mind was foggy.

She was busy pushing strong black coffee down her throat when her DI approached.

Simon raised an eyebrow. 'Couldn't sleep, Guv? You look like shit.'

'Thanks for that, Simon.' Lorrie grimaced and closed her eyes. 'I think I managed about an hour,' she lied. 'Have you anything for me? What did you get from Ricky Boy?'

Simon sighed. 'All ten bodies have been sliced and diced and lots of samples are sitting in a queue with forensics. Ricky isn't confident of learning anything anytime soon but he's definite they were all poisoned.'

'Any idea how?'

He shook his head. 'Only that it wasn't swallowed. Apparently, according to our esteemed pathologist, the poison was on the victim's lips and then their tongues and it then got into their bloodstream via the mucous membranes in the mouth.'

'That's helpful.' Lorrie picked up her coffee cup and winced as a sharp pain leapt from her wrist to her elbow.

'You all right, Guv?'

'Sprained my wrist. I'm okay.'

They were interrupted by DS Baxter.

'Superintendent. You have to see this. I was checking the generic emails. I saw this video attachment and opened it. Sorry... I didn't think. I guess I should have left it alone... not opened it.'

Lorrie said, 'Take a deep breath, Baxter. What video?'

'From him, Ma'am. From the Reaper.' Baxter was quite breathless. 'Sorry, Ma'am. There could've been a virus or anything. I was stupid.'

'Is it still open? Did you shut it down?'

Baxter shook her head. 'No, Ma'am.' She made to turn. 'Shall I close it?'

'No. Leave it and let me see it.' Lorrie followed Baxter back to the computer. Simon and Sonia followed.

The screensaver was on, Baxter moved the mouse and, suddenly, there he was. The image was paused, and the Reaper's face filled the screen.

Lorrie nodded, Baxter clicked the mouse and the image came to life.

The video lasted no more than three minutes, during which the Reaper spoke slowly and calmly and with no giggling this time around. When he finished, Lorrie wished she had managed that hour's sleep after all. It was going to be a long day.

# DAY TWO: AFTERNOON

'EH's pointed us to Manchester, Ma'am.' Lorrie stood to attention in front of Annie Gordon, the Assistant Commissioner.

'He didn't say when or how but insisted it would be soon.'

Commander Scully and Chief Superintendent Connor stood on either side of Lorrie, and both refrained from looking anywhere but at the spot above the AC's head. It was best not to catch her eye. Annie Gordon was apt to put you on the spot with questions designed to embarrass you if you happened to catch her beady eye.

So, the AC directed her questions at Lorrie. 'How? How, Superintendent? Do we know how he's doing this? How can he do this in London one day and be set up to repeat it in Manchester the next?' The Assistant Commissioner shook her head in exasperation. 'How many dead so far, did you say?'

'Ten, Ma'am.'

'Ten dead and he's targeting Manchester? He can't be working on his own, surely?'

'A group, Ma'am? A cell? Something well organised?'

Annie Gordon's ice-blue eyes narrowed. 'In other words, Superintendent Sullivan, you don't know?'

'No, Ma'am.'

Annie Gordon didn't suffer stress or anxiety as a rule. She was a tough nut and proud of her reputation as a hard-nosed bitch, but an unfamiliar sick feeling in the pit of her stomach accompanied by a shortness of breath showed her that she was human after all and could suffer anxiety just as much as lesser mortals. That thought scared the shit out of her and she took a deep breath to steady herself.

She said, 'I have to brief the Home Secretary and that's something no one in their right mind would relish. Just give me something to tell him.'

Lorrie reported the pathologist's findings and waited as the scant information registered in the Assistant Commissioner's brain.

'Brilliant. Just brilliant. So – no suspects? No clues? No ideas?' Her stomach hurt and she hoped she wasn't developing an ulcer. 'Just. Fucking. Brilliant.'

Scully spoke up. 'The good news is that there is nothing so far from Manchester, Ma'am. Perhaps he's bluffing?'

'Do you think he's bluffing, Sullivan?'

'No, Ma'am.' Lorrie cut her eyes at Scully. He wouldn't like her contradicting him. 'Nothing to suggest he's bluffing. He said quite clearly that Manchester would be next.'

'At least there's no more deaths here,' Scully said. 'That's a positive.' He obviously didn't have the sense to keep quiet. 'I mean... Perhaps this is all there is?'

Lorrie groaned inwardly. Scully could be such a plonker at times.

Annie Gordon growled in the back of her throat and, if looks could kill, Commander Scully would be stone cold dead at that moment. 'Are you for real, Commander? Did you just say... perhaps this is all there is?'

Scully had the sense to look away.

The AC turned to Connor. 'What have you to add, Chief Superintendent?'

Connor shook his head. 'Nothing to add, Ma'am. I have every confidence that Superintendent Sullivan is on top of things.'

'Every confidence? Really, Connor? I hope that statement doesn't come back to haunt you.' The Assistant Commissioner's smile was cold as she finally dismissed them with an impatient flap of her hand.

In the corridor, Lorrie had to stand and not only take Scully's angry words, but she had to swallow them and thank him for the privilege of being verbally hammered by him. He'd been humiliated and, like every other bully, he took his anger out on someone who couldn't fight back.

When Scully finished berating her, and he'd stomped off and left her with Connor, Lorrie felt close to fainting. She was exhausted. She was in pain from the wrist that Colin had injured, and she was slowly crashing from her caffeine high.

'You're on thin ice with Scully,' Connor said. 'I actually think he hates you more today than he did yesterday.'

'You don't need to look so pleased about it, sir. I know you run a close second when it comes to disliking me.'

'Careful, Sullivan. I'm your superior officer and you come pretty close to insubordination most of the time. Is it any wonder you're found so insufferable by your betters? Is it any wonder Scully wants to ruin you?'

Lorrie didn't have the energy to retaliate. 'No, sir,' was her only reply.

Pleased with her response, Connor smirked, curtly nodded his head and walked off with a swagger that made his fat arse wobble. Lorrie gave a tired smile. The sight of his backside as he waddled away touched her funny bone.

She followed him and returned to her office.

'ALL HELL IS BREAKING loose along the power corridor,' she told DI Grant on her return. 'I'm telling you, Simon – this will be going all the way up to the Home Secretary where it'll bounce off the walls. The Assistant Commissioner is already gearing up to rip the faces off the lot of us if we don't give her something soon to pacify number ten. We're all well and truly under the microscope and, unfortunately, we don't have either Scully or Connor on our side. Both of them will shit all over us to cover their own backs.'

'The AC isn't a fool, Guv. She knows what we're up against and she knows neither Scully nor Connor are fit to lick your boots.'

She was too tired to get riled up over the dressing down she got from Scully. She was too tired to revel in the fact that the Commander had made himself out to be an ignorant fool in front of Annie Gordon. Simon may be right – and the Assistant Commissioner may realise how much she was hampered in her new role as Superintendent of a squad neither Scully nor Connor wanted – but... and it was a big but... even her mentor and biggest fan would have to swallow her nob if Lorrie fucked the case up.

'The press are camped outside,' Simon said. 'Someone let slip about the Reaper and there's a feeding frenzy.'

'Someone let slip?' Lorrie stared at him for long moments. Her eyes were hard and cold, and for a second, Simon saw how tough his boss really was. Her Barbie doll looks and small stature belied the true extent of her cast iron strength, and he fervently hoped he never screwed up enough to get on the wrong side of her.

'I don't know who it was, Guv, but the phones have been ringing off the hook for hours and I think someone cocked up. I don't believe it was deliberate, but someone on the team let more than a few things slip out to a reporter.'

Lorrie knew that Simon was loath to see the bad in anyone. He was pretty gullible when it came to people he worked with, and he put loyalty above everything. Just because he was as straight as a piece of string, didn't make everyone else as loyal or as honest as him.

Lorrie was a realist. She knew there was always someone in every team who was out for themselves. This wasn't the first time in her career that someone on her team leaked information to the press and she was sure it wouldn't be the last, but she knew she had to nip it in the bud before leaked information seriously damaged their investigation.

'I think it's time I spoke to the troops,' she told Simon. 'Get everyone...and I mean everyone lined up. I'll be out in a minute.'

She followed him moments later. She walked slowly into the major incident room and was gratified to see everyone either standing or sitting to attention. Her voice was low as she addressed them, but no one was under any illusions about the fact that she was furious.

'I'm only going to say this once,' she said. She controlled her anger sufficiently to make sure her words were clear. 'Someone in this room is a Judas. Someone here...' She rested eyes on one and then another of them until she had taken in every person in the room.

'Some idiot... and I'm being generous when I name them idiot because, in fact, this person is a two-faced moron... Well, this person spoke to the press. One of you lot betrayed the hard work of this team.' Her face was sallow with exhaustion and pain, but her eyes were all fire. 'Speaking to the press undermines what we do,' she went on. 'So, who thinks they are so important, so above the rest of us, that they believe that it's okay to go behind my back and blab to the fucking tabloids?'

No one spoke. A few eyes wavered and dropped.

Lorrie looked around the room once more, satisfied they had all got the message. She hoped the fact that she had shown she was onto whoever was yapping to the press would be enough to halt them in their tracks, but just to be sure, she added, 'If one more word escapes this room without my explicit permission, I will hunt the perpetrator down and flay every bit of skin from their body. I may be speaking metaphorically, but I think you all get the gist of what damage I would do to that person when I found them... and I would find them. Don't think of doubting me on that.'

She paused to let her words sink in. 'Solving this case and preventing more deaths,' she went on, 'requires a lot of hard graft and a great deal of dependence on being a fucking team.' Her voice rose. 'I will not tolerate anything other than absolute loyalty to me and to this squad. Do I make myself clear?'

There were urgent nods and a smattering of 'Yes, Guv's' around the room. Satisfied, Lorrie turned and walked slowly away. She'd let them stew on that for a while but would get Simon to read them the riot act himself later. Belt and braces were what was required to stop the mouthy fucker in his or her tracks.

Lorrie's head was reeling. Not for the first time, she felt like a gold-plated fraud. She felt unworthy to be in charge. Someone once told her that a lot of successful women often questioned their right of success. They often believed that they got there by sheer fluke rather than because they deserved it. Oh, she knew she'd worked her arse off for years to get to where she was and that she deserved the promotions she'd achieved, but she found she had to pinch herself at times as she didn't quite believe it. She didn't get the fact that it was only after a particularly bad time with Colin that self-doubt reared its ugly head. Luckily, for Lorrie, she could compartmentalise like the best of them and always managed to pragmatically soldier on.

At the door, she turned and looked towards the far end of the room where she noticed Simon having a go at one of the uniformed officers. It seemed that he might have found their culprit and she was happy enough to allow him to deal with it. She pushed open the door and stepped out into the corridor, glad to be on her own for a moment. Alert to the fact that the press knowing about the Reaper was the proverbial cock-up that would finally bring Scully and Connor down on her like a ton of bricks, she sighed and attempted to steel herself for the battering her ears would soon have to take.

CHIEF SUPERINTENDENT Connor strolled through the major incident room as if he was visiting royalty and poked his head over shoulders, rummaged through papers on desks and generally disrupted the natural flow of the team hard at work.

Lorrie got word of his visit and felt like pulling her hair out by the roots. She'd been on the phone to Manchester for the past hour trying to get a heads up on anything unusual that might be happening there and all she needed was for her boss to do a time-wasting, ego- pumping walkabout.

She cornered him and ushered him into a corner. 'You can see we're pretty busy,' she said. 'Is there anything in particular I can help you with?'

'Just showing my face,' he replied, more than a little put out by her waylaying him in mid-saunter. 'Good for morale to see the chief, don't you think?'

'Yes, sir, but...'

'Oh, stop panicking,' he interjected with a flap of his hand. 'I've no intentions of disrupting your precious team. I was just leaving. I've arranged for a press conference, and I'd like you out front with me.'

She raised an eyebrow. So far, there was no mention of the fact that the press had been tipped off about the Reaper. Perhaps he didn't know?

'That's a first.' She couldn't keep the sarcasm from her voice. He had never wanted her at his side before. 'Why do you want me there? Won't I cramp your style?'

Connor chose to ignore her tone. 'You're the lead on the case. It's only right and proper that you're with me when we update the public.'

'There's nothing to tell them, sir.'

'Nonsense. We need to reassure them. You can answer a few questions, surely?'

Before she could respond, Simon approached them at a trot. 'I've got updates, for what they're worth.' He addressed Lorrie and ignored Connor.

Lorrie made a 'come on' gesture with her hand and winced again as the pain in her wrist took her unawares.

Simon reacted to her obvious discomfort, but she gave a curt shake of her head. It was obvious she wanted no mention of her injured wrist.

'What have you got, Simon?'

He cleared his throat. 'The report is back on the envelope that the USB memory stick came in. We've also received full reports back from the techies on both the stick and the email.'

'Okay, what?'

'As near as damn it, we've got nothing on the envelope. Umpteen prints on it – none of them any good. No DNA from saliva or sweat, or anything else. Looks like he used tap water to seal it and probably wore gloves.' He shook his head slowly. 'We've also got zilch on the USB. It's just a bog-standard stick.

'Nothing remarkable about it.' A smile escaped his lips, and he went on eagerly, 'Now the email is a different story. Not much of a digital footprint, but the IP address where it was sent from is the Bannerman Centre.'

'Bannerman Centre?' Cooper was nonplussed. 'What's the Bannerman Centre?'

Lorrie replied before Simon had the chance to. 'It's the library at Brunel University. Ollie goes to Brunel, that's how I know.'

'That's a break, surely?' Connor looked excited and relieved all at once.

Lorrie was not convinced. She pondered for a moment and addressed Simon. 'Am I right in thinking that CCTV won't help?'

Simon shook his head. 'Needle in a haystack, Guv.'

DS Andrew Powell, an older, shorter version of Richard Gere, hurried over to where the three of them stood huddled in a corner. 'Sorry, Guv... Ma'am.' He avoided looking at the Chief Superintendent. Acknowledging the Chief Super' was above his pay grade and DS Powell was always very mindful of his place in the food chain.

'What is it Powell?' Simon asked.

'There's another death, sir. Supermarket in the East End. We've just had the call.'

In the stillness that Powell's news brought, they all stood like mourners around a grave and each contemplated their next move. It was all too real, too awful, and no one immediately knew what to do or say.

Connor was the first to speak. He said, 'I'll postpone the press conference. No point until we know what's happened with this latest one.'

Lorrie wasn't capable of replying. Her mind was going like the clappers. Another death. Another unexplained decimation of a life. She knew she had to give direction, show leadership, but she couldn't form her thoughts into the words that would bring a little order to the madness descending on all of them.

Connor took the opportunity to leave. He scuttled away. It was amazing how quickly his fat little body moved when he wanted to avoid being in the actual front-line. He seemed terrified someone would ask his advice or look to him to tell them what to do. He disappeared through the door and was gone in the blink of an eye.

Simon looked to Lorrie. Lorrie took a deep breath and pulled herself together. She said, 'You best get on with it.'

'I'll take Lovell with me,' he said.

She nodded and waved him away.

'Make sure you cover all the bases,' she called after his retreating back. 'Get back to me as soon as you can.'

As it was, Sonia was already on her way. Simon couldn't fault her for that. He appreciated her using her initiative.

SHE WAS TWENTY-SEVEN years old. A schoolteacher. She'd popped out to the supermarket in her lunch break and died in the frozen food aisle.

Simon took one look at her face and knew she was truly the latest victim. From a distance he saw that her tongue sat almost on her chin and was so swollen that her cheeks bulged grotesquely. She'd been pretty – Simon could see that much – and he felt an overwhelming urge to cry.

Sonia immediately took herself to his side. She handed him latex gloves and plastic bootees. He donned them before approaching the body. Bending down, he took in every inch of her.

'Doctor Burton has gone off duty, so Doctor Singh is on his way,' Lovell said. 'I've got officers emptying the place of customers and I've secured the scene.'

Simon nodded absently. He couldn't tear his eyes away from the abomination that had been the pretty young woman.

'What do we know about her?'

Sonia replied, 'Not much. I haven't touched the body or did any search of her belongings. I wanted to wait on Dr Singh.'

'Yes, right. Of course.'

'But a member of staff knows... knew her. Apparently, she came in here quite a lot. She was a teacher at the primary school about three miles up the road. Her name is Amber Watson. Her car is parked somewhere on the multi-storey round the corner. Forensics will search it as soon as we can put our hands on her keys.'

Simon hunkered down and looked at Amber's face from all angles. Her eyes were open, and death had placed a grey glaze over them.

'He is one sadistic bastard.' He pushed himself to his feet and retreated a few steps. 'It seems he doesn't care who he kills. There's a randomness about this that is obscene.'

Sonia couldn't think of a reply, and she was glad when the crime scene forensic lot arrived.

Doctor Singh arrived on scene, and everything became routine. He did what he had to do. Members of his team began to painstakingly search the area immediately around the body and soon, the young Amber Watson was in a double body bag on the way to the morgue.

Simon and Sonia stayed to interview the staff and the few customers Sonia had instructed to wait behind.

The forensic officers continued to bag and tag as they saw fit. and everything was done in a quiet, subdued manner.

'She comes in here once or twice a week,' the member of staff who had spoken to Sonia earlier, said. 'She never buys much. Shopping for one, I'd say. I told this officer here,' she gestured with her head, 'that she's a schoolteacher.'

'I bumped into her trolley, and she was the one who apologised to me,' a customer said. 'That was just before she went down on her knees.' Simon could see panic suddenly flare in the customer's eyes. 'I touched her. Do you think it's contagious? Should I see someone...a doctor?'

Simon reassured her and moved on to the next person on his list – the final customer to be questioned.

'Amber was a lovely person,' the elderly woman said. 'Taught my grandkids last year. That school will miss her, for sure.'

'You spoke to her, I understand?'

'Yes,' she nodded. 'Just to say hello. She was in a hurry. Said she only had half an hour.'

'When was this?'

'When we collected our trolleys. We walked in together and then she went off to get something from the fruit and vegetable section.'

'How did she look?'

'How did she look? Well, okay, I guess. Tired... She looked tired.'

'Apart from that?'

'She kept licking her lips. I thought it was a nervous thing.'

'She didn't complain of feeling unwell?'

She shook her head.

'Did you see her again?'

'Not really. I caught a glimpse of her once or twice amongst the aisles.'

Simon concluded the interview and walked with Sonia over to where the store manager was attempting to keep customers from entering. He was having a hard job explaining why they couldn't just walk in, and his temper was beginning to get the better of him.

He spied Simon and Sonia approaching. 'When can we reopen?' he asked. 'This is our busiest time.'

'Not today,' Simon returned. 'Lock the doors and send your staff home. Our forensic team will finish up in a couple of hours, but you have to stay closed until we're satisfied there's no contamination.'

'That's ridiculous. Do you know how much money I'm losing?'

'I can't help that, sir.'

'What with online shopping, I'm barely keeping the wolf from the door as it is.'

'We'll be as quick as we can,' Simon said.

'Will I be compensated for lost takings?'

'Someone died, sir,' Sonia interjected. 'A little respect wouldn't go amiss.'

The manager refused to look sheepish. He glared at Sonia but buttoned his mouth.

'We'll leave you to it.' Simon walked away and Sonia was quick to follow.

'Some people...' she said.

'I know,' Simon agreed.

They headed back in their separate cars. Simon planned to attend the post-mortem examination of Amber and hoped Dr Singh would get around to it sooner rather than later. He was hoping to get home at a decent hour. He was shattered and he didn't cope well on so little sleep.

A telephone call to Simon scuppered both of his plans. He wouldn't be attending after all and his plans for an early night were well and truly kyboshed.

He put his hazard lights on and hand-signalled Sonia to pull over behind him.

'It never rains, but it pours,' Sonia commented. 'Where this time?'

'Two hospital visitors - The London hospital,' Simon said.

'Any connection to any of the others?'

He shook his head. 'Not that I've been told.'

'I'm starting to worry.'

'I've been worried from the get-go.'

'Forensics have to give us something. Can't they get their fingers out before the body count goes through the roof?'

'Ricky Burton is the best. He'll figure it out.'

Sonia wasn't convinced. 'I'm not so sure.'

'Me neither,' he reluctantly agreed.

# DAY TWO: EVENING

The first deaths in Manchester were reported to Lorrie at two minutes past six.

Lorrie assembled her whole weary squad in front of a huge board placed against the far wall of the major incident room. As her team gathered, she was busy pinning up all the photographs of the dead around the central photograph of the Reaper taken from a video still. As she pinned the photographs, she tried to mask the throbbing pain in her wrist.

When the last photograph was on the board she stood back and moved her eyes slowly across each and every one of them, before finally resting on the Reaper. This man – this creature – was responsible for seventeen deaths. There were the eight from the plane, two from the airport, Amber from the supermarket, the two from The London hospital and now four from Manchester Royal Infirmary.

'Seventeen,' Lorrie said. 'Seventeen dead so far.' She turned to face her team. 'Let's take a moment to summarise and list all the common denominators. Who wants to start us off?' At the lack of response, Lorrie shook her head and said, 'Come on, you guys. Shout out. Don't worry about it, just shout out what you see or what you know.'

Like any good leader, Lorrie wanted her team to think. She wanted to hear their thoughts. She wanted to give them the opportunity to contribute to the information that would lead to evidence, and eventually lead to solving the case. She didn't want to stand in front of them and tell them or lecture them. It was important that they understood.

DS Sonia Lovell was the first one to shout out. 'Ten died related to the airport... the eight on the plane and the two at arrivals. Is the airport a common denominator?'

Lorrie nodded and moved the ten photographs of the ten airport victims so they were bunched together, and drew a red asterisk next to them.

'Six died when visiting various hospitals,' this from DS Andrew Powell. 'Our two and the four from Manchester.'

Lorrie used a green pen to draw an asterisk nest to those six victims.

'Amber is the outlier so far,' Lovell added.

'Is there anything to tie her to either of these two groups?' Lorrie looked around the room, her eyes resting on each of her officers. 'No? Okay, then. Amber starts her own group.' With that, Lorrie moved Amber's photograph so that it sat alone and drew a blue asterisk next to it.

She nodded solemnly and continued, 'Although it looks like Amber is an outlier with her own group, she has something in common with all of the other sixteen victims. We can't assume that we are actually looking at three distinct groups.' Lorrie drew interlocking circles around the group of photographs. She shaded in the areas where the circles overlapped. 'These shaded areas represent other common denominators. We just have to find what they are. We have to find what links them all.'

'We need some help with this, Guv,' Simon said. 'We're all running on fumes at the moment.'

Lorrie nodded her understanding. 'Two officers are on their way with the four bodies from Manchester. It's been agreed that we will work to our full remit, taking the lead nationally, and all evidence – including the bodies – will be dealt with by us and our forensic team.' She waited a beat. She knew that the next piece of information would not be welcomed.

'The Assistant Commissioner has requested two transfers from Counter Terrorism and two officers will be temporarily seconded. They will report to me, but it is understood that they will also liaise directly with S015.'

'SO15?' Simon was visibly displeased. 'We don't need Counter Terrorism muddying the waters, Guv.'

'Their secondment isn't up for debate,' she replied curtly. 'Working alongside us, as part of the team, makes perfect sense. They have different brains... different resources. We need all the help we can get.'

Simon dropped his eyes. She was right, of course.

'Who is coming from Manchester, Guv?' Powell asked.

'I don't have their names. All I know is that it is a DI and a DS.'

'Didn't you work Manchester a few years back?' Simon asked her.

Lorrie nodded and smiled wryly. 'A lifetime ago.' She turned back to the board. 'What else have we got? Let's get as much information up here as we can.

# DAY TWO: NIGHT

They worked until eleven updating the board. They included personal information on the victims, times of death and as much of a chronology as they could determine from witness statements. By the time Lorrie stepped back and surveyed their work, there were multiple lists in black ink and multi-coloured lines, like a psychedelic spider's web stretching and weaving across the whole board.

Back in her office, just before midnight, Lorrie sat on the chair behind her desk and rolled up the right sleeve of her jacket. *Christ,* she thought, as she surveyed the swelling of her wrist and the dark red finger marks biting into the skin. They would soon turn into ugly purple bruises. Good job it was winter, and she could keep covered up.

Bloody Colin. Part of her wanted to have him arrested, but the wiser part – the self-preservation part – wanted to brush it aside and forget it.

She rolled her sleeve back down over the evidence of Colin's attack and rested back in her chair. When this was all over – when the murdering bastard was caught, and she could close her first real case as Superintendent - she would think about what to do about Colin. It bothered her, though, that she was so entrenched in building a career for herself that she allowed her husband to abuse her, but what choice did she really have? She would lose the respect of her team. The men who dictated her future in the force would shake their heads and say that they'd been right all along. They'd say that she was weak. Weren't all women weak? They'd congratulate themselves on their decision to side-line her, saying it was what was best for the force. Worst of all, everyone would feel sorry for her. They'd pity her. They wouldn't be able to meet her eye and they would wonder how they ever thought she would be able to have their backs. It didn't matter that this was the first time Colin had ever laid hands on her.

It would all come out – the years of psychological and emotional abuse, the years of cowering under a constant onslaught of vile words and the endemic erosion of her confidence.

Yesterday had been different. She'd swore at him. She'd walked out on him and refused to phone him or text him with the ritualistic reporting of where she was and what she was doing. She'd been impulsive. She knew how to play the game and, yet, she had deviated from her normal strategy. Colin's drunken tirade in her bedroom, his attempt to have sex with her, the grabbing and twisting of her wrist – were all the consequence of her impulsiveness.

'My, God,' she mumbled to herself. 'I'm actually blaming myself.'

She'd met Colin when Ollie was four years old. He'd been sweet and charming and, although he seemed rather overprotective of her and a bit possessive, she was flattered when he singled her out. She really thought he cared.

Ollie's father was a married colleague. Although he never made her any promises, she had truly thought he loved her. Ollie was conceived and he abandoned her.

She remembered how worthless and soiled she felt when he chose his wife over her and their child. It took her a long time to learn to trust a man again.

At first, Colin seemed to be totally understanding of the circumstances of Ollie's conception. He said that her past had nothing to do with their future. He didn't blame her for the affair with a married man. He said that it was none of his business. What she'd done before he met her was entirely her concern.

Colin was good, she gave him that. He knew exactly what buttons to press. He lulled her into a false sense of security. He built up her sense of worthiness as a human being and as a mother. He created an illusion.

She married him and, for the first time, she met the real Colin.

'Guv?'

Lorrie was startled by the sudden appearance of her DI. She quickly put her right arm under the desk and looked across the room to where Simon was standing framed in the doorway.

'You looked miles away,' he said. 'I told you the Manchester and Counter Terrorism lot are here.'

'Oh? Already? I didn't think they'd make an appearance until the morning. Okay. I'll be out in a minute.'

Simon drew her a quizzical look before turning and walking away. He thought of how preoccupied she had looked, and – what was that injured arm all about?

Lorrie gathered her wits and shook off her thoughts. Time enough to sort Colin out. All her attention had to focus on the case and nothing else.

When she walked into the major incident room and saw who was standing in the middle of the floor, all thoughts of the case exploded from her mind and she almost fainted.

Detective Inspector Sean Kelly's gaze never wavered for a second when he saw her. If there was recognition in his eyes no one noticed.

If his shoulders just happened to straighten ever so slightly, if his fists tightly clenched by his sides - no one noticed. What they did notice was Superintendent Sullivan's sudden pallor and the tremble in her hand as she swept her long blonde hair away from her face.

Simon saw that something was amiss. The Guv looked ill. It didn't look as if she was making any move towards them, so he stepped forward and took charge of the introductions.

'Detective Inspector Kelly and Detective Sergeant Friel from Manchester,' he said to Lorrie, indicating Sean and the small brunette by his side. 'And Detective Sergeant Higgins and Detective Constable Wilson from S015.'

Higgins and Wilson – the two tall, broad and gangster-like counter terrorism officers – nodded at Lorrie. Lorrie absentminded-ly nodded back. She avoided looking at Kelly and Friel.

To Simon, she said, 'Get them all up to speed. I'll be in my office.' With that, she turned and walked briskly back the way she'd just come. Her legs held out just long enough to carry her back to her office where she was grateful to collapse into her chair.

'You all right, Guv?' It was Simon once more framed in the doorway. He'd obviously immediately followed her.

'Not now, Simon.' She dismissed him with a flap of her hand. 'Just get on with everything. You don't need me holding your hand.'

He hesitated. Seeing an expression on her face that he couldn't quite fathom, he wisely retreated.

What the fuck? What the fuck? What the fuck? She was so bloody angry. How dare he be here? How dare he agree to come to London? To her squad... To her case? She felt sick to her stomach. She hadn't clapped eyes on him for eighteen years – a miracle consid-ering the circles they both moved in – and now the very sight of him was enough to nearly cause a nuclear proportioned panic attack.

Her heart was hammering in her chest. Breathing was like inhal-ing razor blades. She felt sick. Sean fucking Kelly, large as life. She couldn't believe it. How many DIs were there in Manchester? There must be dozens, at least, and they sent him? What the Hell was she going to do?

Although eighteen years had gone by, she recognised him immediately. The glimpse she snatched of him, before shock had caused her eyes to dart away, was more than enough to see that he was just as tall, just as broad and just as handsome. He had gone a little grey at the temples, and even from across the room, in that brief few seconds, she could see the crow's feet at the corners of his eyes. By God, she could still feel the pull of him.

The bastard! The low down, dirty bastard! He must have known she was leading the investigation. What in Hell's name was he playing at? The case was going to be tough enough without him at her shoulder.

The feeling of panic subsided somewhat. She suddenly felt the heaviness of the loss of him, of his betrayal and his abandonment bear down on her again. She had never fooled herself. She had never once told herself that she was over him. In eighteen years, she had continued to love him.

He should have been willing to leave his wife. It couldn't have been a happy marriage. You don't cheat on someone you love and who makes you happy. Her pregnancy should have been the clincher for him. He should have stood by her, no matter the cost to his marriage or his career.

He didn't choose her. He didn't choose their unborn baby, and for a while she had struggled to go on loving him but love him she did. It only took that quick glance in his direction to realise that he was dangerous to her. His presence would ruin her.

Why did he come down from Manchester and risk seeing her again?

Only one way to find out. Lorrie picked up the desk phone and called through to the major incident room. 'Send DI Kelly through to me,' she ordered sharply. Replacing the phone, she dragged in a deep breath, steadied herself and prepared for a confrontation she didn't believe she would have the strength or the wits to survive.

She waited five minutes and then ten and he didn't put in an appearance. She picked up the phone once more and this time her voice brooked no nonsense. 'Send DI Kelly through to me right now or tell him to fuck off back to Manchester.'

She only just stopped herself from ripping the phone cable from the wall and hurling the whole thing at the door.

He arrived mere seconds later. He entered the room, closed the door behind him, and without invitation, seated himself opposite her at the desk.

He could see that she was pissed at him. Her demeanour suggested she was on the verge of leaping across the desk and ripping his eyes out. He couldn't help it – he smiled.

'Hello, Lorrie.' Sean's voice was as she remembered – soft but with a hint of steel. 'Good to see you.'

Lorrie opened her mouth, but no words came out. This man was the love of her life, the father of her beloved son and the man who had mercilessly torn her heart from her chest and stomped all over it and he had the audacity to be smiling at her, telling her it was good to see her. Was he out of his fucking mind?

Sean cleared his throat. He removed the smile from his face. Her silence was disconcerting. 'You wanted to see me?' he said.

At last, she found her voice. She amazed herself by how steady it was. She said, 'Not really, Sean. You are the last person I wanted to see. What are you doing here?'

'Here? Well, you summoned me to your office, Lorrie.'

'In London, Sean... What are you doing in London?'

He shrugged. 'Someone had to come. I was available.'

'You knew I was heading up this squad?'

He nodded.

'And, you came?' She couldn't keep the incredulity from her voice. 'Did you think I would welcome that?'

He shrugged once more and his laid-back, nonchalant attitude began to grate on her. She stared at him, and he stared right back at her.

'How's your wife these days? She can't be too happy with you scampering off down here.' She hoped that would rattle him.

A shadow cast across Sean's eyes and he said, 'I won't talk about my wife, Lorrie.'

'Superintendent Sullivan to you.' It was petty, but Lorrie couldn't help it. 'And, I don't give a flying fuck about what you will and won't talk about. You being here is an insult.'

'Look, Superintendent,' He rolled forward so his elbows were on his knees and his head was encroaching across the desk. 'If I admit I was a prick and said I was sorry, could we forget the past and just get on with the job?'

'You, what?'

'I was a prick. I hurt you. I'm sorry. Can we move on?'

Lorrie was annoyed with his attempt to trivialise the past. A flippant, thoughtless apology wouldn't cut it. Did he not know her at all?

Her blue eyes sparked with irritation. 'Oh, I know you're a prick and I know you're probably sorry, but I don't give a shit. Did you think that sorry excuse for an apology would somehow eradicate eighteen years of abandonment?'

It was probably too much, but she was now on a roll. 'I don't want you here. I don't want you on my team.'

Sean's eyes never wavered. Her anger seemed to simply bounce straight off him.

'Just what the fuck are you doing here, Sean... and don't give me that shite about you just happening to be available? Wasn't there anyone else who could come?'

For the third time, he shrugged broad shoulders and fixed her with the exact same eyes as her son. 'Okay, cards on the table - I wanted to come.'

'Are you out of your fucking tree?' Her voice held more than mere disgust. It held astonishment. 'After everything? You wanted to come... after everything?'

'Look,' he began, 'What if I stood up and let you knee me in the balls? Would that make a difference?'

Her lips thinned. 'Still think you're a comedian?' She forced a smile. She had to maintain some semblance of control. 'You weren't funny then and you're certainly not funny now. I want you gone. Immediately. Get on the phone to Manchester and find a replacement.'

He noted that her smile didn't quite reach her eyes. His demeanour suddenly changed. He was no longer contrite. Standing up and pushing the chair back with his legs, he looked down on her. With a seriousness that belied his previous manner, he said, 'Superintendent Sullivan, if you want me back in Manchester then go through the proper channels yourself. I'm here because I want to help find the fucker that murdered four citizens of Manchester and I'm prepared to work round the clock. I'm going nowhere unless someone with more wellie than you orders me to.' He paused and watched her as his words sank in. He saw her swallow and drop her eyes. 'You get on the phone. You make arrangements to replace me. Get my boss to order me back. Meantime, I've got a job to do, so – if there's nothing else – then, please excuse me.'

With a straight back and great dignity, he left the office.

When he was gone, and after he had gently closed the door behind him, Lorrie had to fight extremely hard to prevent herself from swiping her arm across her desk and knocking everything to the floor. Sean Kelly was back in her life and that terrified her. It terrified her because, for eighteen long years, it was all she had ever wanted.

Why couldn't she hate him? He had treated her badly, she should hate him. But, she still wanted him. How stupid was that? He had almost destroyed her once before and she was sure that his very presence in her life would be the catalyst for completely destroying her now.

She decided that she wouldn't make the call to Manchester. Self-preservation kicked in. How would she explain her request for an alternative Detective Inspector? No one knew of their history. No one knew that Sean Kelly was the father of her son. She had kept that knowledge secret for eighteen years and she wasn't prepared to let the cat out of the bag now. She wasn't sure if admitting a past affair with a superior officer would have any repercussions. She wasn't sure if any potential consequences of such an admission would include an undermining of her current position. The ramifications could adversely affect her career and she wasn't prepared to take that risk.

Simon – her ever faithful DI – was once again in the office. He had sensed something amiss, and it had brought him to her.

He was shocked at her appearance. She was always so controlled – emotionless even – and he was at a loss for words.

Lorrie saw the shocked expression on his face, and it sobered her and brought her to her senses.

'I'm having a moment, Simon. No need to worry. I'm all right.'

He stepped in and closed the door. 'Is it him? Is it Kelly? What's he done?'

'Please don't ask, Simon. Trust me. I'm okay.'

'You know I'd never betray your confidence, Guv. If there's anything...?'

'No,' she shook her head emphatically. 'There's nothing.'

'Fine.' He wasn't convinced but he accepted what she said.

'Why don't you show the videos to the new lot, and I'll be out in a minute. I just need a moment and I'll be right there.'

Alone, once more, Lorrie placed her forehead on the desk and cried. They were restrained tears. Although she had broken down, she had the wisdom to realise that she had to maintain some control. If she gave in, if she succumbed to the true depth of her emotion, she would completely disintegrate. She would sob and weep and have a hysterical breakdown. The restrained tears, therefore, told her that she was capable, after all, of coping with Sean Kelly waltzing into her life.

# DAY THREE: MORNING

'Can you give me a lift to university please, mum?'

'What's up with your bike?' Lorrie swallowed her third cup of coffee and avoided looking at her son. He was so much like his father and her emotions were still so very raw and she was afraid he would read the pain in her eyes.'

'I've got a couple of boxes of stuff to take to the lab and they won't fit on the bike.'

'Sure, Ollie, but we have to get going now. I can't be late this morning.'

With the boxes loaded in the boot and Lorrie and Ollie both strapped into their seats, they were soon off to Brunel.

'Colin's acting a bit weird,' Ollie said matter-of-fact. 'You two had another falling out?'

'Course not,' Lorrie lied. 'Anyway, I thought you'd be off to work with him this morning? He changed his mind about you working with him I gather?'

Ollie nodded. 'I'm going in this afternoon. Just got a bit of catching up to do first.'

'Are they pleased with what you're doing...? Your research?'

'I guess so. I'm left pretty much to my own devices. I think I scare the professors off. They're not that smart. They may have doctorates and other qualifications coming out of their arses, but I can run rings around them. Except for Professor Napier. He's the only one with more than two brain cells to rub together.'

'You enjoying life at university?' she asked. 'Only you very rarely talk to me, Ollie.'

He was a little discomfited. It seemed she wasn't going to give up on the concerned mother act. 'You're always too busy,' he replied, masking his impatience. 'No need to sweat it, mum. I'm doing okay. All is well with the world.'

His words sank in, but Lorrie wasn't about to let it go. He was a captive audience, for once, and she was going to take the opportunity to talk to her son.

'What's it all for, Ollie? What do you want to do afterwards?' She was genuinely interested. It was usual for Ollie not to give much away. He had always been a very introverted boy. He never shared his feelings, and Lorrie couldn't remember the last time he had spoken to her about his desires, his dreams, or his plans. Perhaps the short journey to the university was the wrong time for a heart to heart, but it was an opportunity not to be missed.

'I don't know,' he replied. 'I've not given it much thought.'

Lorrie could see his mind was elsewhere. She determined to make more time for him and to try and pin him down about his future. He will have finished his PhD this time next year and then what? It pained her to realise that she hadn't the first clue about what her son wanted to do with his life.

Lorrie pulled the car over to the side of the road but kept the engine running.

Ollie made to get out. 'Will you be home for dinner tonight?' he asked.

'I don't think so, love. Things are a bit hectic.' She couldn't fail to see the disappointment and resentment in his eyes as he closed the door and turned away.

THERE WAS NEWS FROM Ricky. Preliminary toxicology results had, at last, given them their first clue.

Lorrie arranged to meet the two DIs at Ricky's lab and quickly drove over to the large glass and shiny steel building that housed the state-of-the-art autopsy suites and forensic facilities owned and run by him.

Inside, Lorrie made her way through security towards the rear of the building - where the dissecting tables with integral downdraft systems, grossing stations, hydro-aspirators and rows of stainless steel sinks lived - where she found the pathologist and her two officers waiting.

'Don't get your hopes up too high,' Ricky warned as she strode towards them. 'It's not much.'

'I'll take anything you can give me, Ricky.' Lorrie purposefully avoided looking at either of the DIs at his side and focussed her full attention on the pathologist.

The smell in the room wasn't nasty – the high-tech ventilation system removed much of the recognisable smell of death – but it was unpleasant, and Lorrie regretted not asking Ricky to meet at her of-fice.

'We got a hit on botulinum toxin,' he said. 'Surprised the hell out of me, I can tell you.'

'Isn't that what's used in Botox injections?'

Ricky nodded at Sean. 'Difference here is that the levels are through the roof.'

'Why are you surprised?' Lorrie asked.

'It's too easy and we found it too fast.'

'But, surely, you would expect initial screening to find the common toxins? That doesn't usually take too long.'

Ricky nodded. 'Exactly, but I'm flabbergasted that botulinum is one of the culprits.'

'One of the culprits?' Lorrie arched a brow.

'It's obviously been used as a carrier of sorts because what's not explained is the time frame from contamination to death. There are a couple of other molecules at play. There's evidence of some sort of a chemical reaction with the botulinum that might explain the rapid devastation and sudden deaths. Botulinum can be deadly in its own right - a tiny amount can go a long way - but it kills a lot more slowly than this bastard.'

'What are these other molecules?' Lorrie was fascinated, despite the horror.

Ricky shrugged. 'Don't have a fucking clue... Pardon my French.'

'Just how clever is this fucker?' Sean asked.

'Very clever, DI Kelly. Very clever indeed. I'd go so far as to say he or she is a bloody genius. You can't help but admire the sheer creativity of the work.'

'I don't think the families of the victims have much admiration,' Simon said, 'And, tell me, doctor – what is there to admire about the grotesque way the bodies are demolished by this super poison?'

Ricky was nonplussed. Simon Grant wasn't usually so confrontational. Surely, he must realise that he'd only been talking from a scientific point of view.

Lorrie saw the danger. An argument was about to break out. She interrupted and brought the subject back on point. 'You've done the PMs on the four from Manchester?' she asked Ricky.

Ricky brought his eyes swinging round to Lorrie. 'I've overseen them all. Didn't do any cutting myself, but I'm doing what I can to be the common eyes and ears between all the victims. The Home Office has confirmed me as lead pathologist and I'm meeting with the operations co-ordinator in half an hour to make sure everything is dotted and crossed.'

'So, anything new on these latest autopsies?'

'Nothing from the bodies. Same old, same old I'm afraid. Preliminary reports on all the victims are up on the system but I'm going to go through everything with a fine-tooth comb before I sign off on any of them.'

'Okay. Thanks, Ricky. Keep us in the loop.' Lorrie signalled to Simon and Sean to follow her from the room.

The fresh air in the corridor smelled sweet and delicious after the stale unpleasantness of the autopsy suite. She spoke as she walked towards the main reception. 'Higgins and Wilson can go through the various databases that counter terrorism has access to and see if any of what Ricky said triggers anything. Perhaps they'll pick up on some chatter.' Lorrie tried to avoid eye contact with Sean. She couldn't trust herself. She feared she would either punch him on the mouth or kiss him. 'Let's cover all the bases. We still can't rule out terrorism.'

'You think this might be run of the mill La La land Jihadists?' Sean asked.

Simon answered before Lorrie could respond. 'We can't rule anything out. There's no point having Tweedle Dum and Tweedle Dee sitting twiddling their thumbs when they can run down a lead.'

'Play nice, Simon. Our colleagues from SO15 warrant a bit of respect.' It was a slap down, though a gentle one.

'Yes, Guv.'

'What do you want me to do, Superintendent?'

Lorrie knew exactly what she wanted Sean to do but she bit back the honest retort and said instead, 'Go check on what Ricky's forensics have come up with on all the belongings. We're still looking for whatever it was that got the poison into their system. Find me something.'

That wasn't the job for a DI and Sean's expression spoke volumes.

Lorrie chewed on her bottom lip. She knew what he was thinking, and he was right.

She halted in mid stride and looked directly at him for the first time. 'Look,' she began. 'This is important, and I need your experienced eyes on it. You won't miss it if it's there. I know I'm sending you off to do a little bit of grunge work, but...'

Sean grinned easily. 'Okay. Okay. I get it.'

'I don't want anyone else looking,' she persisted. 'I need you to go through everything.'

'It's okay. I said that I get it,' he reassured.

'Thanks.' She lost the battle with herself and found herself staring deep into his eyes. She was aware that something had changed with him. There was a tortured sadness there.

Sean stared right back at her, and something ignited between them. It took both of them by surprise.

Sean cleared his throat and dropped his gaze. 'I'll get right to it.'

Simon watched Sean's retreating back as he made his way past the reception and back along the corridor. There was something going on. He turned to Lorrie. 'You two got history?' he asked. He was still convinced that Sean Kelly was the reason for Lorrie's behaviour of late. 'Only...'

'Not your business, DI Grant.'

'It's just...'

'Not your business.'

Simon took the direct hint. 'Sure, Guv. Not my business.'

Back at New Scotland Yard, and fifteen minutes standing over the sink in the toilet, staring at her reflection in the mirror, had calmed her down sufficiently to engage her brain. Sean being back should mean nothing. One of the first things she'd noticed about him was the wedding ring. He was still married. She was married, for God's sake. So, what was that thing between them – that spark? She knew that he'd felt it too.

That spark was a threat. She had to get everything into perspective, or she would be no use to anyone, least of all her team.

Eighteen years was a long time to get over the hurt that someone caused. It was more than enough time to eradicate the pain and humiliation of rejection. She had been twenty years old then – nothing more than a child – and now she was a full-grown woman with responsibilities. There was no way on God's green earth that she was getting mixed up with Sean Kelly again. But, it still hurt, and she still felt the bitterness of his rejection, but there was that something to now contend with.

She attempted to harden her heart. She forced herself to remember. He'd wanted her to get an abortion. His voice had been cold and hateful. When she'd refused and begged him to leave his wife, Sean Kelly had laughed. The bastard had laughed at her. If he'd punched her, she couldn't have felt more pain than she had at that moment. So, why had she thought of him constantly over the years? Why had she lain under Colin as he took her and thought only of Sean?

She absently rubbed her injured wrist and stood back from the sink. She could certainly pick them, she thought ruefully. Sean and Colin were the antithesis of each other. Sean was tall and dark and built like the proverbial brick shithouse, whereas Colin was slim and fair and at least four inches shorter than Sean. But, there was a similarity – they both knew how to be selfish, cruel bastards.

At that precise moment, she made up her mind to leave Colin. If there was an unconscious thought that it would make the way clear for Sean, then she wasn't aware of it. All she knew was that she was fed up with the daily anxiety of living with a psychopath. Sean Kelly being back in her life had absolutely nothing to do with it.

The phone trilled in her pocket. The caller ID showed Colin's name. Screw him, she thought, and rejected the call. It rang again immediately and, this time she accepted it. Far better to get it over with, she thought on a sigh.

'I can't talk now, Colin. I'm busy,' she almost barked into the phone.

His voice was conciliatory on the other end of the phone. 'I'm just worried about you,' he said. 'We haven't had a chance to talk after...'

'After what, Colin? After nearly breaking my wrist?'

'Don't be like that, Lorrie. You know I'd never intentionally hurt you.'

Lorrie didn't answer him.

'Let's go out for dinner tonight and I can make it up to you.'

How many dinners had there been over the years, she thought? How many bunches of flowers? How many pieces of jewellery used to try and show how sorry he was for the damage done by his words and his behaviour?

'I don't want to go to dinner with you. I don't want to talk, and I don't want to hear how sorry you are.' Lorrie kept her voice low, fearful someone would walk in and overhear her. 'Leave me alone, Colin. I've taken a lot from you over the years, and I'm fed up. I'm fed up with being your emotional punch-bag and, now that you've actually laid a hand on me...'

'Do you have to be such a cow, Lorrie?' Colin was now on the verge of blowing up. His mood could always flip instantly. 'I hear Sean Kelly is down from Manchester. Is that why you're being such a fucking bitch?'

Lorrie was so shocked that, instead of replying, she disconnected the call. It didn't surprise her that her husband knew about Sean. He had an uncanny way of finding out everything. It was almost as if he had a camera following her wherever she went. No part of her life had ever been private from Colin.

That settled it. As far as she was concerned, Colin was history. She should have felt a sense of relief but, instead, a feeling of dread washed over her. Who knew what her husband was capable of?

# DAY THREE: AFTERNOON

S ean Kelly surveyed the evidence bags and compared each bag with the information already available on the individual forensic reports. There weren't very many items with results attached. There were just too many things to test. It would be at least a week before they could be reassured that everything had been forensically examined for any and all trace evidence including poison and drugs. Sean put his brain into gear and tried to, through a process of elimination, identify items that ought to go to the front of the queue.

The majority of the possessions came from the suitcases of the eight people who died on the aeroplane and consisted of items you would expect to find in suitcases headed for somewhere warm. There were no surprises. Suntan lotion and various toiletries had either got the all clear forensically, or results were still pending. These specific items appeared to have had a lot of attention but, so far, there was nothing to show for the effort. Of the other items from the suitcases, Sean had no feel for anything being particularly relevant. The same applied to items bagged from the carry-on luggage.

Evidence bags holding items found in twelve cars were a little more interesting and Sean took a little more time looking through them. He wondered why the items from only twelve cars were available. He knew that the total of thirteen London victims had all been driving at some point directly before their deaths. So, why only twelve cars? He made a note to himself to chase that up as soon as he was finished.

There were no sets of car keys kept with the belongings. The keys for all the cars were with the teams at the forensic pounds at Charlton and Perivale. He would check with both pounds later to determine how the examination of the cars was progressing.

He turned his attention back to the evidence collection. Although he could find nothing in the evidence bags to suggest anything out of the ordinary, a picture was beginning to form in his mind regarding a potential link. It was tenuous at best, but it was something worth running past Lorrie. That's if she would listen to him or even give him the time of day.

He had been shocked at just how much she seemed to hold against him. To his mind, there was nothing wrong with him being in London. He had felt no qualms about the temporary transfer. He had, in fact, been looking forward to seeing her again. Over the years, he had heard good things about Lorrie Sullivan. He felt more than a little bit proud of her. Not for a minute, did he imagine that the events of eighteen years earlier would still be affecting her.

He didn't understand what the big deal was. People have affairs. Women get pregnant. She should've been over it by now.

Even as Sean thought those things, he knew he was being unfair to her. She had been young and quite vulnerable. It was only supposed to be a little bit of fun, but he thought that she might have fallen for him in a big way. To compound matters, he could have lost his job for having a relationship with her. She was a rookie PC, and he was an experienced sergeant. He had thought, at the time, that the pregnancy was bound to doom the pair of them but, as it happened, it ended their affair and put an end to any risk.

Thankfully, Lorrie never told anyone about their affair or that he was the father of her child.

She was still beautiful, he mused. Older and a bit fuller in the figure, but still quite the loveliest woman he'd ever seen. He knew that she was happily married to some rich businessman.

He smiled ruefully to himself and packed away the evidence bags. The fact that she was happily married was just as well, because he might have been tempted to find out if the old chemistry was still there.

When he arrived back at the major incident room, he found her busy scribbling on the board, adding snippets of information and drawing multi-coloured lines from the photographs to the new pieces of information.

He watched her for a moment. Although the room was full of people, she seemed to stand alone, and she gave the impression that she was oblivious to everything but what she was doing. Her hair had been shaken loose and hung in untidy tendrils around her face. Her features were screwed up with concentration and her little pink tongue protruded between her teeth. He felt his heart skip at the sight of her.

She didn't hear him approach above the hustle and bustle of the room and only became aware of him when he picked up a red marker pen and began drawing a car-like shape next to each photograph.

Lorrie immediately ceased her activity. 'What are you doing?' she asked.

'I'm drawing cars.'

'Why?'

'Because, I think that cars are an important link.'

'You do?' She looked sceptical. 'Owning a car isn't a link, Sean. That's like saying...' She pondered a moment. 'That's like saying wearing a hat is a link.'

'Exactly.'

'I'm afraid that you'll need to explain yourself.'

'About the hat being a link?'

'They weren't wearing hats.'

'I know. So – that's not a link.'

'But, the cars are?'

He nodded. 'They are.'

Lorrie shook her head and called across the room. 'Simon, come over here.'

Simon dutifully trotted over.

'DI Kelly has a theory,' she said, with evident scepticism. 'Tell Simon about the cars, Sean.'

'I've not said that I know anything specific about the cars – not yet anyway. All I'm sure about, at this juncture, is that there are cars.'

'Yes, and we're having the cars examined,' Simon said, confused as to where this was leading.

'It's not unusual for the victims to have been in a car, Sean.'

'In a car? No, I guess not, but don't you think it's strange that every single victim had been driving a car shortly before they died?'

'Not really,' Lorrie said. She was getting bored. 'But, if it will please you, we'll keep the drawings on the board for now.'

Sean nodded, but he was obviously annoyed that he wasn't being taken seriously. 'It's tenuous, I know, but I'd like to give it a bit more thought. Is it okay if I run with this a bit?'

Lorrie had no opportunity to reply.

'Guv?' DS Lovell approached at a gallop. 'There's a victim in Glasgow.'

Lorrie turned from Sean and faced Sonia. 'Glasgow?'

'Yes, Guv. No real details as yet.'

'That's eighteen,' Simon said through gritted teeth. 'Glasgow? It beggars belief.'

Lorrie, to Lovell – 'Get me everything on it and then get Doctor Burton to liaise directly with Glasgow. I want him involved from the get-go.' To Sean and Simon – 'You two get your fingers out and find me something. And, Sean?'

'Yes, Superintendent?'

'Run with the car theory. I trust your instincts.'

'Thanks.' Both Sean and Simon were a little confused at her change of attitude. One minute she was dissing the very idea that driving a car was important, and now she was intimating it might very well be a viable theory.

Lorrie read the confusion in their eyes and shrugged. 'We've got nothing else. May as well see where it takes us.'

Lorrie wasn't convinced about the cars being a lead, but the one thing she was above all else was a good copper. She always followed up on every hint of clue, every whisper of evidence.

Lorrie gave them both a curt nod, excused herself and headed back to her office. She left behind two DIs wondering what their next move would be.

Sean wondered if he ought to head straight to the car pounds or wait to see what there was from Glasgow. Simon wondered what he ought to do and say about the obvious tension between his Guv and Kelly.

'You two obviously know each other from before,' he said to Sean. 'Only, I don't think she likes you very much.'

'That, my friend, is probably the understatement of the century.'

'She's a good boss, although she does have a habit of taking a hard-line.'

'I don't doubt it. She's certainly taking a hard-line with me.'

'Any particular reason for that?'

Sean shrugged. 'Beats me.'

'She worked in Manchester when she joined the force. Do you know her from back then?'

'I knew her for a few months.'

Simon wondered why Sean wasn't elaborating. It was unusual not to make the most of past acquaintances in the force.

Sean moved the subject along. He said, 'I'm pleased that she got this gig. I hear that there were a lot of names in the hat. Major Crimes with a national remit is a nifty job. Good on her, I say.'

'She earned it.'

'This her first real case?'

Simon nodded. 'And, if we don't catch this fucker, and soon, I think that it, very well, may be her last.'

'Then,' Sean smiled, 'we'd better help her catch him.'

WHEN RICKY WALKED INTO her office later that afternoon, Lorrie could see the worry on his face.

He came straight to the point. 'The death in Glasgow caused a pile up at junction 28 of the M8. Fourteen seriously hurt and three dead. The woman... our victim... was driving her car and she lost control and veered across the carriageway. She was found with hardly a mark on her. I think the loss of control and the accident that followed was the direct result of her collapsing and dying at the wheel. I had the officers and paramedics who'd been at the scene describe to me how she'd looked when they pried her out of the wreckage.'

'And?'

'And,' Ricky frowned. 'She's a dead ringer for the others.'

Lorrie waited a beat, digesting his words. She then asked, 'Where had she been?'

'That's the kicker...' Ricky sat down. His feet were killing him. 'She'd just flown from Heathrow to Glasgow, had picked up her car and was on her way home. She'd parked at Glasgow. We've no information on whether she went straight to the car park or if she had a coffee or if she visited the toilet. CCTV will give us that, I suppose. Anyway, she collected her car and, within minutes of hitting the motorway, she was dying at the wheel and lost control.'

'Heathrow to Glasgow. Heathrow again?'

'Maybe a coincidence?'

'I don't believe in coincidence, Ricky.'

'You may have to, because I don't see how the timeline fits.'

'You have a timeline on the poison?'

Ricky pushed himself forward in the chair and explained. 'I still don't know a great deal, but I do know one thing. I know that, for all of our victims, death occurred between fifteen and forty-five minutes from ingestion of the poison. I know that because I've painstakingly tracked the poison's journey from the lips and meticulously measured and timed each cellular disruption. There's a fairly big window, but that's down to individual variables.'

'Okay, I think.' Her brow furrowed. 'What variables?'

'The amount of poison. How soon the person licked their lips. The physical condition of the victim. I could go on?'

Lorrie shook her head. 'I get it, thanks. But, no more that forty-five minutes?' He shook his head. 'Not that I've determined.'

'So, not Heathrow on this occasion?'

'Not Heathrow.'

'But, another airport... Glasgow... and a car. Sean's running with a theory... No, theory is too strong a word. Sean is running with a hunch about the fact the victims had all been driving.'

Ricky threw her a confused look. 'None of the other victims were driving when they died,' he reminded her.

'No. That's true.'

'You're thinking there's something?'

'Not me... Sean. He has a bee in his bonnet about cars being a possible link. I think he might be right.'

'Maybe it's something on the steering wheels? Hands on the wheel and then fingers brushing the lips?'

'Could be. I suppose all the steering wheels have been swabbed?'

'Soon,' Ricky replied. 'I'll chase them up... Get my lot down to the pounds. I'll insist that they prioritise. If they find something, it shouldn't matter if we can't immediately identify it. What will be crucial is finding something... anything that definitely shouldn't be there. That would certainly give us a heads up.'

'We could do with a breakthrough. Morale is plummeting with every new victim and I'm about to get my marching orders.'

'They wouldn't dare get rid of you.' Ricky was scandalised. 'You're a breath of fresh air.'

Lorrie laughed. 'Scully and Connor would have something different to say.'

'Those pair of arseholes?' He shook his head in dismay. 'Dinosaurs, the both of them.'

'Thanks, Ricky.' Lorrie's face was now straight. 'It's good to have you in my corner.'

'Always, Lorrie.'

SEAN VISITED THE FORENSIC pound at Charlton and systematically searched each of the eight cars personally, despite being told there was no need as the forensic team had already gone through them all with a fine-tooth comb. He had to admit they'd done a fine job. He found nothing. He then travelled across to Perivale pound and did the same with the other eight cars. The outcome was the same.

Swabs had already been taken of the steering wheels, so he had no need to concern himself with that. He was gratified that Lorrie and Ricky Burton had taken him seriously. It might only be a hunch, but his hunches had stood him in good stead over the years.

There was a car missing. There was a total of sixteen cars across the two pounds, but there should have been seventeen. Which one was missing? He checked his list and then he rang Simon.

'Only sixteen cars?' Simon was at a loss. 'Do you know what car is missing?'

'I thought you might know,' Sean returned. 'I've checked the list, but there are no names attached.'

'I don't know, then...Not off the top of my head. Leave it with me.'

He rang back moments later. 'I think it belongs to the girl who died in the supermarket. Looks like the stupid bastards left it in the multi-storey.'

'That's a bit of a cock-up, and no mistake.'

Simon sighed on the other end of the phone. 'I'll have their guts for garters.'

'Text me the address and I'll head over there and take a look.'

'Okay. I'll send Lovell and a couple of the forensics bods. They'll meet you there.'

'See if you can find the keys from evidence. I didn't come across them when I went through everything earlier.'

'Will do.'

The car – an old Ford Fiesta – was obviously a well-cared for and a much loved vehicle. It was immaculate both inside and out and, peering in the windows, Sean couldn't see even one piece of litter.

Sonia arrived with the keys, a forensic investigator trailing behind carrying a large case and with several pairs of white overalls draped in polythene over an arm.

'Where did you find the keys?' Sean asked Sonia, putting on a pair of gloves and taking an overall.

'In her coat pocket of all places. Someone isn't doing their job right.'

The investigator handed an overall to Sonia.

Sean said, 'Let's get the steering wheel swabbed before anything else.' He donned his own overall, pulled up the hood and pressed the key fob. The door unlocked with a double beep.

One of the two forensic investigators opened his case and extracted the equipment necessary to take and secure a swab.

To Sean, Sonia asked, 'Anything in the other cars?'

He shook his head. 'No, they did a good job on them. Let's hope the swabs flag something.'

'Fingers and toes crossed.'

'Let's have a quick look through the car before recovery takes it to the pound.'

The investigator secured the swab in his case and stood back to allow Sean and Sonia to approach the car. He then turned to his colleague and they both did a fingertip search of the garage floor immediately around the vehicle.

Sean bent at the waist and pushed his head through the front door of the car. He kept his hands folded across his chest and took a few moments to simply use his eyes to take in the interior. It was spotless. On the passenger seat were two items – the only two things visible – a class timetable and, on top, the parking ticket the victim had extracted from the barrier on entrance to the car park. He bagged and tagged both items, stepped back from the car and straightened up.

Sonia concentrated on the back seat and found nothing. 'Clean as a whistle,' she said.

'Okay,' he said to Lovell. 'Let's get back.'

NOTHING YET ON THE email?' Lorrie asked Simon. 'Or either of the videos?'

Simon shook his head.

'Anything from either of our Counter Terrorism colleagues?'

Simon shook his head once more.

'Anything from witnesses?'

Just as Simon made to shake his head again, Lorrie glowered and snapped, 'Stop shaking your head, Simon. I want answers.'

Simon subconsciously ran a hand through his mop of unruly hair. 'I'm sorry, there's nothing, Guv. Witnesses all say much the same - sudden breathing problems, clutching at throats, tongue swelling, panic, death.'

'CCTV at Brunel library? I know it's a long shot but who is going through it?'

'Annie Baxter. She's been at it for hours.'

'And...? Don't tell me... nothing?'

'Nothing.'

Where next, she wondered? What else is there to look at? What was she missing?

'Perhaps DI Kelly's hunch will pay off?'

'He doesn't have a hunch. It's not a hunch.'

'Sounds like a hunch to me.' Simon waited a beat and then asked, 'What is it with you two?'

Lorrie felt Simon's eyes on her. He really didn't have any right asking her about her private business but, for all she knew, he might think something had happened professionally. She decided to give him the benefit of the doubt.

'He was my boss, once upon a time.'

'Your boss?' Simon looked sceptical. 'He's not travelled up the ranks much, has he? Why is he still a DI at his age? Did he fuck up?'

Lorrie said nothing.

'That's it, isn't it? He fucked up and you don't trust him. I thought there was something. What did he do?'

'What did who do?' Sean walked the length of the room and raised an eyebrow at Simon.

Simon thought about it and almost replied but he stopped himself. It really wasn't any of his business. He said, 'I need to go and have a word with DS Baxter. Find out how she's getting on with the CCTV.'

Sean stood still and watched him walk away. He then turned to Lorrie.

'He was talking about me, wasn't he?'

'It was no big deal, Sean.'

'You tell him about us?'

'No!' Lorrie was shocked to her core. 'Of course not.'

'Have you told anyone? Have you told Ollie about me?'

Lorrie shook her head. 'He never asked.'

'I shouldn't have insisted on an abortion. I'm sorry.'

'For fuck's sake, Sean. I don't want this all dragged up. You have your life and I have mine. Ollie is a fantastic, clever, wonderful boy and that's all I'm prepared to say about him. He wouldn't be alive today if I'd listened to you. I don't want to discuss Ollie or the past with you again.' She waved him away. 'Just do your job and go back to Manchester and your wife.'

# DAY THREE: EVENING

The squad had a well-deserved early finish. Everyone had their orders on what to pick up in the morning and Lorrie saw her whole team out the door by six-thirty. She hoped Colin wouldn't be home from work yet. All she wanted was a quick shower and then bed. Colin being home would probably scupper that plan.

As it was, Colin wasn't home. The house was in darkness and neither Colin's car nor Ollie's bike were in the drive. Colin hadn't attempted to get hold of her on the phone again all day and she hoped he'd decided to keep out of her way for a while.

The shower, although a short one, revived her somewhat and she decided to postpone her early night until she had a glass of wine. Alcohol was what the doctor ordered, and she poured herself an extra-large Merlot.

Her mind wandered to Sean and mulled over what Simon had said. Why was he still a DI? It didn't make any sense. Sean Kelly had always been a highly ambitious officer. He should, technically, be her boss and not the other way around. It certainly was a conundrum and it piqued her interest because she wondered if his penchant for screwing young female subordinates had marked his card? Perhaps the fact that he couldn't keep his cock in his pants ruined his career prospects? The police force was, after all, quite a hypocritically puritanical institution. He was an excellent detective and had top notch leadership skills – except for screwing junior female officers, that is.

She drained her glass of wine and contemplated another. Glancing at the clock and seeing it wasn't quite nine o'clock, she allowed herself a second, small glass. She fell asleep on the sofa after the first sip.

# DAY THREE: NIGHT

Ollie arrived home and woke her just short of midnight.

Lorrie woke with a start. 'Hello, love. What time is it?' she asked on a yawn. 'I must've dropped off.'

'It's midnight.' Ollie's voice sounded strained to Lorrie's ears. 'I didn't mean to wake you.'

'You're back late. Have you been with Colin? Is he back?'

Ollie shook his head and pushed onto the sofa next to his mum. 'I saw him earlier. I don't know where he is or what he's up to.'

'What he's up to? That sounds ominous.'

'Yeah, well...'

Lorrie smiled. 'No need to worry about Colin, Ollie.'

'I'm not worried about him,' he replied curtly.

'That's okay, then.' She made to pull herself up from the sofa. 'I'd better get up the wooden stairs to bed. I'm knackered.' She got herself to her feet, but Ollie put a hand out and gently pulled her back down.

'I want to talk to you, mum. Sit a minute.' Ollie's deep set eyes sparked with something akin to anger.

'Are you mad at me for something?'

'I don't know... I might be.' He bowed his head, suddenly afraid to look at her. 'I want to ask you something and I need you to be honest with me.'

She was intrigued and a little anxious. 'I always try to be honest, Ollie. What is it? What do you want to ask me?'

'It's about my father.'

Had she heard right? 'What? I don't understand.'

He turned to face her. 'My father. I want you to tell me about him.'

Lorrie was suddenly overwhelmed, and all the air left her body. 'You've never asked about him before. Why now?'

Ollie's expression changed and his eyes shifted. 'Because...'

Oh, she got it. 'Colin told you?'

'That he's here in London? That he's working with you? Yes, Colin happened to mention it. He thought I knew. He thought you would have told me.'

'I bet he did.' Lorrie reached for her glass and swallowed the remaining wine. She waved the empty glass at Ollie, gesturing for a refill.

Ollie pulled himself to his feet and obliged. He handed her back the glass.

She took a sip and said, 'I don't know what you want me to say, darling. He appeared out of the blue. I had no idea he was coming down from Manchester.'

Ollie bowed his head once more so she couldn't see the flash of mixed emotions flit across his face. He struggled to keep his composure. Up until the moment when Colin let slip that the man who was responsible for his very life was working with his mother, he had never allowed himself to give him a moment's thought for most of his eighteen years. Now? Well, now his father was all he could think about.

'Does he want to see me?' Was that hope Lorrie heard in his voice? 'Has he even asked about me?'

Lorrie stalled. She didn't want to discuss Sean with her son, and she didn't want to have to lie. 'Can't we talk about this in the morning? I'm really tired, Ollie.'

Ollie was having none of it. 'Just answer me, mum. Does he want to see me? Did he ask about me?'

*Shit. Shit. Shit.* What was she supposed to say?

'We've been busy. The case...'

'Fuck the case.' Ollie threw himself to his feet. 'Just, for once, can you please put me first?'

'Ollie!' To say she was shocked was an understatement. He had never spoken to her like that before.

'Sorry. I'm sorry.' He sat back down next to her on the sofa and took her hand. 'It was just such a shock when Colin mentioned him to me. I've been thinking about him – my father – all afternoon. It's been doing my head in.'

'Look, Ollie.' Lorrie removed her hand from his and turned to fully face him. 'I would've told you all about him, but you never asked. You never seemed interested. I tried to bring him up a few times over the years, but you were happy and content and it didn't seem right... Not if you really weren't all that bothered.'

He had been bothered. What young boy wouldn't wonder about his father? Truth be told, he had never permitted himself to bring him up to his mother. He could see – even from very early on – that he would hurt her if he asked. He chose not to bring him up out of fear of the consequences.

It was true - his mother had briefly mentioned him a few times - but Ollie always had the distinct impression that she didn't want Ollie to know anything about him. He felt obliged to push him totally from his mind.

'I thought it would hurt you. I didn't want to hurt you,' he said – which was wholly true.

The wine she'd consumed was hot and bitter at the back of Lorrie's throat. She had to swallow hard to stop herself from vomiting. This boy – this much beloved child of hers – hadn't wanted to hurt her. He'd smothered his natural curiosity about his father, his need to know, because she might be hurt by his questions. She could actually feel her heart breaking in her chest.

Ollie avoided looking at her. He didn't want to make eye contact with her. He was angry and hurt and disappointed.

She could see the anxiety in the thinning of his lips and the clenching of his jaw. She was heart sorry. How could she tell him that his father probably wanted nothing to do with him? How could she tell him that he'd wanted her to abort him? She couldn't. She started to lie and soon, the lies took over.

'He wants to see you, Ollie... of course he does. He's always wanted to see you. It was me... I stopped him from having any contact with you. I'm so sorry.'

Ollie's head reared up and he stared her straight in the face. For a fleeting moment Lorrie thought she saw pure hatred in his eyes. But no. She'd been wrong. Her son didn't hate her. That wasn't hate in his eyes.

'I'm sorry, darling. He hurt me. I just wanted to hurt him back.'

Lorrie determined right then and there that her son was going to meet his father, and, by God, his father was going to like it. She'd kill Sean Kelly before she allowed him to reject her boy a second time.

Ollie left her drinking in the lounge and went up to his bedroom. He thought she had just lied to him. He thought that every word out of her mouth had been a lie. He knew her so well and he was confused as to why she felt the need to be so dishonest with him. Did the lies matter? He thought not, but it probably meant that his father didn't want to see him. He probably had never wanted to see him. He thought he could live with that, but not before he looked the man in the eye and not before he asked him why he had abandoned him.

# DAY FOUR: MORNING

Ellie struggled to bend and pick up the scattered toys on the floor. Being thirty two weeks pregnant with twins was proving to be quite a trial, especially when her two year old daughter refused to pick up after herself.

Peter, her harassed husband, walked into the room carrying a struggling bundle of energy in his arms.

'Can you take this little monster so I can shave and finish getting ready for work?' He deposited his daughter onto her feet and smiled as she tore off across the floor and began emptying the toy-box her mother had only recently filled.

'I'm having a scan this morning, remember?' Ellie sighed and plopped down onto the soft sofa. 'You will be there, won't you?'

Peter nodded. 'I have a meeting first thing, but I promise I'll meet you at the hospital. What time is your mum getting here?'

Ellie glanced at the clock on the mantle. 'Twenty minutes or so. She has to get the bus.'

'Okay. So... ten thirty at the hospital?'

Ellie nodded. 'Don't be late.'

THE MAJOR INCIDENT room was heaving. Lorrie's team had grown since the day before – the Assistant Commissioner having seconded twelve additional officers to help with the case – and everyone was busy introducing themselves and catching up.

Lorrie called for silence, and, after a few seconds, the noise abated, and all eyes turned to her.

'Right,' Lorrie said. 'Let's summarise for the newbies.' She turned to the photo board. 'We have, as of now, eighteen victims. We know that they were all poisoned. The toxin of choice for the Reaper has Botulin somewhere in the mix, but there are a couple of other nasty little fuckers in the mix as well.' She let that sink in. 'All of our victims died horribly. All died within forty-five minutes of ingesting the toxin.' She turned to Sean. 'How has the examination of the cars gone?'

'Still in progress, but trace has been found on steering wheels, seatbelt buckles and the inside door handles. The boffins say the traces are minute, but it's definitely traces of our poison.'

'So,' Lorrie went on, 'all the victims had already made contact with the toxin before they got out of their cars. That should narrow it down for us a bit. We know, then, that it didn't come from inside the aeroplane, wasn't somewhere in the hospitals etc.' She flicked her gaze to Simon. 'I want you and DS Lovell to re-interview all the witnesses and the family members.'

'Guv?' Simon looked confused. 'We've already got detailed statements.'

She nodded, agreeing, 'But, we don't have the answers yet, do we? Concentrate on that fifteen to forty-five minute window. I want exact chronologies of where the victims were and what they were doing. I want every second accounted for.'

'That's a big job, Guv.'

'Take four of the newbies with you. I want it done and on my desk by tonight.'

She turned back to the photo board. 'I don't think he is going to be satisfied with eighteen victims,' she said. 'Our profile of the killer leaves a lot to be desired, but one thing we can all agree on is that he's a clever bastard. He has created a poison that has our boffins scratching their heads. Botulin... Botulism... Whatever, is a very dangerous toxin but it takes hours, sometimes days to kill. This kills within forty-five minutes. As far as we know we have one hundred percent mortality. You get it on your lips, and it will kill you.'

A hand went up and Lorrie gestured for the officer to speak.

'There are victims in London, Manchester and Glasgow? How...?'

'We don't know how,' Lorrie interjected impatiently. 'You'll note the coloured asterisks next to the photos?'

Heads nodded around the room.

'So far we have three groups... Airport, hospital and supermarket.' We don't think the supermarket death is particularly related to the actual shop as we now know the victim was poisoned before she entered. I'm not ruling out the airport or the hospitals as the majority of victims have these locations in common.'

Lorrie picked up a folder from the table in front of her but her injured wrist couldn't tolerate the weight and she dropped the folder to the floor, scattering its contents. She bent to retrieve the papers, and everyone took the opportunity to converse with those around them. Everyone was anxious to discuss their hunches, their thoughts.

Lorrie straightened up. 'Quiet down.' Her eyes panned around the room, and she then turned and looked once more at Sean. 'DI Kelly, I want you to take DS Baxter and some newbies and run through the forensics on the belongings again. I know it's a pain, but you're familiar with where we're up to with them and you know what's still pending. I want you to further prioritise. It's taking much too long to identify what poisoned them.'

Sean nodded.

'Two of you newbies... I don't care who...will go through the two videos. I want fresh eyes on them. Find me something no one else has noticed.'

The briefing ended and everyone went about their allotted tasks. An hour later Sean knocked on Lorrie's office door. She was distracted and it took her a few seconds to notice him standing in front of her desk.

She blushed at the sight of him – out of pure embarrassment at the promise she had made on his behalf to her son the night before. She didn't know how she was going to broach the subject with him.

If Sean noticed her heightened colour, he made no show of it.

'I notice you're in a lot of pain with that wrist of yours,' he said. 'I think you ought to go get it x-rayed.'

'My wrist?' She automatically tugged her jacket sleeve further down her arm, hiding the bruises. 'It's fine.'

'It's not fine, Lorrie. I'll run you to hospital. I don't think you should be driving until you get it looked at.'

Her temper flared. 'Who died and made you my keeper? My wrist is fine.'

'It's not,' he repeated, choosing to ignore her annoyance.

'You don't have time to run me anywhere,' she said. 'I gave you a job to do and that's more important than my wrist.'

'I've left Baxter in charge of my lot of newbies. They'll be okay for a few hours. I really think you should go to the hospital.'

Lorrie considered his words. She really didn't think she needed an x-ray, but she liked the idea of being alone with him for a couple of hours. It would give her the chance to bring up Ollie.

'Okay,' she said, surprising him with her sudden change of heart.

'Okay? Right. Come on, then.'

ELLIE WAS SO VERY GRATEFUL to her mum. She was a God-send. Without her, Ellie didn't know how she would cope. Peter was a brilliant husband and a fantastic father, but only her mum knew exactly what was needed to ensure she rested or had a little bit of time to herself. This pregnancy was taking its toll. She was tired almost all of the time and she couldn't wait until the twins were born.

Getting in and out of the car was bad enough, but squeezing her enormous bump behind the steering wheel was almost an impossibility. Her trip to the hospital for the scan was probably going to be the last time she got behind the wheel until after the babies were born.

The journey to the hospital took forty minutes. It was a pleasant drive and she arrived in good time. She drove towards the car park, took a ticket and waited until the barrier rose before driving through. A car at the barrier next to her stalled as it made to move forward and caught Ellie's attention.

She turned and caught sight of a stern-faced but beautiful blonde sitting in the passenger seat next to an irate male driver. It looked as if they were arguing.

SEAN DROVE THROUGH the barrier and then turned to look at her. She had just told him that Ollie wanted to see him and he could see that she was desperate to read something in his face that would give her an idea of what he felt at her words.

'Say something,' she demanded.

'I don't know what to say,' he replied.

'I've just told you that your son wants to see you and you're stuck for words?'

'I certainly wasn't expecting you to say that to me. It'll take me a moment to digest it.'

Sean focussed once more and found an empty space and reversed the car into it. He shut off the engine and turned fully in his seat and waited.

She said, 'I think it's a bad idea but it's what Ollie wants.'

'Okay.'

'Okay?'

'If that's what he wants.'

Lorrie resisted the urge to slap him. He was being so unemotional about it all. Her anger felt like a bitter pill, and she had to swallow it down before she did something so terrible, she'd probably lose her job.

'You could at least look as if you give a shit,' she spat.

Sean felt a flash of shame. Truth be told, he was in shock. He knew he should look pleased, should show some enthusiasm, but her words had astounded him.

'You told him I was down from Manchester?'

Lorrie shook her head. 'My husband told him.'

'He did? Why would he do something like that?'

Lorrie refrained from answering. It was none of Sean Kelly's business why her husband told Ollie.

'So, you'll see him?'

Sean shrugged. 'I suppose so.'

'Good.'

DESPITE THE FRIGID cold of the winter morning air, Ellie felt hot. As she made her way from the car park, her heart began to hammer in her chest and she felt breathless. She reached the main entrance and stopped to attempt to catch her breath.

Ellie saw the blonde again at the main entrance. She was impatiently tapping her foot waiting on her companion to catch up with her. When she struggled through the automatic doors, Ellie felt the blonde's eyes suddenly rivet on her face. The woman looked worried.

Everything started to feel strange. Ellie felt her lips burning and her mouth was suddenly parched. She was finding it difficult to breathe. In a mad panic, she clutched at her huge belly and went into a mad panic.

'My babies, my babies,' she managed to gasp before her legs gave way.

Lorrie caught the woman before she hit the ground. The woman's weight snapped Lorrie's injured wrist and it was now, definitely, broken. She lowered the desperately freaked and terrified woman to the floor and knelt beside her.

Lorrie struggled to keep her on the floor. She was bucking and simultaneously attempting to rip open her own throat. Lorrie lifted her head and screamed for Sean.

Sean loped towards them and hunkered down.

'Call nine, nine, nine,' Lorrie ordered. 'She can't breathe. Her tongue...'

'We're at the hospital,' Sean argued. 'I'll find a doctor.' He made to move off.

Lorrie screamed his name again. 'Sean, no! Call 999. Paramedics will be at A&E. It's quicker.'

Sean understood what Lorrie was trying to say. She had realised that the 999 dispatcher would immediately send the paramedics parked outside A&E straight over. They could get there in under a minute.'

Lorrie saw that the woman had stopped breathing. She was unconscious.

As Sean made the 999 call, Lorrie struggled to force a finger into her mouth in an attempt to shift the swollen tongue sufficiently to open her airway. She took a handkerchief from her pocket and placed it over the woman's mouth and tried to blow air through it and down her throat, but it was obvious from the get go that no air would get past the grotesquely swollen tongue. She then felt for a pulse and, finding none, began rapid chest compressions. The bones in her injured wrist jarred and the pain was unbearable, but she kept pressing, kept pumping.

Her voice was shrill as she ordered the onlookers back and, without pausing and, whilst continuing the compressions, screamed at Sean – 'I need something sharp. I need a knife.'

Sean – his mobile phone still held to his ear – turned quizzical eyes on her.

'She's not breathing. Her babies are dying.' Lorrie could no longer shout or scream out the words. She panted with the exertion of the task at hand. 'Emergency tracheotomy,' she gasped. 'Knife and a ball point pen.'

A woman on the edge of the watching crowd emptied the contents of her handbag onto the floor and picked out a ball-point pen. Another onlooker knelt by Lorrie's side and handed her his Swiss army knife.

Ellie was cyanosed. Her lips were blue, and her chest was still. The two tiny babies in her womb battered and kicked against her abdomen and Lorrie knew they truly were dying - suffocating inside their failing mother. It was all very well for Lorrie to keep the heart pumping, but if the blood wasn't oxygenated then the chest compressions would be to no avail.

'Put the phone down, Sean, and take over from me.'

Sean immediately obeyed and Lorrie made a grab for the knife and broke apart the about to attempt an emergency tracheotomy. She didn't think twice about it. She'd never attempted such a thing before, but she'd been at the emergency aid training and had a general idea of what to do. She knew she could get it wrong, but those two babies needed oxygen. She didn't believe she could save the woman, but she would be damned if she wasn't going to attempt to save the babies.

Sean felt a rib break under his hands. He didn't give it a second thought. A fractured rib was the least of their worries. He looked to Lorrie and said, 'They're on their way. There's no need to do this. It's too dangerous.'

'We can't wait,' Lorrie said calmly back at him. 'I have to do this.'

And, she did it. No hesitation. No fumbling.

Lorrie found the area over the cricothyroid membrane on the woman's neck which was the soft spot on her throat. She knew that women as well as men have an Adam's apple but that, in women, it was sometimes difficult to locate. She didn't take the time to worry. She just got on with it. She located the Adam's apple, felt for the cricoid cartilage and quickly used the Swiss army knife to make a small incision to expose the membrane into which she pushed the empty tube of the pen. It took mere seconds.

Getting air into the woman was Lorrie's only priority.

'Stop compressions.'

Sean ceased and leaned back.

Despite the danger of being exposed to the poison, Lorrie placed her lips over the pen and blew in two rapid breaths. The woman's chest rose and fell, and Lorrie blew the precious air in again. She nodded to Sean, 'Ten compressions and then stop.'

Between them, in the two minutes it took for the paramedics and the A&E consultant to arrive, they gave the woman and her babies a fighting chance. Their survival was now up to the hospital staff.

Sean explained the whole situation – including that the woman was probably the latest Reaper victim – and they took her away on a trolley.

The onlookers dispersed and went about their business.

Sean sat beside Lorrie and they both scooted back so they were leaning against the wall. Both were breathless and both were shocked to their core. Lorrie had no idea how long they sat there being looked at by the seemingly never-ending line of people entering and leaving through the hospital reception doors. It was only when Ricky Burton arrived and loomed over them that both of them snapped out of their reverie and stood up.

'I'm glad to see you're not dead,' he said to Lorrie.

Lorrie's brow furrowed. 'I think my wrist is broken, that's all.'

'You'd be dead by now if your heroics had resulted in a transfer of poison.'

'I used my hankie.' Lorrie wasn't in the mood to contemplate what might have been. 'I'm not completely stupid.'

'No?' Ricky's eyebrow shot up. 'But you are lucky.'

Lorrie shrugged. 'Whatever.'

Sean asked, 'What about the woman and the babies?'

'Problematic. Obviously, there were concerns about cross contamination and it delayed the caesarean. There was a certain reluctance to perform the operation in case the surgeon or the staff got themselves poisoned.'

'But?' Lorrie felt deflated. Had it all been for nothing, she wondered?

'Both babies were delivered by caesarean ten minutes ago. The woman was pronounced dead immediately thereafter.'

'How are they?' Lorrie held her breath.

'Critical, I'm afraid. They both need steroids for their underdeveloped lungs, but they're having to hold off until all the blood results come back. The fear is that there's poison in their systems.'

'Poor little mites.' Sean bowed his head. 'I'll kill that murdering bastard if I ever get my hands on him.'

'How did it happen?' Ricky asked Lorrie directly. 'You were on the scene immediately?'

'She came off the car park at the same time as us. We walked through the doors together and then I saw it?'

'Saw what?'

'I don't know.' She shook her head. 'Just something in her eyes... On her face. It was fleeting but, then, she was gasping for air and down she went.'

'I need to get her to A&E,' Sean said to Ricky. 'She needs to have that wrist x-rayed.'

'I'm fine,' Lorrie protested. 'We need to ...'

'Shut up and do as you're told,' Sean admonished. 'I'm tired and there's things we need to be getting on with and – until you get that wrist seen to - we're not budging from this hospital.'

Ricky gave a sardonic smile and said, 'I guess I'll leave you both to it and see you back at the ranch later.'

Lorrie watched the pathologist waddle away and then allowed herself to be led by Sean towards A&E where they both sat in silence for ninety minutes before being seen by a doctor and then trundling off to radiology where two fractures of her carpal bones were diagnosed.

# DAY FOUR: AFTERNOON

They didn't speak all the way back to the car park. Sean had been considerate and attentive, and Lorrie now found his presence at her side disturbing. As they approached the car, she was suddenly reluctant to get in beside him. She halted in mid stride and turned full circle, as if looking for somewhere to escape to.

'Lorrie?' There was concern in Sean's voice. 'Are you okay?'

She took several steps back. 'No, I guess not,' she said.

'Come and get into the car.'

She stepped farther back, and Sean took two strides towards her and reached out a hand.

Lorrie jumped as if she'd been electrocuted. 'Don't,' she said.

Sean's arm dropped at his side. He looked at her and saw how close to tears she was.

'The shock is setting in,' he said. 'You need to get in the car, Lorrie.'

Then, she was crying. The tears were soft and slow at first and, just as he grabbed her, and just as he enveloped her in his arms, she was sobbing so hard that she jerked violently against his chest.

Sean rubbed her back and drew her ever tighter against him. He ran a hand through her hair and kissed the top of her head.

Lorrie kept crying. She couldn't stop.

'Lorrie? Lorrie, look at me.' Sean drew back and placed a finger beneath her chin, pulling her head up. 'You're in shock. Just look at me and try to calm down.' He gripped her by the upper arms to steady her.

Lorrie hiccupped through the tears and took a series of deep breaths. Slowly, the tears subsided, and she leaned her forehead against his chest.

'I'm sorry,' she spluttered.

In response, he wrapped his arms fully around her and pressed his lips once more on the top of her head. They stood there, still and silent, for long minutes until Lorrie pulled back and out of his embrace.

'We'd better go,' she said.

Sean nodded. 'Yes.'

In the car, Lorrie scrubbed at her face with the sleeve of her jacket and let out one breath after another.

'I was so scared,' she said. 'Cutting into her with the knife.'

Sean started the car. 'You did good Lorrie.'

'I couldn't let those babies die.'

'I know.'

'They might die anyway.'

'But, you gave them a chance.'

Lorrie turned in her seat so she was facing him. 'I'm sorry I sprang that on you... about Ollie.'

Sean was momentarily thrown by the change of subject. 'Ollie?' He shrugged. 'Hardly seems important.'

'It's important to Ollie.'

'I didn't mean it that way. I just meant...'

Lorrie placed a hand on his arm. 'I know what you meant,' she said quietly.

'I really do want to see him, Lorrie. You just took me by surprise earlier.'

Lorrie was profoundly pleased. 'I can go ahead and arrange it, then?'

Sean nodded.

'What...' Lorrie struggled with her next words. 'What about your wife? Does she know that we... that the two of us...?' She cleared her throat. 'Does she know we have a son?'

It was Sean's turn to clear his throat. 'My wife never found out about our affair. I never told her. She never knew about Ollie.'

'Eighteen years is a long time to keep a child a secret. Will you finally tell her now... well, now that you're going to see him? Won't she have a right to know?'

He shook his head and avoided looking at her.

Lorrie let it pass. 'Do you have any other children?' she asked.

'No.'

'I'm surprised. I thought... I thought you wanted children?'

'My wife.' This time he looked at her. He stared directly into her eyes. 'She couldn't have children.'

'I'm sorry.' And, despite what a shit he'd been and despite him choosing his barren wife over his son, she was sorry. 'That's a bummer.'

He nodded. 'She's dead - my wife. She died thirteen years ago.'

'What?' Lorrie almost choked on the word.

'Suicide. She was Bi-Polar.' He had no idea why he was telling her that. He never spoke about his wife – not to anyone – particularly not with ex-lovers.

'I had no idea.' Perhaps it all started to make sense. A little of the hurt at his long-ago betrayal eased and she felt a shift in her chest. Perhaps he had no choice? Living with someone with manic-depression, or Bi-polar disorder as it was now more commonly known, was probably hell on earth. Leaving someone like that, someone so dependent on you – even for a pregnant lover - would not be an easy decision.

It was as if he'd read her mind. 'When... when you and I were together, I had to choose her, Lorrie. The marriage wasn't easy, but I couldn't walk out on her.'

'No, I see that.' And, somehow, she did see it, but it wasn't enough to entirely forgive him.

'Please, understand that I didn't have my head screwed on straight back then. I was married to a woman who desperately needed me. She'd already tried to take her own life and by the time we... well, by the time we started our affair, she was a wreck.'

'That was very noble of you... Staying with her.'

Her sarcasm wasn't lost on him. 'I never professed to be anything other than what I was. I don't recall ever making you any promises. We had an affair, Lorrie. We had fun. I kinda fell in love with you but...'

'But, when I got pregnant, it brought you to your senses?'

'It scared the living shit out of me, to be honest.'

'You told me to get an abortion.' The memory of that night, when Sean had cruelly told her to get rid of her baby, still caused her great pain. When he'd said it, she'd thought she had imagined it. Her Sean couldn't demand such a thing. He was sweet and loving and she'd felt so safe with him. But, his eyes had been hard and his mouth had been set, and no amount of pleading with him to stay with her had moved him. He repeated himself and said those hateful words a second time. 'Get rid of it,' he'd said, and she'd finally seen that he'd meant it.

'I'm sorry.'

Lorrie was pulled back from thoughts of the past. 'You're sorry?' She gave a bitter laugh. 'Really?'

'Actually, I am sorry. I was a prick. I've already admitted that.'

Lorrie bit her lip and reined in her anger. What was the point of dredging it all up? Sean Kelly turned out not to be the man she'd thought he was. He'd let her down, broke her heart and walked away without as much as a backward glance, but – so what? She wasn't the first woman to be scorned and she was sure she wouldn't be the last.

She nodded. 'You're right... You did admit that you were a prick and you did apologise.' She sighed. 'It's all water under the bridge. Perhaps it's not too late for you to get to know your son. There's no need for him to know that you wanted me to flush him down the toilet.'

'Oh? Okay... thanks, I guess. I'd like to get to know him. I realise that I need to apologise to him too.'

Sean switched off the engine. They needed to talk some more. A great deal of air needed clearing and they might not get another opportunity.

Lorrie shifted uncomfortably in her seat. 'We do need to get back,' she said.

'Let's talk for a minute,' he said. 'There's things that I need to say.'

'Go ahead. I'm listening.'

'I've thought about you over the years.'

Lorrie felt her eyes sting. She pressed the fingers on her good hand to her eyelids. She really didn't want to hear that he'd thought about her.

She voiced what was in her mind. 'I don't want to hear that, Sean. What good does it do me to know you'd thought about me?' She lowered her hand and looked at him. 'I got on with my life. I had Ollie. That was all that mattered to me. You turning up like this has sort of thrown me. I don't need to hear anything about you thinking about me over the years. As I said - what good does it do me?'

'I simply needed to say it. I'm sorry if my words hurt you.'

'I'm used to it.' She turned away once more. She knew the power of words and how they could be used to inflict pain. She had been on the receiving end of her husband's words for years. Sean's words, in comparison, were tame.

'I wanted to get in touch when my wife died. I wanted to see my son.'

'Why didn't you?'

'You'd married by then. I didn't want to rock the boat. I didn't want to be selfish.'

Lorrie didn't want to contemplate the life she and Ollie could have had if Sean had got in touch. Judging by the timeline, Ollie was five years old when Sean's wife died. She had only just married Colin but, already, she'd known what a huge mistake that was. She didn't want to hear that Sean had stayed away because he didn't want to intrude in her marriage. How ironic was that?

'How many affairs?' she asked. 'I don't presume I was the only one.'

He said, 'A few.'

'A few?' Her voice trailed off. Her eyes glistened with fresh tears.

He could see she was hurt, and it confused him. 'I didn't cheat on you. I cheated on my wife, Lorrie. I'm not proud of that, but I'm not a saint. I couldn't survive my marriage without some respite.'

'That's pretty despicable.' Her voice was a mere whisper.

He nodded. 'I agree, but that's not really any of your business.'

He was right. Of course, he was right. Why did she believe she had the right to judge him on how he behaved towards his wife? She knew he was married when she allowed him to bed her, after all. The fact that he'd used other women before and after her was well outside of what was her concern. Perhaps she was simply disappointed in him? Perhaps she wanted to think that she'd been his only transgression and that she had actually mattered to him?

She pulled herself together and said, 'We'd better get back.'

'Are we okay? It's important that we're okay, Lorrie.'

'Finding this killer is more important. Nothing else matters at the moment. Let's go, Sean.'

Sean started the engine and put the car in gear. They exited the car park and drove in silence.

As they got closer to New Scotland Yard, Lorrie began to feel a sense of panic. She was so conflicted. They had to work together and there were still so many things that remained unsaid. Could she honestly carry on as normal knowing there was this thing between them? They had to lay some ghosts to rest, especially now that Sean had agreed to see Ollie.

Lorrie dragged in a breath. 'Stop the car,' she said hurriedly.

Sean frowned but kept the car moving.

'Please,' she said. 'Pull over.'

'What's wrong? Do you feel sick?'

She shook her head. 'I don't want to go back just yet.'

Sean nodded and moved down the gears, gently applied the brakes and pulled the car to a halt by the kerbside.

How could she begin? What could she say? She found, at least, some words. She didn't know if they were the right words, but she said, 'It wasn't fair to her... what we did.'

'Sorry?' Sean looked at her and raised his eyebrows. 'Are we talking about my wife?'

'Your dead wife? Yes.' Lorrie realised that there was a huge boulder sitting on her chest. She had expected to feel some sort of righteous indignation at him cheating on his sick wife but, in fact, what she felt was shame. She was ashamed of herself, and she was ashamed of what they had both done.

Sean felt the slow release of his muscles. He hadn't realised how tense he was. 'I'm not proud of myself. I made sure I never hurt her. Nothing I did ever touched her.'

'You don't know that.'

He groaned and shook his head. 'Look, Lorrie, with all due respect to the fact that we once had a fling that resulted in me being an utter prick, I don't really think you have the right to interrogate me. My marriage is my affair. I've tried to explain why I acted the way I did. I wasn't making excuses by telling you how ill she was, but that was then, and this is now.'

'I don't mean to interrogate you. I just want to understand. I feel I need to make peace with you and peace with what we both did.' She sensed his reluctance to take the conversation any further and added, 'If you and Ollie want to be in each other's lives, then I want to understand what happened between us. It wasn't a fling, Sean. I don't care about your other affairs... I need to know that I was different.'

'You were different. Can't we leave it at that?' It was a heartfelt plea. 'I betrayed my wife. I don't want to betray her any further by discussing her with you.'

'Can you at least tell me how she died?' She rested a hand on his shoulder. 'It can't hurt to tell me that.'

Sean kept his hands on the steering wheel and stared out the windscreen at the busy road. He wished he had never left Manchester to come to London. What had possessed him? He could feel his usual calm and cool persona begin to erode as his emotions began to amplify inside of him.

He leaned back and took his hands from the wheel. He would just tell her. He'd lay it all out for her and let her judge him further. It mattered, though. It mattered what she now thought of him. Well, his chickens were about to come well and truly home to roost.

He considered his words and said, 'I hardly spent any time with her. What with work and...'

'The women?'

He nodded. 'I used my work and the affairs to keep me from going home to her. I couldn't bear to watch her destroy herself.' He sighed and pulled at the neck of his shirt. 'Her depressions were terrible. Sometimes she would go days without getting out of bed. She believed... I mean, really believed, that she didn't deserve to live. She thought she was worthless.'

His hands clenched into fists. 'She'd taken so many overdoses over the years that her brain was mush. Oh, she could function and during the manic episodes she ran rings around me. Although I hated every minute I was with her, I couldn't leave her. I couldn't abandon her completely.' He gave a bitter laugh. 'Funny thing is – if I'd walked out on her - she might have got better help. Social services... the health professionals.... they might've been more supportive and kept more of an eye on her if she'd been abandoned by her husband.'

Lorrie sat in silence and let him talk. She could feel the guilt and the shame coming off him in waves.

'She threw herself under a train. I can't even remember the name of the woman I was screwing when I got the news.' He turned and looked Lorrie straight in the face. 'There you have it. All the gory details.'

It was horrific and tragic and sad. Lorrie had no words. She had loved this man and, whilst she was loving him, his wife was suffering an unimaginable torment. She hoped he'd been telling the truth when he'd said she knew nothing about her or Ollie.

She reached for his hand and, finding a clenched fist, she slowly peeled back his fingers until she felt the hand relax and open to her.

'I'm sorry,' she whispered. 'I'm sorry I made you tell me.'

'Did telling you help?'

She nodded. 'In the way that it needed to, I suppose.'

'We can't turn back the clock. I wish...'

Lorrie placed a finger to his lips. 'No more, Sean.'

He drew back. 'Don't feel sorry for me, Lorrie. I was a bastard to my wife, and I was a bastard to you. I don't deserve your sympathy and perhaps I don't deserve to get to know my son.'

'I'll let Ollie be the judge of that. It's not up to me.'

There was nothing left to say. Both realised they had brokered a mutual truce. Neither had any expectations of the other and all that was left for them was to get on with their jobs and catch a killer.

# DAY FOUR: EVENING

Simon noticed that, since Lorrie and Sean's return from the hospital that afternoon, there was something different between them. He couldn't quite put his finger on what it was and decided that he couldn't be bothered thinking about it. There was too much going on and too much to worry about without getting preoccupied with the pair of them.

The whole team was extremely proud of Lorrie's heroics with the pregnant woman, but Lorrie played the whole thing down and seemed almost deflated. She adamantly refused to indulge Scully and Connor when they requested she speak to the press about performing the emergency tracheotomy and saving the babies, and they both continued to pester her to agree. It got so annoying for her that she took herself off out of the building for an hour to get away from them.

Thankfully, on her return, Scully and Connor had made themselves scarce.

Simon spied her the minute she walked into her office and made a beeline straight for her.

'Guv? Where have you been? I've been ringing you.'

Lorrie scowled and snapped, 'For fuck's sake, Simon. Can't I have an hour to myself? What do you want?'

'To tell you there's been four more deaths.'

She halted in mid stride. 'Four more?' She couldn't quite believe it. 'Where this time?'

'Manchester.'

'Christ. That's...' She counted in her head. 'Twenty three.'

Simon nodded. 'I'm afraid so.'

'Have we any details?'

'DI Kelly is going to get on the blower to his DCI in Manchester to get what he can. Everything's a bit hazy at the moment.'

Lorrie was at a loss. Four more deaths and she was really beginning to feel as if she was being buried alive. Her head would probably be handed to the press on a platter by Scully and Connor, and who could blame them? She refused the good PR opportunity and now they would use the latest deaths to hang her. She had no clue who the killer was. She had no knowledge of how the victims were being poisoned and the body count kept growing.

She ran a weary hand through her hair. 'You must know something, Simon? Where did they die?'

'Hospital again... All four. Ricky says there's no need to bring the bodies down here just yet. He wants the post-mortems done up there and the reports sent direct to him. He says there's probably fuck all else to learn from them, but he'll decide later if he needs to take a look for himself.'

'Is it the same MO? Is there anything different about these four?'

Simon shook his head. 'I'm not sure.'

'Okay.' She thought for a moment. 'Get whatever information you have on them up on the board and update it as soon as Sean gets off the blower with Manchester, then get everyone assembled. I'll join you in a minute.'

Simon did not immediately leave. 'One more thing. The Chief Super was here looking for you.'

'Not the bloody press statement again?'

He shook his head. 'No... another press statement. He says the Home Secretary is going to speak to the press himself later on this evening. He wants you to brief him so he can brief the Home Secretary.'

'Brief him?' Lorrie gave a strangled laugh. 'What is there to say?'

'I'm sorry, Guv. We're letting you down. We just can't find the fucker.'

She sighed. 'I guess we just have to try a little harder.'

Simon nodded. 'One more thing, Guv. I've been given a heads up on one thing that the Home Secretary is going to include in his statement.'

'Oh?'

'He's going to say that they are going to close down all the affected hospitals to all new admissions and will be temporarily cancelling all discharges. No visitors will be allowed at any of these hospital for the foreseeable future.'

'God, that's a logistical nightmare.'

'Yes, it's absolute madness, and that's not all... they're locking down Heathrow.' His expression of incredulity said it all. 'Can you imagine the pandemonium that will cause?'

'Oh, fuck. That's serious. Okay. I can understand why you were pissed at me. I should've been here.'

Simon shrugged. 'No harm done. I've got your back.'

'You're a star, Simon. Don't let me ever say otherwise.'

Sean walked through the office door. 'Chief Superintendent Connor and Commander Scully are in the major incident room and blasting everyone to Hell,' he said. 'You'd better go pacify them before there's a mutiny. Everyone has been working themselves into the ground and those two pricks are tearing strips off them. It's not on, Lorrie.'

'Bastards.' Lorrie's dander was up. 'I'll not have it.'

She wasted no time in marching along the corridor and straight to the incident room. She took in the bowed heads, the angry atmosphere and stomped straight to her two superiors.

Neither of them witnessed her approach. They were too busy playing to a browbeaten audience.

Heads came up all over the room at Lorrie's approach. Every eye in the room turned to look at her.

Scully was the first to notice the change in atmosphere in the room and the first to realise that the attention of his audience had shifted. He looked to Connor and they both turned and saw her, and they were just about to vent their spleen on the woman they held responsible for the debacle of an investigation when she stalled them with a simple raising of her hand.

With her temper held precariously in check, she said, 'May I see you both in my office, please?'

Scully wasn't sure if he had heard correctly. He looked to Connor to ascertain if he had just heard the same.

Connor cleared his throat and lowered his eyes. There was going to be a bloodbath. Sullivan had put her foot well and truly in it again.

'We're not finished here,' Scully said. 'There's things that still need to be said and you can just bloody well stand there and hear it as well, Sullivan.'

Lorrie continued to keep a tight rein on her temper. It wasn't the time to tear the moron's face off.

'Please, sir,' she said, with feigned respect. 'I'd appreciate it if you would speak to me in private. My team need to get on with their investigations. They're all very busy. Some of them have had very little sleep in four days.'

Connor and Scully scowled. They were angry. They were pissed at Sullivan and her whole motley crew because they were making the two of them look bad. The latest four deaths had sent the Assistant Commissioner apoplectic with fury, and she'd been taking it out on them instead of the one person who was fucking up – Sullivan.

Lorrie turned and walked back the way she had come. She hoped that they had the sense to follow her. If not, she would tear them both a new arsehole in front of everyone and be damned to the consequences.

They reluctantly followed her back to her office. She had put them on the spot and, anyway, they had lost the momentum of their tirade.

Scully took Lorrie's seat behind the desk and Connor began pacing the room. Lorrie stood with her back against the door. She clenched her fists, set her face and waited.

Scully said, 'Do you know what the Assistant Commissioner said to me not half an hour ago?'

'No sir.' Lorrie placed and kept her eyes on a spot on the wall just above Scully's head.

'Well, Sullivan - she said to me exactly what the Home Secretary said to her. She said... and I quote... this fuck up of an investigation has us the laughing stock of the civilised world. The idiots running it should be put up against a wall and shot.'

'The Home Secretary said that, sir?' Lorrie was shocked. 'And the Assistant Commissioner repeated it to you?' Disbelief flared in her eyes.

Scully cleared his throat and back-peddled. 'Perhaps not those exact words, but the meaning is the same. You and your team are failing and doing sweet FA to prevent more and more deaths. We've now got hospitals closed and Heathrow at a fucking standstill.'

'We're doing our best with what we have, sir.' Lorrie looked to Connor for some support.

'Don't look at me. Superintendent,' Connor snapped. 'I'm not going to come to your rescue. We're all in the mire here and it's up to you to dig us out. Do you actually know what you're doing? Do you have a single fucking clue?'

'We're making progress.' Her words sounded weak, even to her own ears.

'Progress, my arse,' Connor spat.

Scully said, 'You have forty-eight hours to find this bastard or you're off the case.' He stabbed a finger in her direction. 'Forty-eight hours, Superintendent and then Counter Terrorism takes over. The Assistant Commissioner had to convince the Home Secretary to give you and your team this extra time. Fuck knows why she's got any faith left in you. Take note, Sullivan - every minute is now borrowed. You'd better make good use of the time you have left. Am I making myself clear?'

All Lorrie could say was, 'Yes, sir.' All she could do was her best and, if that proved not to be good enough, then they wouldn't need to fire her - she would willingly step down.

# DAY FOUR: NIGHT

Lorrie shared a coffee with Simon in her office. She looked at him as he sat across from her, and she noted just how much character was in his face. He had strong, intelligent eyes and a firm but compassionate mouth. He was quite a few years younger than her and had done well to reach the position of DI before he was out of his twenties. She realised just how much she depended on him. He looked out for her. She knew that he respected her and would probably take a bullet for her. He was nothing like Sean. They were opposite ends of the spectrum, but she sensed that they could be a formidable team. She was beginning to realise just how lucky she was in having them at her side.

'Penny for them, Guv.' Simon smiled. 'You look well away.'

Lorrie returned his smile. 'You're a good lad, Simon. I'm lucky to have you.'

'Less of the lad, please, Guv. Anyone would think you were in your dotage.'

'I feel it, I can tell you. My weary bones think they're a hundred years old.'

'What's the occasion?' he asked.

'Occasion?' Her brow puckered.

Simon raised his coffee cup. 'I'm not often invited in for coffee.'

Lorrie closed her eyes. To avoid spilling coffee, she placed the cup on the desk with a shaky hand. 'I guess I just need a moment with a friend,' she said.

She had never called him a friend before. Simon was a little taken aback.

'Sorry if that sounds presumptuous, Simon.'

He gave his tousled head a violent shake. 'No, not at all. I'm glad you see me as a friend.'

'We've known each other a few years,' she said. 'You've followed me to more than one assignment.'

He shrugged. 'I want to work with the best. I'd follow you anywhere.'

'Am I the best, Simon? Am I really?' There was a child-like, desperate note to her voice.

This was the first time he had ever witnessed his boss being insecure. It scared him a little and that fear was all too clear in his eyes.

Lorrie reacted. 'Sorry. I'm sorry. Ignore me.' She forced a grin onto her face and said, 'Listen to me... all maudlin. What must you think?'

'I think you're exhausted and need a good night's sleep.' Simon placed his cup on the desk and stood up. 'I think you need to be a little more selfish. Put yourself first for a change.'

'It's not in me,' she sighed. 'The case always comes first.'

'You have to, Guv. How can you look out for us if you don't look out for yourself? You've had a hell of a day. Give yourself a break.'

'Yes. Yes. I know you're right.' She picked up her coffee cup once more and drained it.

He stood up, turned and made towards the door where he twisted his head back around on his neck. He said, 'Go home. Get right to bed. We'll crack this in the morning.'

She nodded. 'I will and, Simon...?'

'Yes, Guv?'

'Thank you.'

'You're welcome, Guv.'

Simon disappeared through the door and Lorrie was left alone with her thoughts. She should never have put Simon in such a spot. She was just grateful that he was trustworthy and loyal, and not likely to go gossiping with the others about how insecure and neurotic she was. What had possessed her? It wasn't as if he was the ideal person to be confiding her thoughts to. He was her subordinate, and there was a reason for the hierarchy they all worked within. Simon, and the others, had to have confidence in her. They had to feel secure in the knowledge that their boss had their backs and would be sound as a pound in any given situation. She had made Simon doubt her and she could only hope he truly believed that it was simple exhaustion and not the beginning of a nervous breakdown.

IT WAS TEN O'CLOCK and Lorrie was just putting her key in the front door when she heard Ollie arrive on his motor bike.

He gave her no time to push the door open before asking, 'Did you speak to him? Will he see me?'

'Yes and yes,' she replied. 'We'll sort a meeting out in the next day or so.' It was all she needed – this thing with Ollie and Sean – but what could she do? She would have to find some time in her hectic, frantic life for her son to meet his father.

They walked through the front door together.

Ollie said, 'I don't want you to say anything to Colin.'

Lorrie threw her car keys down onto the hall table and sighed. She had Colin to think about as well. How would she find the time to leave him?

'I won't tell him, not if you don't want me to, but he has the right to know.' She looked up at her son and frowned. 'Why don't you want him to know?'

'Because he'll be funny about it.'

'He'll be even funnier when he finds out. He'll be hurt that you did it behind his back.'

'I'll cross that bridge when I come to it. No point upsetting him any earlier than needs be.' He bounded up the stairs, calling down, 'What's to eat? I'm starving.'

'You're always starving,' she called after him. She tried to smile at his retreating back, but she failed miserably. She didn't have the energy.

Colin joined them for a meal of pizza, chips and salad an hour later.

All three ate in silence. Ollie left them as soon as his plate was cleared and went up to bed.

As Lorrie was washing up the dishes at the sink, Colin approached her from behind and put his arms around her waist. He felt her stiffen, but persevered, drawing her back against him.

She felt his hardness and swallowed back a mouthful of bile.

'You okay?' he asked. 'I want to apologise again for hurting you. Did I do that?' He lifted up her injured arm and gently rubbed at the cast.

She could have lied and not mentioned that the fractures were a result of what happened at the hospital, but she wasn't a liar. She pulled away from him and said, 'You certainly sprained and bruised it, but I broke it myself.'

'I'm sorry.'

'You're always sorry, Colin.'

'I know the best way to make up.' He pulled her back against him, kissed her neck and reached up to cup a breast.

Lorrie twisted to the side and broke fully out of his embrace.

'I'm not having sex with you, Colin.' She threw down the dishcloth and walked round the table, putting distance between them.

Colin kept hold of his temper. 'You're my wife. Is it too much to expect you to have sex with me once in a while?' He sounded pathetic.

'Always the romantic.' Her voice was hot with sarcasm.

'You're a bitch, Lorrie.' Colin spoke with the minimum of rancour. He was still keeping his temper in check.

'And, you're my husband. Is it too much to expect to be treated with respect and not tortured every day of my fucking life?'

'Always so melodramatic, Lorrie. The wrist thing was an accident.'

'I'm not talking about my bloody wrist.'

'What, then?' He was genuinely perplexed. 'I've been a good husband to you. How many men would take on a whore and her bastard?'

'Don't call him a bastard, Colin. Keep Ollie out of it.'

'What else is he, but a bastard? It's not a swear word, Lorrie. Look it up in the dictionary.'

Lorrie refused to rise to the bait. She'd learned over the years to let his words wash over her.

'I'm tired. I don't want to argue.'

'Then, let's not argue. I want you in my bed tonight. It's been months. I have rights.'

'You don't have rights. It would be rape.'

Colin actually laughed at that. 'Rape? I'm your husband.'

'I don't want you to touch me. I don't want you inside me. I'm saying no. It would be rape.'

A look of calculated malice touched his eyes. 'Is it Kelly?'

'Is what, Kelly?' She felt the blood rush to her face.

'You fucked him yet? Oh, I get it... that's it, isn't it? You've fucked him and now you won't fuck me?'

'You're being ridiculous, Colin. I'm tired. I can't take this crap from you.'

'Come on, answer me, Lorrie... have you fucked him yet? I'm really curious. I mean, you were at it like rabbits behind his wife's back. Are you at it like rabbits behind mine?'

'Stop it.' Lorrie pushed passed him. 'I'm going to bed.'

He made a grab for her. 'Don't you walk out on me, I'm not finished.'

She'd had enough. 'Fuck you, Colin. Touch me again and I'll have you arrested. Fuck the consequences to my job, my career. You'll be in a cell before the night is out if you lay another finger on me.'

They locked eyes and Colin was the first to lower his. Lorrie nodded once and turned to leave.

He let her go. Ollie was in the house so he couldn't follow her and take her by force. He'd never forced her before, but he knew he was pretty close to doing just that very thing. It wouldn't be rape. She was quite wrong about that. She was his wife, after all. He could do what he wanted.

Lorrie locked the bedroom door. The last thing she wanted was a repeat of the night before. She was wound tight and wished she could switch off – disengage completely from everything – but Sean and Colin and Ollie and the Reaper twisted at her gut, and she was reminded of just how precarious her sanity was. She had lived a life on tenterhooks ever since she could remember and, in lots of ways, it had shaped her in a way that made her nothing more than a coward. She was afraid of everything. She was afraid to remain married to Colin, afraid to leave him. She was afraid that she was a lousy mother and an even worse police officer. She was terrified that the Reaper would ruin her career and equally terrified that he would actually make it. And Sean? She was afraid to see him, to be near him. She was afraid that the love she had for him – a love that she had hoped would fester to hate over the years – would ruin her.

She made her way through to the en-suite and bent over the sink. She turned on the tap and splashed cold water on her face. She felt sick and dry heaved. Being afraid really did take its toll on the mind and body and she wondered just how much sleep she'd manage that night.

Her mobile rang and she quickly dried her hands and made a grab for it before it switched to voicemail.

'It's me,' the voice said. 'I just wanted to check that you were okay.'

The sudden euphoria that reared up from her belly took her completely by surprise and she found that couldn't breathe.

'Lorrie? Are you okay, Lorrie?'

The genuine concern in Sean's voice moved her to tears.

'I'm sorry to phone so late.'

'No. It's fine. I'm glad you called.'

'Are you crying?'

'No,' she lied. 'I'm just tired.

'I'll say goodnight, then. You need to get some rest. I just... I just had to make sure you were okay.'

'Why Sean? Why do you care so much?'

'Well, that's quite a question. I wish I could explain.'

She didn't comment for a moment. She wondered what it all meant –the phone call, the concern. 'Please try,' she said. 'Please try and explain.'

When he replied, Lorrie could hear the longing in his voice. 'Love, I guess,' he said.

'I love you.'

And, at that moment, all her fear dissipated.

# DAY FIVE: MORNING

Fake news spiralled out of control all across social media. What wasn't known as fact was made up, and the public was being perversely jack-knifed into wild panic. The twenty-four hour coverage on all the main television news channels didn't help. So-called experts were brought on to pontificate on everything from the characteristics of a psychopath to directing the viewers on how easy it was to concoct a poison from items they could find in their kitchen cupboards. Then there were the interviews with the victims' families. The poor souls were wrung for every raw emotion purely for the gratification of a terrified audience. Throughout it all, the police were slated for ineptitude.

Journalists were camped outside the barriers erected around the hospital where the twins still clung to life and dozens of paparazzi were swarming around the entrances to New Scotland Yard. They were desperate to get a photograph of Lorrie. Ever fickle, they had turned her from the heroine who had single-handedly saved two unborn babies, to the idiot cop who was personally responsible for the growing number of dead.

It was absolute Hell and no one on Lorrie's team had any hope of the furore subsiding any time soon.

The Home Secretary made his statement to the press, and it did nothing but fuel an already roaring fire. He had been forced to say very little and he was livid. He had no answers to give, and he could make no reassurances. Just like everyone else in the country, he blamed Lorrie. As far as he was concerned Superintendent Lorrie Sullivan was doing a very bad job and he wanted rid of her. He made his feelings perfectly clear to everyone who would listen and, at his instruction, both Scully and Connor were poised to strip her of her job. What none of them banked on was the strength of character of the Assistant Commissioner. Annie Gordon was having none of their histrionics and, despite the risk of making an enemy of the Home Secretary, she told them to piss off and let her Superintendent do her job.

Lorrie was humbled by the older woman's continued faith in her. That faith bolstered her, and, in turn, it bolstered her struggling teams' confidence.

Despite there being no direct evidence of terrorism, the Prime Minister had held a COBRA meeting and Counter Terrorism were now taking much more of an interest in the investigation. Lorrie was under strict orders to afford them every courtesy and to not only keep them in the loop, but to permit them access to every piece of information. She had no qualms about their increased profile. She had the sense to realise that they were very likely to be handed the case in approximately thirty-six hours. The clock was ticking, and she had very little time to make a breakthrough. Annie Gordon had insisted she have all of the forty-eight hours promised her and she needed all the help she could get, even from SO15.

THE SHIT HIT THE FAN at eleven o'clock when the BBC informed Lorrie directly that they had an exclusive video message from the Reaper. They wanted to air it and were kicking up an almighty fuss because they were being threatened with legal action if they did.

Lorrie rammed the law down their throats and the BBC had no option but to co-operate and hand the video over to be forensically scrutinised.

That wouldn't be the end of it, though. The fly in the ointment was that the killer promised that – if the BBC did not air it by six o'clock that evening – he would put it online with no holds barred.

Discussion and debate had taken place all the way up to the Prime Minister and it was decided that it was better to air the video on the BBC, rather than have it go viral online. The reasoning was that, at least, there would be some control if the BBC aired it. The public could be warned of the content beforehand. The BBC could add comment and play down the message somewhat. It was agreed that it was the lesser of the two evils.

Once forensics had their look at it, viewing of the video took place at twelve minutes to twelve privately in the small incident room at New Scotland Yard. In attendance were the Assistant Commissioner, Commander Scully, Chief Superintendent Connor, Lorrie, Sean and Simon. Also in attendance was Brian Matthews - the profiler newly brought onto the team with the hope of getting some insight into who the killer was.

The room was hot, and the aroma of predominantly male sweat was overpowering. Lorrie opened a window and purposefully sat in the cold draught. Both Scully and Connor ignored her. The Assistant Commissioner drew a chair over to the window and sat down beside her. They were the only two women in the room and Sean thought to himself that it would be a fool who thought that the power lay with the men.

Simon took charge of the remote and, once he assured himself that everyone was comfortable, he pressed 'play'.

There he was – the Reaper – in all his demonic glory. His image filled the small screen and almost escaped into the room itself. At the sight of him, the hair on the back of every single person's neck stood up.

The costume was still the same. The voice was still electronically disguised. The message was still as chilling. They all listened in absolute silence. Lorrie remained convinced that there was something familiar about the character on the screen. She ran through the first video in her head – the one she had been goggle-eyed scrutinising - and recalled a similar conviction that there was something, but it was an elusive something.

She didn't think that the familiarity she felt with the image of the Reaper was irrational, but she couldn't help but wonder if she had, perhaps, seen too much of him? She had lost count of the times she'd sat in front of him and listened to every nuance of the distorted voice and watched for every gesture and every tell-tale inflection. It would be so easy to doubt herself. The way she had been feeling, and her diminishing confidence, made her question her instincts, but that something bugged her.

'Hi there, good people,' the Reaper began. 'Thank you for allowing me into your living rooms to speak to you. Please do not switch off your televisions. Please do not press the mute button. It's important that you listen to what I have to say.' He waited a beat before continuing, 'This is a relatively short message. I want to tell the father of those two tiny babies fighting for their little lives that I'm sorry. I am not a killer of babies. Please believe me when I say that I hope they live. As for the other victims? Well, I'm glad all those people are dead. How many are there, now?' He pondered a moment. 'I'm not keeping a running tally of the numbers, but I'm guessing that it's a lot.'

'Pause it,' the Assistant Commissioner said. Simon complied. 'Why doesn't he know how many are dead?' she asked.

'There's a randomness about the deaths,' Lorrie replied. 'In the first video he made it clear that he doesn't have any control over who or when they die. He sets something in motion, and it seems he then lets the dice roll.'

The Assistant Commissioner turned to Brian Matthews. 'He has some guilt about the babies. Is it genuine?'

Brian nodded. 'I would say so.'

'Why would he feel guilty?'

The profiler shrugged. 'Hard to say at this juncture.'

'I don't think he has a guilty bone in his body,' Lorrie put in.

Brian turned curious eyes on her. He asked, 'You have a psychology degree, Superintendent?'

Scully smirked and covered his mouth with a hand.

'No,' Lorrie replied. 'But, I know an amoral psychopath when I see one.'

'Indeed? Perhaps I'll learn something from you, then?'

'Perhaps you will.'

Annie Gordon interjected into their verbal spar. She asked, Brian, 'Anything else so far? Anything jumping out at you?'

Brian thought about it. 'He's being polite... saying thank you and please... but, on the other hand he's relishing the deaths.'

'And?'

Brian shrugged once more.

Lorrie didn't like him, and she liked shruggers even less. She guessed that the Assistant Commissioner didn't like shruggers any more than she did.

'Let us hope you will be able to offer a little more than a shrug, Mister Matthews or you'll be wasting our time.' She nodded to Simon, and he restarted the video.

The Reaper continued. 'They've closed a couple of hospitals and Heathrow airport. Well, bully for them. They think they're being clever... that it will make a difference. It won't. I promise you that there will be more deaths.'

He paused for a beat then, 'Did anyone tell you how they die? No?' He laughed. 'I thought not. Shall I tell you?'

A full minute passed without another word being said. His image remained frozen on the screen and Lorrie had to check that the video was still running.

Finally, 'I may tell you next time,' he said. 'It will give you something to look forward to. Meantime, keep safe.' He laughed once more. 'Of course, you all know that I don't really mean that.'

The screen went black.

No one spoke. Every eye turned to Brian.

'He's younger than you first thought,' he said. 'I'd say younger than thirty.'

'Why do you think that?' Lorrie asked. 'Everything points to someone older. It's a sophisticated crime spree. The whole thing smacks of intelligence and someone very clever is behind it.'

'It's possible to get a sophisticated, intelligent and clever person below the age of thirty, Superintendent.' He was obviously still smarting from her earlier challenge of his opinion.

'Yes, I understand that, Brian. What I don't understand is your conclusion.'

'Well, I've studied the other videos. I've now seen this one and his language, his costume, his demeanour? It all points to a younger person.'

'Anything else?' Scully prompted.

'Superior education. A privileged upbringing, but he doesn't think he mattered growing up. He lacked control. He's taking control now. Rebelling... again, another sign of youth.'

'Rebelling?' Lorrie scoffed. 'You make him sound like a spotty adolescent.'

Scully cut her with a look. 'Brian is here for a reason,' he said. 'You've not progressed very far, despite your obvious insight into the killer, so let us give the actual expert a chance.'

It was Conner's turn to hide a smirk behind a hand.

'How many thousands of suspects does Brian's profile give us?' Lorrie asked sarcastically.

'Not many,' Brian replied, ignoring the sarcasm in her voice. 'Factor in access to a laboratory, a means of distributing the toxin. That should narrow it down somewhat.'

Simon joined in. 'If we knew how it was distributed... how the victims came into contact with it.'

'I can't help you with that, I'm afraid.' Brian looked a little smug as he turned and stared at Simon. 'That's your job.

# DAY FIVE: AFTERNOON

'Tell me you've found something, Sean? How long are the boffins going to take analysing the belongings? It's been four days.'

Sean refrained from reaching out and touching her. There were too many eyes and, anyway, he wasn't sure how Lorrie felt about him. He had confided in her – told her that he loved her - and he had sensed that he had touched something in her, but that did not necessarily mean anything. For the first time ever, he didn't feel in full control of himself nor his emotions. He had not consciously intended to fall in love with her again. His brain and his heart were constantly expressing memories and feelings and thoughts of that previous life - when they had been lovers - and, no matter how hard he tried, he could not totally divorce the past from the present.

'What's left to do?' she asked, interrupting his thoughts.

He threw her a look of concern. She was panicking. He could see it in her eyes. 'I don't know what's left to do, Lorrie. Give me a minute and I'll check.'

Lorrie gave no thought to how she was coming across. Time was sprinting along, and she was desperate for any lead, any single clue. Her voice was a ferocious bark as she demanded, 'Go, check, then. Now!'

Sean stood where he was. 'In a minute, Lorrie. First, I want you to sit down and take that panic-stricken look off your face. Everyone is watching you.'

Lorrie turned and looked around the room. Everyone – all the dozens of officers – were surreptitiously staring at her. Their expressions clearly said that they didn't appreciate their boss having a public melt-down.

'They're taking the lead from you,' Sean whispered. 'You panic and they panic. You fall to pieces, and they follow.'

She gulped and turned her back on the room. 'Sorry. Yes, sorry.' She ran a weary hand through her hair and forced a smile onto her face. 'I think I'm losing the plot somewhat.'

Sean returned her smile. 'I've got your back,' he said.

She nodded and turned once more to the team. To the room, she said, 'Okay everyone. Let's take a moment to wrack our brains. Everyone stop what they're doing and turn to the photo board. Study it. Look at the photographs and run your eyes along the red lines linking the photos to the information. Now, look to the board on the right where the lists of belongings are.' She turned to Sean. 'Thank you for putting that information up there. It'll help.' Eyes back on the room. 'We're missing something very important... the means. We need to find how the poison manages to find its way onto the lips and into the mouths of the victims.'

She flapped her good hand at the possessions' board. 'There are over eight hundred pieces of information on this board... Over eight hundred items found in suitcases, pockets, handbags, wallets, cars. Sean, Dixon, and the newbies have begun to group them, but those groups might not be kosher. Forensics are systematically working their way through them, and it'll be days before we have everything analysed. We've been trying to prioritise... trying to find groups of items to jump the queue to be tested. Everything that's been under the microscope so far has come up clean.'

Sean took a step towards the board. 'As you know, trace of the poison has been found on all the steering wheels of the cars driven by the victims prior to their deaths. Traces have also been found on the inside door handles and on the seatbelt buckles. We've been told that this was transference as opposed to the toxin being placed there deliberately. Conclusion is that the victims were exposed to the toxin before they got into the car.'

'Then why wasn't any found on the handle outside of the car... on the driver's door?'

'Good question, Lovell. I don't have an answer, I'm afraid. We're pretty much guessing.'

Lorrie let the information sink in before walking to the middle of the room and turning full circle, her look taking in each and every one of her team.

She said, 'I know we're all struggling. I know I am, but we are making progress. We know things today that we didn't know yesterday. We have to keep our noses to the grindstone and carry on.' She turned to Simon and gestured him to her side. She did the same to Sean. 'Let's regroup in my office.'

'I want to explore the Brunel angle,' she said as soon as they walked into her office. 'Brian said a few things that are worth following up.'

'Like what?' Simon asked. 'The guy is an ass-wipe.'

'Yes, but some of what he said warrants investigation. He mentioned access to a lab. Brunel has a state of the art lab. Ollie is there all the time and he praises it to the heavens. Plus, the second video and this latest one was emailed from the university. Coincidence? I think not.'

'You think it might be one of the professors or a student?' Sean's attention was well and truly grabbed.

'Could be,' she replied. 'I don't think it's a student... I don't buy the young person conclusion, but...'

'One of the professors?' Simon liked the idea.

'Still leaves us with a huge question mark over how it gets out there,' Sean put in.

'One thing at a time,' Lorrie said.

They agreed to keep the visit to Brunel to themselves. The last thing they wanted was a stampede of journalists breaking down the university doors.

'Sean and I will go,' Lorrie told a disappointed Simon. 'I need you here pushing through the last of the interviews and keeping everyone on track.'

'Where will I say you both are if anyone... Scully or Connor for example... ask?'

'You'll think of something, but keep Brunel under wraps for now.'

LORRIE DIDN'T CALL ahead. She didn't warn anyone at the university that they were going to visit. This was purely a recognisance trip. They were going to have a nose around, ask a few inconspicuous questions and see if they could shake anything loose.

Sean drove. The usual twenty minute journey from Westminster to Kingston took over an hour. Traffic was horrendous and an accident on the Hammersmith flyover meant they were virtually stationary for thirty minutes. They spent the time talking, but not about the case.

Sean beat about the bush and then plucked up the courage to say, 'I'm sorry. Telling you I loved you must have seemed like I lobbed you a grenade. I'll understand it if you can't say that you love me back.'

For reasons that she could not fully articulate, Lorrie suddenly felt very shy. She hadn't been sure how they would pass the time on the journey to the university, but the last thing she had expected was for Sean to bring up what he'd said during the phone call.

The day had turned out to be unseasonably warm, yet Lorrie didn't believe that the heat surging through her body had anything to do with the weather and more to do with the proximity of the man in the seat next to her.

She refrained from responding to him immediately. When Sean offered no more words, she said, 'It's hard for me to admit that I love you, Sean. I'm scared.'

'I won't hurt you again, Lorrie.'

She knew that he meant it. 'I know,' she said quietly.

'Do you?'

She nodded. 'You didn't mean to hurt me the first time.'

'No,' he agreed. 'I was just selfish... Thoughtless.'

'We were both selfish. I had an affair with a married man. I wasn't blameless.'

'Can we put it behind us?'

Lorrie wanted desperately to say that, yes, they could put it behind them. She felt a tear form in the corner of one eye and absent-mindedly blinked it back.

'Lorrie?'

'I don't know,' she said. 'We're different people now.'

'All the more reason to believe that we know what we're doing this time.'

Lorrie could no longer feel the warmth of the day. She was suddenly cold. A sense of foreboding swept over her as she contemplated a future with him. She turned and met his eyes. 'I don't really know what's happening. It seems so...'

'Soon?'

She nodded. 'I can't really think straight right now. How do I know that I can trust you? How do I know that this is actually means anything?'

Lorrie knew that she loved him. She knew without a shadow of a doubt that he loved her, but what did it mean? What future could they have?

'I need some time,' she said. 'Can you give me some time?'

'I can't help how I feel about you, Lorrie. I need you. I know I have to earn your trust so – yes – I can give you all the time you need.'

They drove in silence for a while. Lorrie then said, 'This time it's me who is married. I can't cheat on him. I can't be that person for a second time.'

'I understand.' Sean nodded and kept his eyes straight ahead. 'Do you love him?' he asked, a trace of fear in his voice. 'Do you love your husband, Lorrie?'

'Good gracious... No.' A pained expression settled on her features. She had never loved Colin. She sighed. 'That sounds awful. It makes me seem so shallow.'

'You're far from shallow. If he was worth loving, then you'd love him.' Sean was relieved. The thought of her loving another man was inconceivable to him.

'Colin...' She absently nestled her injured wrist against her chest. 'Colin isn't a nice man. I don't like him, I don't respect him and I certainly don't love him.'

Sean noticed the way she held her plastered wrist and a sudden anger erupted from his chest. 'Did he do that? Did he hurt you?'

Lorrie shook her head. 'That's not the problem. He really didn't mean it.' She eyed him intently. 'Don't go jumping to conclusions, Sean. He's never abused me physically. This was the first time. It was my fault.'

Traffic was at a standstill once more and Sean applied the handbrake and turned fully in the seat. The seatbelt restricted him somewhat, so he removed it and leaned in towards her.

'Jesus Christ, Lorrie. Can you hear yourself?' He used both hands to pull her around so that he faced her. 'You sound just like every other battered wife... It was my fault. How many times have you heard a bruised and battered woman say that?'

Lorrie couldn't help herself. She laughed. 'You look ready for murder,' she said through the hilarity then, noticing the genuine concern on his face, added, 'Honestly, Sean, Colin is too much of a coward to hit me. He knows I would rip his balls off.'

'What, then? What has he done to you?'

Lorrie shrugged. 'Emotional abuse, I suppose. Psychological torture.'

'You?' Sean was frankly amazed. 'You let a man get so far inside your brain that he could do that to you?' He shook his head. 'That's a difficult one to comprehend.'

'He got to me when I was vulnerable.'

Realisation dawned and Sean felt a surge of shame. 'It's my fault. I made you vulnerable.'

'Oh, stop it,' she scolded. 'It's Colin's fault... and mine.'

Sean closed his eyes. He wanted to shut out the expression on her face. He swallowed deeply and tried to eradicate the picture in his head of a single mother, deserted and alone, falling into the clutches of a man like Colin. 'I'm sorry,' he said.

Lorrie shook him and he opened his eyes. She saw that they were wet and her own eyes filled. 'I'm going to leave him,' she said. 'It has nothing to do with seeing you again. I just know that it's time.'

'Just like that?' He didn't believe her.

'He hasn't broken me, yet, Sean, but - if I don't leave - then I'm sure that he will.'

They lapsed into an uncomfortable silence. Traffic on the flyover was beginning to move again and Sean settled himself, put his seatbelt back on, and concentrated all his attention on the road.

As they drew closer to the university, Sean spoke. He said, 'When this is all over, I want to be with you, Lorrie. I'll move to London if that's what it takes.'

'Don't make me any promises,' she responded quietly.

He ignored her words. 'I'll put in for a transfer. I'll do everything in my power to be with you.'

Lorrie sighed. It was what she wanted more than anything, but she was frightened. 'Let's see,' she said. 'Wait until after the case is closed. Wait until you meet Ollie. Wait until after Colin.'

'Okay, I understand, but you have to tell Colin about us. No secrets, Lorrie. We won't skulk around as if we're dirty.'

The traffic stalled once more, and Sean shifted down a gear. He looked out the windscreen and waited on her response.

'We have to wait. Ollie has a lot to deal with in meeting you. He's a sensitive boy and it's important that we put his feelings first. I don't want to confuse things by leaving Colin just as the both of you are trying to establish some kind of relationship. It will muddy the waters. Let's see how things go with you and Ollie first.'

He saw that she was right. 'Okay. I guess that makes sense.'

THEY FINALLY ARRIVED at Brunel and immediately found somewhere to park.

Sean switched off the engine and unfastened his seatbelt. 'How do you want to play this?' he asked.

'I know where the lab is. Ollie showed me around last year. Let's head over there.'

'What if Ollie is there? It could be awkward.'

'Not really. It would be opportune and the perfect excuse to introduce you to him.'

As it was, Ollie wasn't there. In fact, no one was there. The lab was locked and, peering through the window of the large, double doors, Lorrie saw no movement and no evidence that anyone was inside.

Sean stepped back from the doors. 'What now?'

'Let's see if we can find someone to talk to.'

Lorrie led the way all the way back to the administration offices where she knocked on the first door they came to.

'Can I help you?' A small, round woman greeted them with a wary smile.

Lorrie produced her warrant card. 'Superintendent Sullivan,' she said. 'And, this is Detective Inspector Kelly. We're wondering who could provide us with a list of the professors with access to your biochemistry laboratory.'

'I could help you with that,' the small, round woman said. 'But I don't think I'm allowed to... not just like that.'

'What about your manager? Would it be better if we spoke to him?'

'Her.' The small round woman wasn't pleased by the reference to her manager being a man. 'Ms. Phillips is busy at the moment. Perhaps you could come back later? Perhaps with a document or something.'

'A document?' Lorrie showed her confusion.

'A search warrant. I think Ms Phillips would want to see a search warrant.'

'There would be no need for that,' Lorrie said. 'It's an informal request and we have no immediate plans to search anywhere.'

'May I enquire as to what this is about?'

'Just routine.' Lorrie turned to Sean and said, 'We'll come back later when the manager is free. I don't want to take up any more of Miss...?' She looked down at the woman with an arched brow.

The woman bristled. 'It's Mrs. Atkins.'

'Okay... We won't take up any more of Mrs. Atkins' time.'

Lorrie and Sean made to turn away but were stopped by Mrs. Atkin's next words.

'If you told me what this was about then, perhaps, I could get you that list? Ms Phillips is a very busy woman, and she would probably thank me for keeping yet another task off her desk.' She looked expectantly at the two officers.

Lorrie shifted to confidential mode and lowered her head so she could speak quietly into the woman's ear. 'Can I rely on your discretion?' she asked.

Mrs. Atkins nodded enthusiastically. She was suddenly feeling quite important.

Lorrie turned and looked over her shoulder, searching for eavesdroppers. 'This is in the strictest confidence, you understand?'

'I can be trusted, Superintendent. I have access to a great deal of confidential information.'

'Thank you. Well,' Lorrie spoke as if to a fellow conspirator, 'The Met is looking to send some lucrative forensic work to one of the London universities. Obviously, we have to screen all the people in charge and ensure there aren't any skeletons in their cupboards. We can't take any chances and we don't want word to get out because of the risk of sabotage. You understand?'

'Yes. Yes.' Mrs Atkins was almost hyperventilating. She was an insignificant cog in a very large wheel, and this was the first time anyone was looking to her for something secret and important. 'I'll be happy to get you that list. Tell me... will there be an administrative role in this new venture? Only, I'm looking for something more suited to my skill-set.'

Lorrie smiled. 'I'm sure there will be.'

The woman scurried away and Lorrie gave Sean a saucy wink then, list in hand, they made their way back to the car.

'Cleverly done, Superintendent,' Sean praised. 'Quite the actress.'

Lorrie acknowledged his words with a smirk and a curtsey. She said, 'Let's get back and go through this list and then we'll sit down in front of the telly with the rest of the squad and watch the Reaper on the six o'clock news.'

# DAY FIVE: EVENING

The introduction to the Reaper's video was well done. The familiar face of the BBC newsreader was reassuring to the public and it was hoped everyone watching would believe him when he said the police knew about the video and that they had everything under control. It was a bare-faced lie, but the last thing anyone wanted or needed was mass panic.

Baxter served a round of hot coffee to everyone huddled around the screen and, if it wasn't for the content of the video and everyone's severe expressions, you could have been forgiven for thinking it was an evening at the movies.

'He's a cocky bastard,' Simon commented at the end of the viewing. 'I can't wait to nick him and rip that bloody mask off his face.'

'You and me both,' Sean agreed.

DS Baxter collected the empty coffee mugs and hesitated a moment before walking off with them. She returned almost immediately and approached Simon. He could see she was itching to say something and raised an eyebrow at her.

'Spit it out, Baxter,' he said. 'I don't bite.'

'Well,' she said. 'It's just that I've been thinking.'

'Thinking is good, Baxter. We pay you to think,'

**153**

'The costume... you know – the Reaper costume? Has anyone looked into where he got it?'

Simon's brow furrowed and suddenly he was up and out of his seat. 'Bloody Hell, Baxter. I don't think so. Fuck, no!' He looked around the room for Lorrie. Spying her standing with Sean, he turned once more and hugged the DS saying, 'I could kiss you, Baxter. You're a fucking marvel.'

Lorrie walked towards them and asked what all the commotion was about.

Simon explained and Lorrie's jaw dropped. 'That's a cock-up of monumental proportions,' she said. 'How could we have missed something so obvious?' She glanced at her watch. 'It's too late to contact the fancy dress shops tonight. Let's get online... Google it and run through Amazon and, what's that other main online shopping thing?'

'Ebay, Ma'am,' Baxter volunteered.

'Yes... Ebay.' She stood and spoke to the room. 'I want everyone to listen up.'

Everyone gave Lorrie their full attention.

'I want a full list of outlets for this Grim Reaper costume. I want High Street shops identified and a rota drawn up to visit them as soon as they're open in the morning. Lovell and Baxter... you two lead on the High Street outlets and pick your teams. Get your questions synchronised and ready for the off. Simon, you take all the newbies and find all the online outlets and get straight onto as many customer services as you can tonight. Shake a few trees and get information on orders and deliveries in the past...' She considered a moment. 'Let's start with six months.'

'That takes in Halloween,' Simon said. 'Let's hope the Grim Reaper costume wasn't a popular purchase.' He sighed. 'Never mind... soon as we start the sooner we'll finish.' He strode off, gathering several officers as he went.

'Sean, you and I will finish off on that list of Professors. I want to knock on one or two doors tonight.'

THERE WERE EIGHT NAMES on the list, but it was clear that the majority only accessed the laboratory on an ad-hoc basis. They decided to prioritise the three who spent most of every day – when not lecturing – working in the lab.

'Ollie mentioned this Professor Napier a few times. He sort of looks up to him, which is something in itself because Ollie doesn't normally look up to anyone. We'll start with him. He lives in Battersea. Let's head off now and have a chat with him.'

'What about the other two?'

'Napier first. We'll think about the other two later.'

PROFESSOR NAPIER WAS an enigma. Both Lorrie and Sean had expected to be confronted by what they imagined a typical professor in bio-chemistry would look like. They expected someone small and thin, probably bald and wearing spectacles. In reality, he was a bear of a man. He stood well over six feet tall, had a full head of ginger hair and his equally ginger beard reached almost to his chest.

His voice was cultured, and it was strange to hear it coming from underneath so much hair.

'Do come in,' he said. 'I've just put the kettle on. Can I tempt you to a cup of tea?'

Taking tea from a man they suspected might make poison for the thrill of committing murder was too horrifying to contemplate and their dual refusals was almost comical.

'Suit yourself,' he said. 'I'll just be a minute.' He walked through to the kitchen and Lorrie and Sean surreptitiously watched him. They didn't want him bolting out the back door.

Tea made, and everyone made comfortable in the lounge, and Lorrie searched for the right opening.

'You've seen tonight's news?' she asked.

The bear nodded. 'I always watch the tea-time news... that is, when I'm not held up at work.'

'What did you make of the video on the BBC?'

'That Grim Reaper nonsense? I didn't think anything of it, truth be told.'

'You don't seem curious as to why we're here,' Sean put in.

'I supposed you'd enlighten me when you were good and ready, but I'm guessing you want some advice about whatever it is that's killing those poor sods?'

'You have an idea about that?' Lorrie moved forward in her chair. 'Anything you want to share with us?'

'Nothing springs to mind, I'm afraid.'

'No thoughts at all?'

'I don't know enough about it. That video didn't give much away. I know something's been happening at a couple of hospitals. I thought, perhaps, some virus or other.'

'No, it's not a virus, Professor Napier.'

'Just as well – I don't know anything about viruses. Poison, then?' His dark eyes flashed with interest.

'We're not at liberty to say, I'm afraid.'

'Okay. I understand. So...' He placed his teacup on the table at the side of his chair and crossed his legs. 'What can I help you with?'

'The laboratory at Brunel,' Lorrie began cautiously. 'We think it might be a place of interest to us.'

'My lab?' The bear laughed. 'That's ridiculous.'

'We might be clutching at straws,' Sean interjected. 'We just want to talk with someone who works there.'

'Well, talk away. I'm all ears.'

Lorrie gave him a disarming smile. 'Do you mind if I run a hypothetical past you, Professor?'

'By all means,' he replied amiably.

'Okay, let's say – for argument's sake - that someone accessed the lab to concoct a poison. Let's say your lab was used by the killer. Do you think that could happen...? Hypothetically?'

'It couldn't happen.' The bear was adamant.

'Why not?'

'Well, there's no way on God's green earth that it would be possible.'

'You understand that by simply saying that it's not possible without an explanation isn't evidentiary? You do a lot of research?'

The bear nodded.

'Evidence is important?'

He nodded once more.

'So?' Lorrie settled back in her chair. 'Why is it impossible? Where's your evidence to support that belief?'

'Well, for starters, access is strictly limited. I'm there, more often than not, and I keep a close eye on what's going on. Every molecule of every single product is catalogued and checked routinely twice a day. We had some pilfering a couple of years ago... Idiot students thinking they could nick MDMA to make ecstasy... so security was beefed up and I now run a pretty tight ship.'

Sean had a thought. 'Could someone bring stuff into the lab and work on it unobserved?'

'Who? Who are we talking about? Some random person off the street?' The bear shook his mane of shaggy hair. 'You really are clutching at straws. Everyone in my lab has a reason to be there. I know everything they're working on.'

'Everything? You check what they're doing?'

'Of course. I have to sign off on different stages of their research.'

'What about when you're not there? What about out of hours?' Lorrie remembered that Ollie was allowed in the lab out of hours. Perhaps other people used the lab when Professor Napier was absent.

'Yes, well, I suppose the lab is accessed when I'm not there.'

'Are you there on your own very often?'

The bear's eyes narrowed. 'Am I a suspect in this hypothetical scenario of yours?'

'No, of course not, Professor.' Lorrie stood up and put her hand out.

'Sorry to have troubled you.' She shook hands with him. 'If you think of anything, please get in touch.' She handed him her card. 'We'll see ourselves out.'

She felt the bear's eyes on her all the way to the car.

'I don't like him,' she said to Sean. 'He's hiding something.'

'I didn't catch that. He seemed on the up and up.'

'He was too cool. Too laid back and he wasn't perturbed by our visit.'

'Why would he be perturbed?'

'Surprised, then. It was as if he was expecting us.'

'Hmmm.' Sean wasn't convinced. 'Why did we leave so abruptly?'

They climbed into the car and Lorrie said, 'I felt we'd spooked him, and retreat seemed best. Next time we question him it will be under caution in an interview room. There's definitely something about him that I don't like. He's squirrelly.'

'Squirrelly? Right. What about the other two on the list?'

Lorrie shook her head. 'No more home visits. This little fishing expedition could have backfired on us big time. I want all three brought in tomorrow and we'll question them in our own back yard where they just might feel uncomfortable enough to let something slip. Get them knocked up at the crack of dawn before they've had their morning coffee and have them brought to us.'

# DAY FIVE: NIGHT

Colin was late leaving the office. It wasn't often that he stayed at work beyond eight o'clock, but he was still there at ten and had plans to spend some time in the warehouse before heading home. He disengaged the alarm and stepped back to pull open the huge metal doors before crossing the threshold and turning on the lights.

There were three large windows, cracked with age, along one wall, and rows upon rows of tall, stacked boxes along the length and breadth of the hanger-like building. Each box was labelled and ready for shipping out. Colin spent thirty minutes checking the labels against information printed on a clipboard in his hand. Satisfied that all was in order, he turned towards a solitary box standing in a corner and, with one last flick through the paperwork, picked it up and placed it on top of a small tower of similar boxes.

He didn't quite want to leave the warehouse. He loved the smell of the place. He also loved the way it sounded in the still of the night. The overhead fluorescent lights crackled. A drinks machine hummed in one far corner. His footsteps echoed as he walked. During the day it was a hive of noisy activity but, at night, it had a voice all of its own. He sat down on the dusty floor – not caring about dirtying the seat of his trousers – and simply allowed the smell and the quiet sounds to wash over him. He would have to go home soon. He would have to pick up where he had left off with Lorrie but, for the moment, he was content to sit there.

# DAY SIX: MORNING

Professor Napier – the bear - was not a happy bunny. He'd found himself unceremoniously woken at six o'clock and bundled into a car and brought to this stark, grey interview room without so much as a single word of explanation. He'd eventually been told that, no, he wasn't under arrest and, no, there was no need for a solicitor, but it was all bullshit. He wasn't stupid... They suspected him of something.

He knew who Lorrie Sullivan was. He'd known her immediately the previous night. She was Ollie's mother. How that bright, clever boy had this woman as a mother defied all logic as far as the bear was concerned. She was obviously one of those women who let power go to their heads. Well, she'd bit off more than she would be able to chew this time. The bear was ready for her.

He kept his voice low and neutral. 'You have no right to hold me here,' he said. 'Unless you're charging me with something?'

Lorrie feigned shock. 'Charging you, Professor Napier? Of course not.'

'Then, I can leave?'

'Absolutely. I'm sure my officers explained that you were free to leave any old time you pleased?'

He remained composed. 'No, they didn't.' He made to stand.

'But,' Lorrie pulled out a chair and sat at the table. 'We'd appreciate picking your brains a little bit more. Please relax. Hang out with us a while.'

The bear was curious, so he decided to find out what was on her mind. He relaxed back in his chair, placed his hands behind his head and stretched out his long legs.

'I guess I can spare you some time,' he said.

'Thank you, Professor. Now... a question for you - do you use the computers in the university library?'

'What?' The bear shifted slightly. 'Of course not. There's no need for me to trail all the way to the library. Do you know how many computers there are in the lab? And, not to mention the fact that I have one in my office and a laptop at my disposal. So, no - I don't use the computers in the library.'

Lorrie thought that he doth protest too much but she let it slide. 'Perhaps you nipped in when passing?'

'Not that I recollect, Superintendent.'

'Not that you recollect? So, you could have, but maybe forgot?'

'I have an excellent memory. I'm quite positive that I didn't nip in.' He sat up straight. He was losing patience. 'You could have asked me this last night.'

'It was late. We'd outstayed our welcome.'

'I think I want to leave, Superintendent. This is boring.'

She nodded. 'Of course. But, what I don't understand is why you don't want to help us with our enquiries.'

'I thought I was helping?'

'Yes, my mistake - of course you are - and that's why I'd appreciate it if you'd stay just a few minutes longer.' She exchanged a glance with Sean who immediately took over the questioning.

'Do you know if any of your PhD students use the library?' he asked.

The bear shrugged his massive shoulders. 'I suppose so. It's what it's there for.'

'And, the computers at the lab... they use them too?'

'Of course. Look...' He placed his elbows on the table and leaned forward. 'Perhaps if you told me what this is all about then I'd be able to help with your enquiries a little better.'

'You are helping, Professor,' Lorrie put in.

'Tell me about your most promising students,' Sean asked.

The bear relaxed back in his chair. 'They're all promising.'

'Anyone worry you?'

'Worry me? In what way?'

Sean shrugged. 'Oh, I don't know... Anyone have any ideas that seem a bit iffy?'

'You think this Reaper person is one of my students?' He let out a great bellow of a laugh. 'None of them have the capability.'

'How do you know what the Reaper is capable of?' That was Lorrie again.

'I watch the news, Superintendent. I told you that.'

'So... Enlighten me.'

'Well,' he avoided eye contact with both Lorrie and Sean. 'I'm assuming you don't know exactly what it is that's killing all those people?' He looked up for a reaction but both expressions were blank. 'I don't have a single student capable of coming up with a poison that would have your forensic scientists baffled.' A look of cunning crossed his face. 'Except for your son, of course, Superintendent Sullivan.'

'My son?' Lorrie was careful to give nothing away.

'Ollie... He is your son?'

'You think Ollie is capable of being the Reaper?'

He back-peddled somewhat. 'I didn't say that.'

'What are you saying?' Sean put in.

'That Ollie is the only one with the knowledge and the skill.'

'To do what, exactly?'

He shrugged once more. 'Whatever.'

'What about you, professor?' Lorrie was trying desperately to keep her temper in check. How dare he raise Ollie as a suspect? 'Are you capable of being the Reaper?'

The bear thought a moment before smiling. He shook his head sadly. 'If you two are the sum total of what the public has protecting them, then God help us all.' He stood up. 'I'm going now. But,' He stepped away from the table, 'Take a good look at me.' He held his thick arms out to the side and turned full circle. 'Do I look like the guy in the video? Do I look like the Reaper?'

There were no words to respond to that and Lorrie nodded to the constable standing at the door and he opened it to allow the bear to leave.

Alone in the room, Sean and Lorrie let out collective sighs of frustration.

'About Ollie...' Sean began.

Lorrie waved a hand in dismissal. 'He's talking nonsense.'

'I know, but we still have to bring him in.'

'What? Are you joking?'

'We have to question all of Napier's students... Ollie included.'

'I can't accuse my son of being a serial killer... Our son!'

'That's not what I'm saying. Anyway... there's no rush. We still have the other two professors to question and then we'll need the up-dates on the enquiries about the costume.'

'Yes. Okay. You're right. Of course, you're right.'

Sean justified himself further. 'Lovell and Baxter can question all of the students who use the Lab. We need to eliminate them, Lorrie.'

She nodded. 'I know.'

OLLIE AND COLIN WERE having a heated argument and it wasn't pleasant. They were in Colin's office and the door was closed.

'Shut up, Ollie and listen to me,' Colin bellowed. 'All this sneaking around is doing my head in. I want an explanation about what you're up to.'

'Get off my back,' Ollie countered. 'You're not my father.'

If Colin had heard that statement once, he had heard it a million times over the years. 'I don't want to be your fucking father,' he spat. 'Your father was a tosser who knocked up your mother and then fucked off back to his wife. Don't mention me in the same breath as that wanker.'

With a face full of hate and disdain, Ollie spat back, 'And, what makes you any less of a wanker? You treat my mum like shit. I don't know why she stays with you.'

Colin's fists clenched at his sides, and it took every bit of willpower not to batter the little fucker. He spoke through clenched teeth. 'I want to know what you've been up to in the warehouse. I want to know why you're there in the middle of the night and I want to know just what the fuck you think you've been doing on my computer?'

Ollie was stumped for a response. He couldn't answer his stepfather. Colin had caught him reading through his computer files and he couldn't think of an explanation.

'Lost for words, you little shit?'

'I'm... I'm sorry. I was just doing some research.'

'How the fuck did you know my password? You can't get in without it.'

Ollie dropped his eyes. He was well and truly rumbled. 'You keep it on a piece of paper in your desk drawer,' he said. 'That's a bit stupid, if you ask me.'

'Well, I didn't ask you. You have no right...'

Ollie raised his hands. 'Okay. You're right. I said I was sorry.'

'And, what about all the sneaking around? What are you up to?'

'Nothing. I'm not up to anything.'

'That's not an answer. I want to know what you've been doing in the warehouse.'

'Look, I'll leave,' Ollie said, deflated. 'I won't work here anymore.'

'That's not good enough.'

'It'll have to do,' he suddenly flared. 'You don't want me here anyway.'

Colin contemplated his options. He was desperate to know what Ollie had been up to. There was something highly suspicious about his actions, but he couldn't call in the police – what would he say to them? What would he accuse him of? He couldn't complain to Lorrie as she'd dismiss his concerns out of hand and have a go at him for having a go at her precious son. Anyway, he didn't want his wife poking her nose into what went on at his place of business.

'Just, fuck off, Ollie. Get out of my sight.'

Ollie didn't need telling twice. He almost ran from the room. It had been all too close for comfort, and he now needed to think carefully about his next move.

Colin watched him leave and walked around his desk and began to explore what it was Ollie had been looking at. He was surprised to see that the boy had been examining the delivery runs. He was nonplussed. Just what was he up to? he wondered.

THEY GOT EXACTLY NOTHING from the other two professors. Neither of them made the hair on the back of Lorrie's neck stand up. They were clueless. No wonder Ollie was so detrimental about his professors. They hardly seemed to have a brain cell between them.

'I think the university might very well end up as a red herring,' she said to Sean. 'And, it has nothing to do with being worried about Ollie.'

Sean said nothing.

'The lab, anyway. The library is still in the equation. Has Baxter found anything yet?'

'No.'

'I might take a look at the CCTV myself.'

'Your prerogative.'

Lorrie narrowed her eyes. 'Are you pissed at me?'

'No.'

'Don't lie.'

He shrugged. 'You're losing focus.'

'Am I, indeed?'

'Superintendent level is supposed to have a strategic focus. I don't think trawling through hours of CCTV is the best use of your strategic brain.'

'Is that right? Well, I'm at a loss as to why the CCTV is giving us zilch. We know where the email came from and we know what time it was sent, so why hasn't DS Baxter found anything? Perhaps it will take a strategic brain to see what no one else can?'

'CCTV cameras don't cover the computer sections. All we have are people coming in and out of the library and some views across areas where the rare books are kept.'

'I still want to look for myself.'

'You're being ridiculous. Baxter knows what she's about.'

'And, you're out of order,' she snapped. 'I won't be told what to do on my own investigation.'

'Jesus, Lorrie. You need to screw your head on straight.'

'You're very blunt. Are you taking advantage me? Just because I told you that Colin...'

The look he gave her could have frozen volcanic lava. 'I'm one of your DIs... albeit a temporary position. I'm doing my job. If I do it bluntly, then that's just the way I bloody well do it. Get over yourself, Superintendent.'

Lorrie was shocked to her core. Gone was the man who told her that he loved her.

Gone was the man who'd offered to up sticks and move to London to be with her. He was acting as if he was mad at her. He obviously regretted his words and had apparently sprouted a pair of cold feet.

She took a moment to compose herself and gave herself a mental shake. Sean was an experienced detective. He only wanted to do his job and he wouldn't let the fact that he was in love with her cloud his judgement. He was simply saying it as he saw it.

'I'm sorry,' she said, chastened.

His expression softened a fraction. 'Do what you're good at, Lorrie. Don't start going off on a tangent or getting weighed down with things you can't influence.'

'I know, you're right. Thank you.' She looked at him, beseeching him with her eyes to understand and forgive her bitchiness. Because that's what it was. She had lapsed into bitch mode and, if she didn't get her act together, she would lose the case and she would lose him.

They both turned at the sound of approaching footsteps. It was Simon.

He said, 'Baxter and Lovell are still doing the rounds of fancy dress shops, but I think it's a waste of time. Most, if not all of these shops, rent out costumes. I don't think our guy rented his. Can I bring the two teams back and get them to help me with the online searches?'

'Sure,' Lorrie nodded. 'If you think that's best, but put Lovell onto finding out details of all the students who use Brunel's lab. Get her to start with the PhD students.'

'Yes, Guv.' Simon turned and made his way back the way he had come.

Sean smiled his appreciation of her instruction to Simon. 'That's my girl,' he said.

# DAY SIX: AFTERNOON

'If we don't have some sort of a breakthrough by the end of the day then Counter Terrorism takes over.' Lorrie paced the length and breadth of her office as she informed her senior officers of Scully's threat to take the case away from them.

'There was no point in me making a big deal out of it and telling you before now because, quite frankly, everyone has been working their hearts out and what else could anyone do that's not already been done?'

'Those fuckwits won't do any better,' Simon gnashed out through gritted teeth. 'They're supposed to be helping us, supporting us, but they're so far up their own arses that they're a fucking hindrance.'

'Have you informed Scully and Connor of the two leads we're following – the PhD students and the Reaper costume?' Sean asked.

She nodded. 'They're both up to speed.'

'They need to let us see those leads through. Pulling us off now would be a big mistake.'

She nodded once more in Sean's direction. 'I hope they have the sense to see that.'

'Unfortunately,' Simon put in. 'It's like wading through treacle. For each enquiry online we're on the phone at least an hour. Bastards keep putting us on hold then transferring us and putting us on hold again.'

'The Reaper mentioned Halloween in one of the videos...the first one, I think.' Lorrie wracked her brain. 'I'm sure he called it a Halloween costume. Narrow your search parameters a bit more, Simon. I've got a feeling he purchased it in the run up to Halloween. Focus on purchases September through October.'

Simon nodded. 'Sure thing, Guv.'

Lorrie turned to Sean. 'Let's go see Ricky. He rang earlier.'

PATHOLOGIST, RICKY Burton, couldn't hide his excitement. Lorrie and Sean had to stand and listen to him go on about genetic manipulation, biotechnology, RNA molecules and proteins, for ten long minutes before he stopped long enough to allow Lorrie to get a word in.

'Slow down, Ricky. How the Hell do you imagine we've got the least clue what you're on about? Do we look like square-headed boffins to you?'

Ricky laughed and Lorrie was concerned at the manic element of that laugh.

'Ricky!' Her voice penetrated Ricky's euphoria and he sobered.

'Sorry. I've not slept for two days and I'm a bit loopy in the head.' He sat down and took several deep breaths.

'What's this all about? What's got you so hyper?'

Ricky smiled at her. 'We've only gone and sussed it. We've only gone and identified what he did.'

Lorrie's heart leapt in her chest. 'Tell me, then... and the idiot's guide, if you please.'

Ricky explained. 'He spliced it. He cut the DNA of the botulinum and inserted a gene. It altered the characteristics. He added a bloody virus. Can you believe it? I can't believe it.'

'And?'

Ricky frowned. 'And, what? Do you understand the significance of what I just told you?'

'Not really.'

He glowered at her. 'Sometimes I wonder about you.'

'Just get on with it, Ricky. Why is this good news for us?'

'Well, we know what that virus is, and we know how the genetic manipulation of the toxin led to an accelerated outcome. In other words – we know what it is and exactly how it works.'

'What else?' Lorrie looked at him expectantly.

'What else?' Ricky looked confused. 'What else is there?'

'How did it get into their systems?'

'Oh,' Ricky flapped a hand. 'I don't know that as yet... Not fully, anyway.'

Lorrie bit her tongue. There had to be more. 'Ricky,' she said calmly. 'What else is there?'

'Right. Right... what else?' Ricky tried to gather his thoughts. His mind was racing, and he desperately needed sleep. 'Paper... we found minute traces of a paper-like substance on one of the victim's tongues. We think it's a thin card... dissolved on the tongue.'

'Okay.' Lorrie encouraged him with a hand gesture. 'What does that tell us?'

'Well, we're re-examining all the other tongues and, if we find the same evidence, then...'

'Chances are the poison was on thin card?' Sean said quickly.

Ricky nodded. 'Could be.'

'That's something,' Lorrie sighed.

'We didn't find it on first examination,' Ricky countered. 'It might be an anomaly. Don't get your hopes up just yet.'

'No,' she conceded, but her mind was racing, and her hopes were well and truly soaring to the stratosphere. 'When will we know if the other victims have that same dissolved paper on their tongues?'

'I've put a rush on, but there are a lot of bodies to re-examine. Everyone is well and truly knackered, and I've had to ask for some help. I've got three more Home Office approved pathologists starting with me tomorrow. I should have the full picture by dinner time tomorrow at the latest.'

Tomorrow was too long a wait, but Lorrie had to content herself with that timeline.

NEWS OF NINE NEW VICTIMS hit the major incident room just as Lorrie and Sean returned from seeing the pathologist. Her first thought was that Ricky wasn't going to get any sleep after all.

'Another three hospitals, Guv,' Simon said. 'All in and around Glasgow.'

All the air in Lorrie's lungs dissipated and she gasped to drag in a breath.

Sean put out a hand to steady her. The news was devastating, and Lorrie took it hard.

'We're just getting the details,' Simon went on. 'Two women at Queen Elizabeth University hospital, three women at the Royal Children's hospital and three men and one woman at Gartnavel General.'

'How... how many does that make it now?'

'Thirty-two, Guv.'

'I... I need to ring Commander Scully,' she said. 'I think it's time we handed this over.' She turned to leave.

'Wait,' Sean said. 'We've got until the end of the day. Give us until then, Lorrie.'

She faced him. 'Too many people are dying. I don't think it's going to stop. I'm... I'm not the person to lead this investigation anymore. Scully was right all along.'

'Bullshit.' Sean grabbed her by the shoulders and shook her. 'No one will do it any better. You're exactly the right person to lead us and lead this investigation. Fuck Scully and fuck Connor and fuck all the other pricks who think otherwise.' He dropped his arms. 'Just until the end of the day, Lorrie. Please.'

'He's right, Guv. You can't give up on us. We've worked too hard.'

Lorrie became aware of the silence in the room. Everyone had stopped what they were doing and were silently watching their Superintendent being given a talking to.

'It won't be up to me,' she said. 'Scully will take these latest deaths as an excuse to be rid of me.'

'Then, go to the Assistant Commissioner. Explain to her all that we've done and all we are doing.'

'I can't go above Scully's head. He'll have my guts for garters.'

Exasperated, Sean threw his arms in the air. 'That's it, then? We stand back and watch as S015 cock it up?'

'Perhaps they'll do a better job. Counter Terrorism has better resources.'

'Well, fuck that for a game of soldiers.' Sean stalked off.

'Where are you going?' Lorrie called after him. 'Don't do anything stupid.'

SEAN DID SOMETHING stupid. He had nothing to lose. He would be on his way back to Manchester soon and Scully's malice didn't reach that far, so he went straight to bang on the Assistant Commissioner's door.

'DI Kelly.' Annie Gordon sat behind her desk and pursed her lips. 'I see they don't breed good manners in Manchester. An appointment is usually necessary to see me.'

'I apologise, Ma'am but it's urgent.'

'Everything on my desk is urgent, Kelly. You're breaching the chain of command by insisting on seeing me. I hope, for your sake, it's worth the five minutes I can spare you.'

Annie Gordon was well known to Sean. They went way back. They'd always respected one another. Sean was counting on their history working together back in the day to gain him a favour.

'I want you to give Superintendent Sullivan another couple of days before transferring the case to SO15.' He noted her frown and went on quickly. 'I'm out of order – I know that. I'm probably well and truly fucking up what's left of my career, but she's doing a good job and that prick Scully has it in for her. We've got two good lines of enquiry at the moment and Sullivan needs to see them through. We've also got confirmation of the exact constitution of the poison and the pathologist has found some paper...'

'Slow down, Kelly. Yes, I can see you've all made progress, but...'

Sean interjected, 'It would be a mistake to take her off the case, Ma'am.'

The Assistant Commissioner bridled. 'I don't make mistakes,' she snapped. 'I take exception to you intimating otherwise.' She stood up and walked to the window where she turned her back on him and gazed out over London. 'What are these two lines of enquiry?'

Sean replied almost breathlessly, 'We're looking into where the killer got the Reaper costume. We're running down every order and tracing every delivery since just before Halloween.'

'And, the other?'

'PhD students from Brunel.'

'Students?' She turned to face him once more. 'You're not serious?'

'The emails were sent from the library at Brunel. The university has a state of the art laboratory. Sullivan's nose tells her there's something going on in that lab. We're just about to start bringing in the students. They're a clever bunch and the profiler said to look for someone young.'

He held his breath and waited as she mulled over his words. He could almost see the cogs turning in her brain.

'I think I've heard enough,' she finally said. 'You'd better go back on the job.' She turned her back to him again.

Deflated, but with hope still in his voice, he asked, 'Will you give her another two days, Ma'am?'

She waited a beat. 'I told you to leave, Kelly.' It was her only reply.

'WHAT DID YOU DO?' LORRIE was far from pleased. 'I've just had Scully ripping the skin off my face and accusing me of undermining him. What did you do, Sean?'

He refused to answer her question. He asked, instead, 'Have you still got the case?'

'Yes, but you know that, don't you?'

He shook his head. 'I hoped, but I wasn't sure if I'd convinced her.'

'Convinced who?' Realisation dawned. 'Don't tell me you went to the Assistant Commissioner? Jesus, Sean.'

'You were ready to throw in the towel and let Scully destroy you. I wasn't about to let that happen.'

'No wonder he's incandescent.'

'He'll get over it.'

'I doubt it.'

'Tell me, Lorrie.' Sean was particularly serious. 'Do you really give a toss about Scully being pissed off?'

She smiled. 'I guess not.'

'I'm glad to hear it. Now, how much longer did the AC give us?'

'Another forty-eight hours. It's all she could swing without giving the Home Secretary a heart attack,' she replied.

'She's got some balls, has Annie Gordon.'

'She's sweet, really.'

'Don't ever let her hear you say that.'

Sean's relief was evident on his face and in his eyes. Another forty-eight hours was a Godsend. He could have hugged her, but it wasn't the time nor the place for such a demonstration of feeling.

He said, 'It's not long, but, by Christ, we'll make the most of every minute. We'll get the bastard.'

# DAY SIX: EVENING

'Eleven PhD students have been identified and contact details are all on file,' Simon said. 'Ollie is on the list.'

Lorrie nodded. 'You interview Ollie with Lovell. It's best if I stay clear.'

When do you want us to bring them in?'

Lorrie glanced at her watch. 'It's gone six. Let's see how many we can round up before bed time. Get who you can picked up and brought here.'

'You really think it's one of them, Guv?' Simon's tone suggested he wasn't convinced.

'I don't know, Simon, and that's the God's honest truth. But, what else have we got?'

'Okay, Guv. I'm on it.'

OLLIE WAS WORRIED. He mentally ran through his options and concluded that something drastic was required. He had to protect himself and, as it was obvious that Colin was onto him, he knew that his next step had to be conclusive. He had to do something that would take Colin completely out of the equation.

It was dark in the house. Ollie liked being alone in the dark. As a child, he never allowed his mother to leave a nightlight on in his bedroom, preferring to give the monsters under his bed the opportunity to crawl out under the protection of the velvet black of the night.

He was never afraid. Until he was a teenager, Ollie didn't even know that the emotion of fear existed. What he grew up feeling the most was loneliness and the monsters under the bed were better than having no one at all.

He supposed he was blunted in some way, but reconciled himself with the fact that, although he couldn't understand real fear, he could associate with anxiety. If he had tried to explain things – to a doctor or a psychologist – they would probably have told him that worry and anxiety were forms of fear, but he didn't see it like that. He worried about things not working out. He became anxious when he imagined that some plan or another would fail. The reason for those feelings of anxiety were all too present in his psyche. In many ways, he grew up worried. He matured with the ever-present weight of anxiety on his chest, but was never frightened that any harm would come to him.

As he sat on the bed and contemplated his next move, he heard a car pull up on the driveway followed directly by a loud knock on the front door. He made a move and stood to go out of the room and down the stairs but something – a sense of curiosity – halted him. He turned and approached the window instead where he peered out into the night.

His bedroom window looked straight onto the front of the house and his view of the driveway was clear. He saw the police car and quickly drew back. He wasn't unduly concerned. There were a whole lot of reasons why a police car would be parked on the drive. His mother, after all, was a police officer and perhaps they were looking for her. Someone could have had an accident or there were some door to door enquiries going on. Somehow Ollie knew that none of those reasons applied. He knew they were looking for him. He checked his mobile phone for missed calls or texts from his mum and was a little surprised to see that there were none. So, he thought – it was worse than he imagined.

The knock sounded again. The fact that the house was in darkness was obviously not deterring the police officer. Ollie's motorbike on the drive was obviously a dead giveaway.

He knew that he had to get out of the house. He had some thinking to do. A little of the familiar anxiety crept over him. His plan was in jeopardy.

He crept stealthily down the stairs and made his way through to the kitchen and to the back door.

There was another, louder, knock on the front door but, by that time, Ollie was out of the kitchen door and over the back fence.

A mile along the road and he was chilled to the bone. A thin shirt and no jacket wasn't the least defence against the cold of the evening, and Ollie made straight for the pub where there was heat. He'd call a taxi and head for the warehouse. He'd decided what his next move was going to be. He was going to burn it to the ground.

DS FRIEL CORNERED SEAN in the corridor and complained, 'No one is giving me anything to do, Guv. I've been hovering on the side-lines watching everyone else do all the work. I don't know why I bothered trailing all the way down here from Manchester.'

Sean was preoccupied and barely heard her. Ollie was on the missing list, and he was anxious to go tell Lorrie.

'Guv?'

'What? Oh, Friel... Sorry. My mind's elsewhere. What's that you were saying?'

'I need something to do, Guv. No one is giving me anything. I'm well and truly fed up.'

Sean gave her his full attention. 'Okay, well I might just have something for you. Can you go find Ollie, the Super's son? I need you to be very discreet, though.'

'The Super's son? I don't understand.'

'He's one of the PhD students we're bringing in, only he's not at home nor at the university. The Super has enough on her plate without wondering where he is and why we can't find him.'

'Sure. I can do that.'

'Do it on the quiet. When you find him, report directly to me. The press are camped outside and I want him brought in surreptitiously.'

'I can do that, Guv.'

'Good. Off you go, then.' Sean turned from her.

'Guv?' DS Friel halted him. 'When can I head back to Manchester? I'm not really needed here. I'm virtually invisible. I don't think anyone even knows my name. I've been unnoticed since the moment we got here.'

Sean eyed her. 'It's not up to everyone here to see you, Friel,' he said. 'It's up to you to be seen.' He tempered his tone. 'Look,' he put a hand on her shoulder. 'There are more than a few strong detectives on this team, but you're good and can hold your own with the best of them. Your problem is that you're not pushy enough. If you have something to say, then say it. If you want to be involved then make damn sure you are front and foremost at all the briefings.'

'Okay, Guv. Understood.'

'I'm sorry if you feel that I've neglected you.'

Friel blushed. 'No, not at all. You're right – I'm a bit backward at coming forward.'

Sean smiled. 'Just find Ollie and then you can sit in on his interview.'

'Okay.' Friel nodded. 'Where should I look for him?'

'Well, according to what I know about the lad, he's usually at the lab at Brunel, at his stepfather's place of work - he has a warehouse and a distribution centre - or at home. The uniforms have already checked at the university and at home.'

'So, no one's checked the warehouse or the distribution centre?'

'I don't believe so. Start there, ring me when you've checked, and we'll take it from there.'

'What does the Super's husband do? What's his business?'

'I don't have a Scooby, Friel. I know the lad works for him in his spare time so I'm guessing he's there. Just find him and bring him in. It's a formality. We don't really think any of the students have anything to do with this nasty business, but we're turning over every stone. For pure appearance's sake, it's prudent to ensure the Super's lad is one of the first to be interviewed. We don't want any accusations of leaving him out.'

'Right, I'm on it. I'll ring you when I find him.'

Sean watched her walk away. He felt guilty. Friel was a good DS, and he should have ensured that she was integrated into the team and given a purpose. He'd keep her on his radar from now on.

LORRIE RECEIVED NEWS from the hospital that the twins were off the critical list. The paediatrician had already cleared them for steroids and, although their condition remained serious, there was hope that they would survive. Lorrie actually cried when she heard the news. It was, at least, one piece of good news to help balance out the bad and the relief she felt was palpable.

She shared the news with her team and the mood in the major incident room lightened immensely. The hope of life amongst all the death was a boost to many a heavy heart.

To add to the euphoria that swept the room, on news of the twins, was the update from Simon on the Reaper costume.

'We've narrowed the search down to three possibilities,' he said. 'Three London addresses all took delivery of the costume the week before Halloween. Unfortunately, one of them is a PO box, but we have the name and credit card details of who rented the box. The other two are residential and I'm on my way to the first of them now.'

Relief tasted sweet. Lorrie exhaled slowly and allowed the anticipation of an imminent arrest and a cessation of the deaths to overtake her.

Simon continued, 'I'll take Lovell and a couple of uniforms with me. Baxter and Powell can head out to the other address. We'll have to track the PO Box owner down later.'

'Bring them both in for questioning,' Lorrie said to Simon. 'No excuses. Don't let their feet touch the ground. I'll put SO15 onto tracking the box holder down. With any luck, we'll have all three with us within the next couple of hours.'

OLLIE ARRIVED AT THE warehouse and avoided the CCTV cameras with ease. He knew the security guard's routine. Colin was too mean to employ someone to be on site and so an outside firm sent a man to do a look-over twice each night.

Ollie waited until he'd done the first of his rounds before approaching the office building.

Colin hadn't alarmed that particular building, so breaking in would be a dawdle. The only alarms were at the warehouse itself and the distribution centre.

Once inside, Ollie headed straight for Colin's office. He left the light switched off and waited as his eyes grew accustomed to the dark before approaching the desk. Before he carried out his plan to torch the warehouse, Ollie had one or two things to find. If he failed to find what he was looking for then he would have no choice but to burn down the offices as well.

COLIN HAD ARRIVED HOME and was slowly working his way through a bottle of Jack Daniels. Three drinks in and he suddenly wondered where Ollie was. His bike was on the driveway and, but for him, the house was empty. It was getting late, and Colin's in-built trouble detector pinged. He suddenly knew that his stepson was back at the warehouse. He didn't know exactly how he knew, but he was absolutely sure that the little shit was snooping again.

He placed his empty glass on the coffee table and pulled himself to his feet. He was going to catch the fucker in the act and woe betide him when he did. He could feel the effects of the bourbon, but that didn't stop him from getting behind the wheel of his BMW and head off to confront the bane of his life.

BAXTER AND POWELL WERE the first to arrive back with their suspect in tow. Convincing him to return with them had been ridiculously easy and, judging by the lad's significantly challenged intellect, both officers seriously doubted he was the Reaper. But, before they could eliminate him from their enquiries, a few questions had to be asked. He could, Baxter informed her colleague, have bought the costume for someone else, so he wasn't quite in the clear as yet.

Simon and Sonia arrived with a more likely suspect minutes later. Bringing him in had been more problematic. He had adamantly refused to leave the house, saying he wasn't predisposed to their Gestapo tactics and, as it wasn't quite a police state yet, he insisted on them buggering off and leaving him alone. When that failed to elicit the desired outcome, he took a swing at Powell and his fist connected squarely with the DS's jaw. A carefully twisted arm up the back and an arrest for assaulting a police officer convinced him that, perhaps, acquiescence was the better part of valour and he arrived in hand-cuffs at New Scotland Yard as quiet as a mouse.

Lorrie staggered the interviews and joined Baxter and Powell first. It took a mere half a dozen questions to ascertain that this suspect was, in fact, innocent of everything. He was a simple lad who had bought the Reaper costume for a party and hadn't the least clue what had become of it.

The Mohammed Ali wannabe was a different kettle of fish. They had to wait on the duty solicitor to arrive before they could interview him, and Lorrie took the time to grab a quick cup of coffee and have a few minutes alone in her office with Sean.

'I'm almost afraid to hope,' she said to him. 'Imagine, Sean, we could have the Reaper banged up and waiting to spill his guts. I'm virtually holding my breath.'

'What do you want to do about the PhD students?' he asked. 'We're still trying to round them all up, including Ollie.'

'Best not to count our chickens. Belt and braces are called for. We'll interview them as planned, unless we get a quick confession from our guest.'

'Okay, boss.'

She smiled. 'It's strange to hear you call me that. You were my boss for a time.'

'A lifetime ago.'

'You were a good boss, Sean. I learned a lot from you.'

'Some things best forgotten,' he countered with a sardonic smile.

DS Powell poked his head around the office door. 'Duty solicitor is here, Guv.'

Lorrie nodded and indicated for Sean to follow her.

Lorrie and Sean took their seats across from George Manners, their suspect. Lorrie made direct eye contact with him but remained silent.

Sean started the tape, which was evidenced by the long, loud tone.

Lorrie spoke for the benefit of the tape - 'Interview with George Manners. In attendance duty solicitor Margaret Bolton, Superintendent Lorraine Sullivan and Detective Inspector Sean Kelly.'

George Manners – his face contorted with affronted dignity – leant over the table and almost snarled, 'You have no right dragging me in here. Who the fuck do you think you are?'

The duty solicitor placed a restraining hand on his arm and shook her head at him. He threw her hand off and made to stand.

'Sit down, Mr. Manners,' Lorrie said, brooking no argument. 'You are under arrest and have been cautioned and you're not going anywhere until I'm finished with you.'

'That copper deserved a punch. I was defending myself.' Despite his ongoing bad temper, he relaxed back down in his chair. 'Ask your bloody questions and be done with it.'

Lorrie took her time. She wasn't about to be dictated to. She finally began the interview.

'I want to be clear, Mr. Manners, that you are being interviewed as part of an ongoing investigation into the deaths by poisoning of over thirty people. Now, if it wasn't for your obvious aggression and downright nastiness, we wouldn't be sitting in a room with a solicitor and with the tape running. If you'd accepted our invitation to join us and help with our enquiries, instead of lashing out and breaking a police officer's jaw, then we would have asked our questions and most probably thanked you and sent you on your way. Now...' Lorrie let out a slow breath and resisted the urge to raise her voice. 'Now, Mr. Manners, I have to wonder why you refused to accept our invitation gracefully. I have to wonder if that aggressive streak of yours makes you more likely to be our murderer. It makes me think that you poisoned all those people.'

George's jaw literally dropped open. His expression changed to one of shock and fear. 'What? Are you having a laugh? Murder? Poison?' He shook his head and turned to beseech his solicitor. 'What's she on about?'

Lorrie ignored his attempt to rope in the solicitor and went on – 'The Reaper, Mister Manners. You saw the video on the BBC? You saw the costume?'

Slack-jawed, he could only stare.

'You own a costume like that, don't you, Mr. Manners?'

He found his voice. 'That Halloween thing? You've got to be fucking kidding me.'

'I can assure you that I'm far from kidding.'

The solicitor piped in, 'You are questioning my client on the basis of a Halloween costume?'

'He's not under arrest for owning a Reaper costume,' Sean put in. 'If he'd come quietly at our request then this could've been done and dusted within ten minutes.' He turned to George. 'You must admit that your aggressive behaviour certainly raises some questions, Mr. Manners.'

'I had nothing to do with poisoning anyone. Where the fuck would I get hold of poison?'

It was a good question and one that Lorrie meant to explore. 'What do you do for a living?' she asked.

'I'm between jobs,' he replied defensively.

'Do you have any qualifications?'

'GCSEs, you mean?'

'Anything more other than a GCSE?'

'Nope.'

'What was your last job?'

'I worked in sales.'

'Selling what?'

'Cars.' He was beginning to relax. 'Where is this leading?'

'I'd also like to know where this is leading, Superintendent,' the solicitor interjected. 'It sounds like a fishing expedition to me. If you have direct questions related to these murders, then please put them to my client.'

Lorrie ignored her. 'Where is the Reaper costume?'

'Fucked if I know.'

Lorrie sucked in a breath. 'Think, Mr. Manners. Where is the costume?'

'I left it in a pub.'

'When did you leave it there and what pub do you mean?'

He shrugged. 'Can't remember.'

'Try.'

He hesitated and then reached a decision. He decided to co-operate. He had nothing to hide, and he really wanted out of there. Being belligerent and stalling would only delay his release.

Lorrie could see the wheels turning behind his eyes and she knew he wasn't their man. Buying and owning a Reaper costume wasn't a crime and he didn't fit their profile. She really couldn't be bothered waiting on his response and she had no further questions, so she stood abruptly and said, 'Interview terminated.' Then, to George – 'You'll be notified of bail arrangements and the date of your hearing on the matter of the assault on one of my officers. Other than that, you're free to go.'

Sean turned off the tape and he walked out behind Lorrie and left behind a stunned George Manners and an equally stunned solicitor.

'That went well,' he said to Lorrie as they walked back to her office.

'I knew it was too good to be true.'

'Are you sure?'

Lorrie tugged at the neck of her blouse and stopped to look up at him. 'Are you seriously asking me that? You saw him. You heard him. He's a Neanderthal. He's so far off the profile it's laughable.'

Sean said, 'We still have the third guy to follow-up on.'

'The one with the post office box?'

He nodded. 'All is not lost.'

Lorrie's eyes tracked across his face taking in the signs of exhaustion. She wondered if she looked as rough as he did. She could count on one hand the hours she'd slept in the past couple of days, and it was obvious that he was getting just as little sleep.

She commenced the journey back to her office. 'Will you get me an update on where our S015 boys are with that?' she asked. 'Let's hope they've tracked him down.'

'Sure.' Sean stopped walking and turned to head off in the direction of the major incident room. 'I'll come find you when I have news.'

# DAY SIX: NIGHT

DS Friel found both the warehouse and the adjoining distribution centre in darkness. There were no cars and no vans in the car park and, although the reception area was also dark, it was unlocked with the door standing ajar.

Her first priority was to find Ollie. She hoped the open door was an indication that he was inside. She had no sense of trepidation as she crossed the threshold. There were indicators that suggested something was amiss – no parked vehicles, an open door, darkness – but her brain failed to connect the dots and she ventured further into the building without the due care and attention her experience as a police officer should have dictated.

She ignored the reception area and went directly to the offices. She called out and identified herself, her voice bouncing off the walls. There was no response, so she called out a second time. Silence was the only comeback.

She thought she saw a movement out of the corner of her eye. She turned her head and stiffened. Nothing. She decided against calling out a third time.

Despite thinking that she had caught a glimpse of movement, there was a continued absence of any unease in her mind. She certainly didn't experience any sense of foreboding.

Hindsight would surely tell her that she was an utter fool, but meantime, she carried on, oblivious to any danger.

One of the offices was obviously the manager's and she entered it with an easy step and without caution. There was no one there. She pushed herself through a line of chairs and approached the desk. It was tidy and free of papers, but she quickly noticed that the computer screen was lit up. Someone had definitely been in the office recently.

The disquiet that had previously alluded her suddenly kicked in. Without knowing why, she was unexpectedly alarmed. The hairs on the back of her neck stood up and a sense of urgency turned her on her heels.

Back in the reception area, she took a moment to look around. Now that her senses were alert to danger, every corner of the large room seemed to harbour something sinister. She was spooked by the absolute silence. The air seemed heavy, and she could hardly catch her breath. She told herself to get a grip. Apart from her imagination and the fact that the computer had been switched on, there was nothing tangible to explain her unease. She began to feel like a fool.

She dragged in a deep breath and took one last look around the room. She concluded that Ollie wasn't on the premises – not in the office building, at least. She would give the other buildings – the warehouse and the distribution centre – the once over before giving up and heading back to HQ.

The buildings were locked, and all the windows were closed fast. She shone her torch around the outside and did a visual search of the immediate grounds. Just as she turned to make her way back to the car, she caught a brief whiff of smoke. She stood still and tried to catch the scent of the smoke once more. Nose in the air and sniffing unselfconsciously, she failed to detect any further hint of fire. It was just something else that she had imagined.

She walked away. Her feet scrunched on the gravel and the sound was loud in the quiet night. Just as she heard a second set of scrunching on gravel, one of the windows of the warehouse exploded behind her. Friel was thrown through the air and crashed to the ground. The blast rendered her unconscious.

When she regained consciousness an hour later, she was hog-tied on a hard floor, blindfolded and gagged.

'THAT'S THE LAST OF the interviews for now,' Simon said, relieved. 'There's just one more student and Ollie to catch up with.'

Lorrie stood up from behind her desk and stretched the kinks from her body. It was fast approaching midnight and they were nearly into day seven of the investigation and she remained dissatisfied with their progress.

None of the interviews so far had elicited anything of worth and she contemplated what other line of enquiry she could open. There was still the owner of the post office box, of course, but identifying him was proving problematic. The Reaper costume had been bought using a stolen credit card and the identity of the PO box's owner also proved to be a non- starter. Documentation was false and there were absolutely no leads as to who the man was.

'I'll bring Ollie in myself tomorrow,' she said. 'You get the other one tracked down in the morning. We may as well get these damned interviews finished and closed down. It wasn't such a promising line of enquiry, after all.' She sighed and shook her head. 'Looks like it's thinking caps on again, I'm afraid.'

Sean entered the office. A concerned expression on his face, he asked, 'Anyone heard anything from Friel?'

'Friel?' Lorrie was momentarily nonplussed.

'DS Friel,' Sean returned. 'I sent her off looking for Ollie, but that was hours ago. Her mobile goes straight to voicemail, and no one's heard a peep from her.'

'Where did you send her?' Simon took out his mobile phone and dialled a number. 'I'll get a search started.'

'Colin's warehouse,' Sean replied.

Simon nodded and walked from the office. He could be heard giving instructions as he walked away.

'Why the warehouse?' Lorrie asked.

'He wasn't at home, and he wasn't at the university. Friel was at a loose end - felt like a bit of a spare part - so I sent her off to find him. You'd already told me that he worked with Colin, so it made sense...'

'Yes. Yes.' Lorrie flapped a hand at him. 'I understand. Let's just find her.'

DS FRIEL REALISED THAT she should have done things differently. In retrospect, she should have taken a uniformed officer with her to look for Ollie. Her actions had all but got her killed and she was under no illusions – death was still, most probably, on someone's agenda.

When not hog-tied and much the worse for wear, DS Friel was a proper English rose. She had a boyfriend of three years and plans to marry in the very near future. A career in the police force, children and a bright future with a man who loved the very bones of her, were on the cards and she wondered what she could possibly do so as not to wholly jeopardise that future?

The ground was cold beneath her, but she welcomed the arctic contact on the skin of her face. It detracted from the agony of her limbs. Her arms and her legs were on fire. The rope securing her was pulled so tight that her heels almost reached the back of her head and her shoulders felt as if they were being wrenched from their sockets.

She was confused and disoriented, and she feared she was about to be sick and choke on the gag in her mouth.

She had no idea how long she had been unconscious. She had no idea where she was or who had brought her there.

Why, she wondered? Why had she been abducted? The better question was who had abducted her? She had not considered the consequences of exploring a dark building on her own and she had certainly not contemplated being dragged off, hog-tied and held prisoner by some nutter. Understandably, Friel was very pissed at herself for being so stupid.

She tried to move and the pain that detonated in her muscles almost caused her to lose consciousness again. She could hear moaning and it took her a moment to realise that the sound was coming from deep in her own throat. She tried to spit out the gag and that only caused her nausea to intensify. There was nothing else for it – she had to resign herself to lying on the floor, blind and dumb, and await her fate.

JUST AS SEAN AND SIMON were approaching the car park to join the search for Friel, Lorrie came hurtling down the stairs towards them.

'I've just been told,' she panted breathlessly, 'that Colin's warehouse is on fire. The call went through to the fire station ten minutes ago and I only heard about it by chance. That's where DS Friel was headed. That's where my Ollie might be. Jesus fucking Christ. They might be...' Lorrie began to cry. She couldn't stop herself. She was absolutely terrified.

Sean took her roughly by the shoulders. 'Calm down, Lorrie and get in the car. We'll be there in twenty minutes.' He threw the car keys to Simon and pushed Lorrie into the back seat where he joined her.

'Stop crying and listen to me,' he told her.

Lorrie closed her eyes and squeezed back the tears. She forced herself to take a deep breath, compose herself and listen to Sean.

He said, 'We don't know jack shit. We don't know if either Friel or Ollie are there. We don't know how bad the fire is, so let's all get a grip and find out what's happened.'

Simon started the car and left the car park at speed. His plan was to get them there in less than the twenty minutes Sean predicted.

COLIN WATCHED AS THE flames lost a losing battle with the fire hoses. He spoke to the senior fire officer and assured him that there were no personnel inside. He then stood and gazed at the destruction of his building and all its contents. Anger was slow to burn but he could feel the heat of it in his chest and he was sure that, by the time his fury reached its crescendo, it would be as hot as the inferno that had obliterated the warehouse.

He was unaware of Lorrie's presence until he felt her place a hand on his arm. He turned, startled, and was shocked at the agony of emotions flitting across her face.

'What's wrong?' he asked. 'Surely, you're not upset that my livelihood is going up in flames?'

Lorrie shook her head, and the tears came again. 'Ollie,' she managed to say. 'Is he...? Is he...?'

'What? What is it? What about Ollie?'

Sean spoke. 'We thought he might be here.'

Colin realised that Lorrie was not alone. He eyed the stranger then looked from him to Lorrie.

Lorrie flinched inside. 'This is Sean,' she said.

His head snapped around and he was face to face with the devil. So, he was finally meeting the man who had turned his wife into a whore. He wanted to say something clever, something cutting, but his brain wouldn't engage with his mouth.

Lorrie watched, wide-eyed, as the two men sized each other up. She wondered who would throw the first punch.

Her voice, thick with emotion, as she tried to get everyone back on track. 'Please - can we find Ollie? Is he in there, Colin?'

Colin dragged his eyes around to look at her once more. He drank in the aura of her distress and felt himself relax. Absolute terror was emanating from her in waves, and it had the effect of further calming him. He glanced to his left where his warehouse lit the dark sky in a crimson cloak of fire, and he had to chew on his lip to prevent the smile from appearing.

Lorrie squeezed her eyes tight closed. She couldn't believe that Colin was enjoying her distress. Did he honestly think that she didn't see the corners of his mouth twitch as he supressed a smile? She opened her eyes once more and saw that Colin was still engrossed in the fire and saw that Sean was staring at him warily. She wondered where Simon had got to.

Colin wanted to laugh. Inside him there was a huge snigger building, but he stifled the urge. It wouldn't do to wrong-foot himself.

'Colin?' Lorrie placed a hand on his arm. 'What happened here?'

He shrugged and turned to fully face her. 'They think arson, but it's too soon to tell.'

'Arson?' Lorrie choked on the word. 'What about Ollie? Have you seen him?'

'No.'

Sean asked, 'When was the last time you saw him?'

Colin's mouth hardened. There were things he wanted to say to this man – this piece of shit – but answering questions about Ollie wasn't included on his agenda of things he wanted to say. He turned away, ignoring the question.

Sean felt the deliberate insult and his eyes narrowed to slits. What an arsehole, he thought. Poor Lorrie.

Lorrie could, to a certain extent, understand her husband's attitude. He obviously felt threatened by Sean's presence at her side. She was shrewd enough to recognise that jealousy was making him act a bigger prick than usual, but she needed answers about her son's whereabouts and Colin was her best bet to get those answers.

'Sean,' she said, 'Go find out what's happened to Simon. I want a word in private with my husband.'

Sean's jaw dropped open, and Colin was gratified when he turned in time to see the look of hurt flare in the other man's eyes.

'Are you sure? Sean asked her. He was afraid to leave her alone with Colin.

'She's sure,' Colin replied in her stead. 'Off you go.'

Sean took a step towards him, and it was only Lorrie's expression that stopped him from laying him flat on his scrawny back.

She watched Sean walk reluctantly away then turned furious eyes on her husband.

'Well?' she barked. 'Where is he?'

Colin sniffed and shrugged. 'I've not seen Ollie.'

Lorrie's eyes showed her scepticism. 'I don't believe you.'

'I don't care if you believe me, or not. It's the truth. Why would I lie to you?'

'Because you like playing stupid mind games. You take pleasure from tormenting me.' She became agitated. The fire was still out of control, and she had a dreadful feeling that Ollie was being burned alive. 'Please, Colin...'

Colin stared at her as if she was a mouse beneath his cat's paw. 'You think he's in the fire, don't you?'

She nodded and gulped back a sob.

He said, 'I'm sorry that I'm too wrapped up in my building burning to the fucking ground to be concerned about where your son is.'

Lorrie reared back as if slapped. The anger in her husband's eyes was vicious.

Sean had worked his way back towards them – keeping in the shadows – and, when he witnessed Colin's cruel words and Lorrie's reaction, he stepped forward and grabbed Colin by the shoulders.

'Have some respect,' he said. 'Can't you see she's sick with worry?'

Colin raised a hand and, with a sideways swing, knocked himself free from Sean's grip. 'Don't you touch me,' he spat. 'Don't you fucking touch me. Who the Hell do you think you are – putting hands on me?'

Sean retreated, his hands in the air, and shook his head. 'Just trying to get you to listen.'

Colin's face was a distorted knot of hate. 'Fuck off,' he demanded. 'Get yourself away from me.'

Lorrie intervened. 'Please, Colin...'

He rounded on her. 'Don't please, Colin me,' he snarled. 'Are you out of your mind bringing him here? You just had to rub my nose in it, didn't you?'

'Rub your nose in what?' Lorrie was genuinely confused.

Colin ran his tongue over his mouth and bared his teeth. 'I'm not a bloody fool.'

Sean had had enough. They were wasting time with all of Colin's nonsense. 'Did you mention to the fire officer that Ollie might be inside?' he asked him, attempting to get the attention back to what was most important.

He turned a malevolent eye back to Sean. 'Why would I have done that?'

Lorrie said, 'Because he's not at home and he's not at the university. Where else would he be?'

'One of our police officers might be in there as well.' Sean deliberately kept an even tone in his voice. 'I'm here looking for her. We only just found out about the fire.'

Sean's conciliatory tone inflamed Colin's senses. He felt, rightly, that the man was humouring him. He pointed a finger at him. 'I know what your game is,' he said. 'Don't think I'm too stupid to see it. Here you come – prancing around my wife like a stud bull – with your smarmy grin and smart mouth and think she's yours for the taking. Well, I'm here to tell you different, mate. You're not welcome in London, and you're not welcome anywhere near my wife.'

Sean met his stare, confident that the other man would recognise he was on a hiding to nothing. There was no way that Sean was going to allow the prick to intimidate him, and he made sure that the expression in his eyes said as much. He smiled slowly and considered his reply.

Colin intrigued him. By all accounts he was very successful in business, was married to the most beautiful woman in the world and yet, he was a prize scoundrel. He pitied him a little and so, his retort turned out not to be as harsh as it could have been.

He said, 'Why don't you toddle off and watch your warehouse burn, Colin? You're obviously not any good to Lorrie, so best to leave Ollie to us.'

'You jumped up little...' Colin made to take a swing at him. 'I'll flatten you.'

Sean stepped easily out of the arc of Colin's fist and grinned back at him.

Lorrie had had enough. She wasn't about to allow her testosterone fuelled husband to start a punch up and delay them any further. 'Cut it out,' she said. 'I'll speak to the fire officer myself. You two can stand here bickering for as long as you want. You can even bash each other's brains in if it floats your boats but do it out of my sight.'

Both men wisely make no further comment, and just as Lorrie made to move off, Simon approached at a run. All three turned at the sound of his footsteps.

'Friel's car is out back,' he gasped. 'It's easy to miss as she parked behind a big rubbish bin.'

Sean wiped a hand across his face and groaned.

'She's still here somewhere. I've had a quick look around the grounds, but I can't find her. She must be inside.'

'Who's Friel?' Colin asked.

'Our DS,' Lorrie said, shocked. Then, to Simon, 'What about Ollie? Any sign?'

Simon shook his head.

Lorrie began to walk towards the fire. Sean tried to pull her back, his hand gentle on her arm. She shook him off and veered towards a fire officer she recognised as being in charge.

'You can't be here, Ma'am,' he said.

'I'm Detective Superintendent Sullivan. We think one of our officers may be inside, and...' her voice faltered, 'and, my son.'

The whole strategy of the firefight changed immediately. Officers with breathing apparatus were summoned and, after they lined up for instructions, they began to enter the burning building.

# DAY SEVEN: MORNING

Pathologist, Ricky Burton, had tried several times to contact Lorrie. His attempts to reach both DI Grant and DI Kelly also failed. He was on the point of telephoning Scully when DI Grant returned his missed call.

'Don't you lot answer your phones?' he asked irritably. 'I've been trying to get through to you for the past hour. Where's Superintendent Sullivan?'

'Busy,' Simon replied. 'What's so urgent?'

'I want to speak to her. Put her on.'

'She's busy, Ricky. Can't it wait?'

'No, it can't bloody wait.'

'Then, you'll have to tell me. She can't come to the phone right now.'

'Well, you tell her that, when she's got a minute, to ring me. Tell her I know exactly how the victims were poisoned. Tell her I've cracked it.'

Lorrie sat in the back seat of the car and slowly clenched and unclenched her fists. She stared straight ahead, unblinking, and quietly unravelled.

The waiting was terrible. So far, no bodies had been found in the rubble of the destroyed warehouse, but there were many hours of searching to be done before she would know if her son and DS Friel were dead.

Colin had finally climbed down from his high horse and had been attempting to support her in her abject misery, but – as far as Lorrie was concerned - it was too little too late. She had banished him to his office where she fervently hoped he would stay.

Sean, not wanting to make an awkward situation worse, had also taken himself away. He had donned protective clothing and was helping with the search. That only left Simon to provide what comfort and reassurance he could. The problem was, the Guv didn't want him comforting her or providing her with any useless reassurances so – in effect – he was the proverbial chocolate teapot.

He had been pacing around the car and running backwards and forwards between Lorrie and the burnt-out warehouse when he noticed the missed calls on his phone.

He opened the car door and scotched inside next to Lorrie. 'Ricky Burton wants to speak to you,' he said. 'He's been ringing us all on and off for an hour.'

'I can't speak to him now.' Lorrie's voice was flat and dead. 'You speak to him.'

'I've tried, but he wants you.'

She shook her head. 'Later.'

'He's got news.'

'Later, I said.' The tone of her voice remained unchanged.

Simon ignored her and continued, 'He knows everything. He's discovered how the victims got poisoned but he'll only explain it to you.'

Lorrie sighed. She was going to be forced to carry on with her job, regardless of whether or not her son had perished in the flames.

'Okay,' she said. 'I'll ring him in a minute. Can you go and check if they've found anything?'

'I'm sure they'll let us know.' Simon had only just asked, and he believed the fire officers were sick of the sight of him.

Lorrie turned cold, lifeless eyes on him. 'Please, go see,' she begged.

Simon looked at her. He could see her swallowing back the grief and fear and felt heart sorry. He reminded himself that she was a mother and, by what he had witnessed earlier, he also saw that she was a wife to an utter bastard. If getting out of the car for the hundredth time and going over to enquire if they'd found anything was what she needed, then he was happy to oblige. He'd do anything to help alleviate her worry and to Hell with making himself a nuisance.

'Okay. I'll be back in a minute.'

He climbed from the car and made his way over to where the senior fire officer was co-ordinating the search. The fire had been fully doused hours before and the remains of the building had been rendered safe. Sean, as well as a dozen fire officers, were painstakingly sifting through the debris but it had been a huge building and Simon knew that it would be well into the afternoon, and perhaps the evening, before the search could be concluded.

There was no news of any bodies. He tried to convince Lorrie that no news was good news, but she was left untouched by his attempt at reassurance.

'Sean is searching like someone possessed,' he told her. 'He's not even taking any rest. They're threatening to haul him physically from the site if he doesn't ease up.'

Yes, she thought, Sean was searching for the body of his son. She was sure he would work until he dropped, but Simon wasn't aware of his motivation so she could understand his confusion at his unrelenting efforts.

'Where's Colin?' she asked. 'Is he still shut away in his office?'

Simon shrugged. 'I didn't see him anywhere about.'

'No?'

'He seems...'

'A bit of a wanker?' Lorrie actually smiled. 'Yes, that about sums him up.'

'It's probably the shock.'

'You don't have to make excuses for him, Simon. He's like that all of the time.'

Simon resisted the urge to take her hand. He didn't think she would appreciate the gesture.

'Can you get Ricky on the phone for me, please? My hands are shaking, and I don't think I'm capable of getting his number.'

'Sure.' Simon took her phone and brought up Ricky's number on the screen. 'Do you want me to stay?'

'No. I'd appreciate it if you would go and insist Sean takes a break.'

She waited until Simon exited the car once more before pressing the green call button on her phone.

Ricky answered on the first ring. 'About bloody time,' he said.

'Sorry,' she returned. 'I'm at the scene of a fire and we may have a couple of bodies to recover.'

'Why are you at a fire? Oh, never mind. I'm sure you've got your reasons.'

'Simon told me your news.'

Her lack of excitement at his breakthrough wasn't lost on Ricky.

'You could sound a bit more pleased. Do you know how absolutely fucking amazing this is?'

'Just explain it to me,' she said. 'I'll get excited about it later.'

And, Ricky told her. His words did not fill her with excitement. They didn't amaze or please her. Instead, his words sent a stiletto of ice through her heart.

DS FRIEL WAS MAD WITH thirst and every nerve in her body was on fire. Bile surged in her throat and burned as she desperately swallowed it back. She felt sick. She felt close to death. She had no hope.

Since she'd awoken – however many hours ago that was – she'd been alone. She was sure Sean was looking for her, but that gave her no solace. He wouldn't find her. No one would find her. She would die and she would be lucky if anyone even discovered her body.

She had no clue as to why she was there. What was the motivation for abducting her? She'd been looking for the Superintendent's son – a task that shouldn't have resulted in her current predicament. Perhaps she'd interrupted a burglary? And, what about the fire? Was it arson? Had she disturbed an arson attack? All those thoughts buzzed and bounced around her brain incessantly and she wished she could go back to sleep to escape for a while.

She groaned and tried to adjust her position on the floor, but it was impossible and excruciating. She needed to find a way to ease the tension on the ropes, but even the slightest adjustment to her position was still too painful.

She gasped through the pain and slowly brought her body back from the brink of hell. In the quiet, she suddenly thought she heard footsteps. Much against her better judgement, hope bloomed in her chest.

Lying there blindfolded and gagged had heightened her sense of hearing and sense of smell. She picked up the stench of stale sweat and knew she was no longer alone.

When two hands pulled at the rope around her bound wrists she tried to scream. Her shoulders felt as if they were being wrenched from their sockets and, when she realised that the rope had been cut, there was a brief moment when she thought the pain would go. The opposite happened. The freeing up of her limbs actually caused greater agony. The pain in her limbs was now so intense that her whole body went into violent spasm. Once again, she tried to scream but, because of the gag, the only sounds she could make was a series of anguished, guttural groans.

Any hope that whoever had freed her was there to save her was quashed when a male voice said, 'You're going to die soon. It won't be pretty but, I promise- you won't suffer for too long.'

He removed the gag from her mouth, and she immediately opened it wide to scream. He rubbed something liquid on her lips. Her immediate reflex was to stick her tongue out and lick.

'Who... Who are you?' she croaked. 'I'm police... I'm a police officer.' It pained her to talk. Her throat had almost closed up and her mouth was like sandpaper. 'Please. Please let me go.'

'Too late,' he said. 'It'll be over soon. I give it fifteen minutes.'

She licked her lips once more. The gummy substance irritated her tongue, and it took a few moments before she understood.

'Poison? Did you poison me?'

'Give the girl a prize,' he laughed. 'I'm impressed.'

She could sense that he was very close to her, and she made a feeble attempt to kick out at him.

'I'd save your energy if I were you. Why make it harder on yourself?'

'You're the Reaper.' It was a statement rather than a question.

He didn't answer her, and she heard him move away.

'Why?' she asked. 'Why are you doing this?'

He ignored her. She no longer held his interest.

'SHE'S LOCKED HERSELF in the car.' Simon grabbed at Sean's arm and pulled him to a private space. 'She's just sitting there like a zombie and ignoring my pleas to open the door.'

Sean shook the soot from his hair. He could hear Simon prattling on about something, but he was too exhausted to understand.

'Are you listening to me? You need to do something.'

'Do what? What are you going on about, Simon?'

'Jesus, Sean. Listen, will you? Lorrie has locked herself in the car.'

'Why? What happened?' Sean still wasn't fully comprehending what Simon was saying.

'She spoke to Ricky and went all pale and shaky.'

'She's been pale and shaky since last night.'

'But, she's locked herself in the car.'

'I'll go talk to her.' Sean took off his protective overalls, steel toe-capped boots and pulled on his shoes and made for the car.

Simon trotted after him and they both arrived at the car together.

'Lorrie?' Sean tapped on the window. 'Open the door, Lorrie.'

If Lorrie heard him, she made no sign. She sat with her eyes fixed on her lap and didn't move a muscle at the sound of Sean's voice. She heard nothing but the thunderous rush of her pounding heart in her ears.

Sean turned to Simon. 'What did Ricky want?'

'He said that he'd found out how the victims were being poisoned but he only wanted to give the details to Lorrie.'

'Phone him. Find out exactly what he told her.'

Simon walked around to the rear of the car and made the call.

Sean stared in the window at Lorrie and attempted, once again, to get her attention. She looked like a ghost.

'Come on, Lorrie,' he said. 'It's me... Sean. Open the door. Whatever it is, we'll fix it.' He pulled at the door handle with both hands. He then checked all the other doors. They were all locked.

Simon returned. He put his phone in his pocket and shrugged. 'He didn't say anything to warrant her going zombie on us.'

'What did he say?'

'Something about parking tickets. Apparently, the poison was on the parking tickets.'

'That's it? Nothing else?'

'Nope.' Simon shook his head. 'That's it.'

They were both startled by Lorrie suddenly pushing open the door. She leant over and, in a voice devoid of all emotion, asked Simon to fetch her a cup of coffee.

'There's a kitchen in the office building,' she said. 'Make it black with no sugar.'

Simon looked from Lorrie to Simon and, at the imperceptible nod from Sean, he left to fetch the coffee.

'Sit in beside me,' she told Sean. 'I need to tell you something.'

Once inside the car, Sean attempted to take Lorrie's hand. She withdrew it sharply and turned so he couldn't see her face.

'What's going on, Lorrie? You're scaring the shit out of me.'

'You were the first person to ever drill into me about motive, means and opportunity,' she said.

'So?' Sean scrunched up his eyes in confusion. 'Look, Lorrie, I know how worried you are about Ollie and Friel, but there's no sign of any bodies. I don't think either of them were caught in the fire.'

'I'm not worried about that.'

'Then, what?' He was becoming exasperated. 'What's all this locking yourself in the car shit?'

She turned her face to him. 'Motive, means and opportunity. All three are important, aren't they?'

'Of course.'

Lorrie thought a moment. 'I think I know the means and the opportunity, but what's really confusing me is the motive. I can't get my head around the motive.'

'Okay. We can work motive out. Ricky told us the means – the parking tickets – but how have you come up with opportunity?'

She didn't answer right away. Then, instead of answering his question, she rummaged in her bag and produced the keys to her house. She said, 'Take these and go to my house with a forensic team. Search everywhere. Pay attention to Ollie's bedroom.'

Sean refused to take the keys. All of the blood drained from his face. He swallowed and whispered, 'What's going on here, Lorrie? What's Ollie's bedroom got to do with anything?'

Lorrie's voice remained cold and detached. 'Have you wondered what it is that my husband does? Have you wondered what was in the warehouse that just burned to the ground?'

'No,' he croaked. 'I guess I haven't.'

'Parking tickets.' The words came out on a sigh. 'He has the contracts to supply parking tickets for the machines you find at barriers to hospitals, airports, city car parks. He delivers them all across the country.' There was more. 'Ollie had the means and the opportunity. He's also brilliant... talented. You remember what Professor Napier said? He said that my son was the only one of his students with the brains to pull this off.'

'That's bullshit.' Spittle flew from Sean's lips. 'How can you think such a thing? It's utter bullshit, Lorrie.'

'Take the keys, Sean. It's important to me that you be the one to find the costume.'

'I'm not taking your fucking keys. I don't want anything to do with this.' He flung open the door and climbed out of the car. 'You're out of your fucking mind.'

Simon arrived with the coffee, took one look at Sean's face, and said, 'What the Hell?'

He bent and looked in at Lorrie and saw her use the fingertips of her uninjured hand to brush away the tears from her eyes.

'Someone want to tell me what's going on?'

The lump in Lorrie's chest was pure ice. It reached all the way up to her throat and she felt it choking her. She couldn't breathe. Now that she'd said those terrible words to Sean, she felt she could happily go to her death.

'Guv? What's happened?' Simon placed the coffee cup on the ground at his feet and joined her on the seat. 'What's got Sean so riled up and why are you crying?'

Lorrie pressed her house keys into Simon's hands. 'Take these,' she said. 'Give Sean a minute or two to get his head around what I've just told him and then go with him to my house. He'll explain on the way.'

It was on the tip of his tongue to insist on an explanation right then and there, but the look on his boss's face and the utter deadness of her eyes stayed his words. He nodded and got back out of the car.

# DAY SEVEN: AFTERNOON

He dumped the body. He left it on the side of the road. He wasn't worried about being seen because it was an ill-used road. Regardless, it would be easily discovered. He had no qualms about the police finding it, because that was exactly what he wanted.

Despite the fact that he had an almost uncontrollable urge to smash in the policewoman's face, to violate her in a bestial manner, he'd refrained from inflicting any damage. It wasn't permitted, but he was permitted to pose her.

He removed her shoes and then her trousers and splayed her legs. He ripped the buttons from her blouse and exposed her bra. He could have done more, but he satisfied himself that it was enough.

He ate a sandwich as he drove away. He wondered if there would be any more deaths. He hoped so, but he couldn't be sure. He wished that the idea had been his but – no matter who had thought of the ingenious way of poisoning random people – he still got to kill them, he still got the hard-on when he witnessed the police, and in particular that bitch, run themselves ragged trying to suss it all out.

It was so simple, really. All you needed were people who habitually put their parking tickets between their lips as they drove through the barrier.

He took a few moments of pleasure going over in his mind the whole process.

Quite a few drivers alone in their cars struggled to adjust the gearstick, guide the steering wheel and make their way under the parking barrier with the ticket still clutched in their hand. Some – not all – threw the ticket onto the passenger seat, or onto the dashboard and some even managed to keep it in their hand. The ones who died were the ones who temporarily put it between their lips.

The plan had been hatched and then worked relentlessly to bring it to fruition. The results were far greater than expected.

LORRIE SAT IN HER DRIVEWAY in the car and waited out the forensic search of her home. She had a sick feeling in the pit of her stomach. Her heart constantly jerked in her chest and her hands wouldn't stop shaking. The enormity of the situation, together with her role in the whole scheme of things, took an enormous toll on her reserves. She wanted nothing more than to curl up into a tiny ball, go to sleep and never wake up. But, somewhere down inside, buried beneath an avalanche of abject misery, a deep-rooted fortitude railed against submission.

She didn't really believe in God. As a police officer, she had witnessed too many horrors, too much evil, to believe in a divine being, so she shocked herself by praying. She prayed to a God - who she thought was a delusion - for the forensic team to find nothing incriminating in her home. Even as she prayed, she knew it was a useless endeavour. Ollie was guilty.

When the penny had first dropped – when Ricky had given her the news about the parking tickets – her first and only thought had been Ollie. She didn't immediately consider anyone else. Ollie, her son, was the Reaper. He had the means, and he had the opportunity, but what about the motive? Why would an eighteen-year old boy go on such a killing spree?

What could his motive possibly be? He wasn't a psychopath. Surely, she would have known if her son was cold-blooded and without conscience?

She had plenty of time to think. Despite the grim realisation of who the killer was, her mind had still attempted to deny it. Sitting in the car, she conjured up and dismissed a whole selection of different possibilities for the identity of the Reaper. Each time she thought of someone, her brain shut it down.

They had been turning her home upside down for hours. She knew that they would be thorough. Sean was in the house, as was Simon and DS Lovell. Colin was on the missing list, and she was all alone with her thoughts and her pain.

Her mobile rang several times during the hours she sat alone. She heard the ringtone as if from a great distance and made no attempt to answer any of the calls. She didn't want to talk to anyone. She didn't care if it was the Commissioner himself ringing her – she had nothing to say to anyone.

Colin arrived just as the forensic team began taking bagged items out of the house. He had changed into jeans, a heavy sweater and work-boots – obviously the only spare clothes he kept at the office – and he had taken the time to shave. Lorrie, clothes sweat-stained and creased, hair a mess and face all crumpled with misery, marvelled at his ability to consider his appearance at such a time.

She watched as he folded himself in beside her and was taken aback when he gave her a sympathetic look. He obviously felt sorry for her, and she didn't know how that made her feel.

'What do you think they've found?' Colin asked her.

Lorrie shook her head. It had been a long time since she had last uttered a single word and, when she did, they came with great difficulty.

'I don't know,' she said. 'The costume, perhaps.' Her voice sounded alien to her ears. It wasn't her voice. Her voice didn't mewl and sound so pathetic.

Colin's voice was soft. 'I don't believe any of this, Lorrie,' he said. 'Ollie's not a killer. I don't understand why they're here searching our home. What's brought them here? What's made them believe that it's our Ollie?'

If Lorrie had never, not once in eighteen years, loved her husband, she found that she truly loved him at that moment. He believed in her son where she couldn't, and she was glad – glad that her boy had at least one person who had faith in his innocence.

She squeezed his hand, leaned to the side and placed her head on his shoulder. Despite the change of clothes, he still smelled of smoke and fire. His presence was strangely comforting.

'Do you know what it was that turned them to Ollie? You're the lead investigator – you would know, Lorrie.'

How could she explain? How could she admit to turning her own son in?

'It's what makes sense,' she replied. 'The parking tickets knocked sense into everything.'

'My parking tickets?'

She nodded against his shoulder.

'Jesus, Lorrie. I still can't believe any of it. None of it makes sense.'

She was reminded that Colin had lost part of his business earlier that day. She wondered how he would feel if she expressed the fact that she also believed Ollie had burned it down.

'I'm sorry about the warehouse,' she said. She felt him stiffen. 'I don't want that to have been Ollie too. I don't want any of this to have been Ollie.'

'It doesn't matter about the warehouse,' he replied gently. 'It's easy to replace things. It's people you can't replace.' He hesitated a beat. 'Have they found your missing police officer?'

'I don't know, Colin. No one is telling me anything.'

'Do you want me to go and ask someone? I can ask Sean if you want.'

That he meant it and, that he was prepared to humble himself and speak to Sean for her, was a revelation.

'Best to leave them to it,' she said. 'We'll know soon enough.'

He squeezed her hand. He wondered how best to broach the next subject and decided to simply go for it.

'I caught Ollie at the warehouse on his own at night a few times,' he said, attempting to sound matter-of-fact. 'I also caught him snooping through my computer.' He felt her draw away from him and went on hurriedly, 'I'm not saying this to upset you, Lorrie. I just thought you ought to know.'

Revelation after revelation. Her boy was becoming guiltier by the minute. She said nothing. She was afraid that her thoughts would manifest into such a betrayal of Ollie that she would never forgive herself.

'Say something.' Colin squeezed her hand tighter. 'I won't say anything to the police if you don't want me to. I'll protect him, Lorrie.'

'I am the police,' she rasped.

'But, he's your son. Can't you stop being a policewoman for a minute?'

Lorrie heard the sharp undertone in her husband's voice. She could tell that he was trying desperately to keep his emotions in check and that he was trying to think of a way her son could be saved. She couldn't quite accept that his motives were pure. This wasn't the Colin she knew.

'What was he up to with your computer?' she asked.

Colin shrugged. 'Damned if I know.' He glanced at the house and noticed Sean standing framed in an upstairs window. 'I don't know what the Hell he was up to, but I can't believe he used the warehouse to spike the parking tickets. Why would he do such a thing?'

'Hate.'

'Hate? Who could Ollie possibly hate that much?'

'Me, I guess.' Lorrie stifled a sob. 'He did it because he despises me.'

If Lorrie had happened to be looking directly at Colin, she would have seen the smile that tugged at the corners of his mouth. Ollie despising his mother was a balm to Colin's soul.

'I've upset you,' he said.

'I was already upset, Colin. There's nothing you can say to make me feel any worse.'

How was she still functioning? Colin wondered. She was in a right state, but she seemed to be holding her shit together like a trooper. It was probably shock and adrenalin keeping her going, but that would wear off and she would crash. She might believe that she knew what her son had done, but, once she fully realised and accepted it, she would be inconsolable.

'Why don't we go to a hotel for the night? I don't think it's a good idea to go back into the house just yet.'

Lorrie pulled her hand from Colin's tight grasp and placed it over her eyes. 'No, I want to stay here,' she said. 'I want my own bed.'

'Okay. Whatever you want is fine with me.'

FROM OLLIE'S BEDROOM window, Sean looked down on the driveway. He could see the two of them sitting in the car and he wondered what they were talking about. Was Colin providing Lorrie with the comfort and support he wished he could give her? Was Lorrie grateful for her husband's presence next to her or was she longing for him?

When, what Lorrie suggested back at the warehouse, had penetrated the thick fog of disbelief, Sean agreed to accompany Simon to the house and supervise the search. He had been adding up the clues and the evidence in his mind and, he had to admit, nothing looked good for Ollie. He hadn't even met the boy yet. He hadn't introduced himself nor apologised for everything. Now... well, now the first time he would meet him would be when he charged him with multiple counts of murder.

Lorrie must be suffering all the ravages of Hell. She was the one who had put two and two together and all but accused her son of being the Reaper. He knew that she must desperately need him to be there for her, but he had a job to do and Lorrie – in her wisdom – had pointed him straight to what he must do. She had tried to give him the house keys. She had insisted he lead the search. She trusted him to do what was right because, above all else, Lorrie Sullivan was a policewoman.

Ollie was his son. No one outside of the family knew that fact.

Lorrie had been hauled off the case, but Sean still had full access. He planned to keep that access and maintain a lead in the investigation. He would tell nobody about being Ollie's father. He was sure it would be what Lorrie wanted.

Simon pulled him from the window and said, 'We've found it.'

'Where?'

'Behind the bath panel in the en-suite. There were also vials of something. I'm thinking...'

'The poison?'

Simon nodded. 'This is shit, Sean. How can we...?'

'We can do our jobs, Simon.'

Sean walked to the middle of the room and turned full circle, taking in everything. Ollie's bedroom was beyond reason. He would never have believed it belonged to a teenaged boy.

Everything in the room was white – from the walls to the curtains, to the carpet. It was a clinical white and, apart from a bookcase with tidy rows of academic textbooks and a desk with an open laptop, there was not a single personal item to be seen. The bed was neatly made with a soft white quilt. A bedside lamp with a white shade cast a muted light over a spotlessly white carpet. There were no photographs, no posters on the walls. To Sean, the room spoke of a lack of personality. It spoke of housing an emotionless person. How could any son of his live in such a bedroom? How could any son of Lorrie's be so austere?

'A maelstrom of white,' Simon said.

Sean turned sharply. 'Sorry?'

'A maelstrom of white,' he repeated. 'This room – it's a frenzy of white. Weird.'

'Have you ever seen anything like it? I mean... look at it.'

Simon shook his head. 'Doesn't scream psychopath to me.'

'No?' Sean wasn't convinced. 'That's exactly what it screams to me.'

'It's too pure. It smacks of innocence.' Simon turned full circle and took in everything once more. 'But, what do I know?'

COLIN GOT OUT OF THE car and walked towards the front door of the house. He walked straight through and was stopped by a uniformed police officer.

'You're not allowed in here, sir,' the officer said.

'It's my house,' Colin barked back at him. 'I need to get a few things.'

'I'm sorry, sir. I'm afraid I'm going to have to ask you to leave.'

Colin attempted to barge past him, but he was no match for the strong arm of the police constable. He found himself unceremoniously propelled back through the door and onto the step and then gently pushed back onto the driveway.

Colin felt the warm sting of humiliation and reacted. He took a swing and his fist landed squarely on the young officer's jaw. The next thing he knew, he was lying face down on the ground with his arms twisted behind his back.

Lorrie was out of the car like a shot.

'Please,' she said. 'He's upset. Let him up. I'll get him out of here.'

'He assaulted me, Ma'am.'

'I know. I'm sorry.'

The PC stood up and rubbed at his jaw. He was quite within his rights to arrest his assailant, but he was the Super's husband, and her life was, at present, gurgling down the plughole. He decided to give her a break because, God knew, she needed it.

'Get him away from here,' he said. 'And I'll say nothing more about it.'

Lorrie helped Colin to his feet. 'Thank you,' she said.

Back in the car, she buckled up behind the wheel. 'I think we'll go to that hotel, after all,' she sighed.

'I GUESS LORRIE IS WELL and truly off the case,' Simon said. 'Scully and Connor will be doing cartwheels.'

'We need to talk to her. We need to tell her what we've found.'

'I don't think we should, Sean. Not yet, anyway.'

'She pointed us here. She knew what we would find.'

Simon nodded. 'I know she did.'

'This is going to kill her.'

'It's pretty unbelievable. I liked Ollie.'

'You've met him?' Sean narrowed his eyes. 'What's your take on the lad?'

Simon shrugged. 'Typical teenager in lots of ways – arrogant, selfish – but, so fucking clever, Sean. I felt like an idiot compared to him. I've known him for four years and I would never... never have believed this of him.'

'Take a look around you, Simon. Look at this bloody room. It's like a monk's cell. What eighteen year old boy has a bedroom like this? Where are the rock posters and where is the game console? Where are the pictures of the girls he fancies? No – he's no typical teenager, that's for sure.'

'But, what about the whiteness of everything?'

'You know what I think.' Sean raised an eyebrow.

'Well,' Simon thought a moment, 'Like I said... white is pure. How many serial killers do you know who surround themselves with a colour that symbolises purity?'

Sean shrugged. 'I can't say I've ever met any serial killers, never mind been in their bedrooms, but I guess black would be a better bet.'

'It's not evidence of innocence, though.'

'No.' Sean shook his head. 'But I guess that it's an anomaly.'

'One that we'll keep in mind?'

'To what end? We've found the costume and probably found the poison.'

Simon had no answer for that.

# DAY SEVEN: EVENING

Scully arrived at the house and was shortly followed by Connor. Both ignored Lorrie's car as it turned on the drive and headed out onto the road. They went straight indoors. Both were cock-a-hoop at the turn of events, and you could have lit up a ballroom from the beams on their faces.

Scully got straight to the point. 'She's off the case as of right now and on administrative leave.' He nodded at Simon. 'DI Grant...you're in charge. Report directly to Chief Superintendent Connor and make sure you don't share anything with Sullivan. She's out of the loop and I don't want even a whisper reaching her ears.' To Sean, he said, 'You can head off back to Manchester.'

'I can't, sir,' Sean responded. 'My DS is still missing.'

'Oh, right.' Scully had the decency to look ashamed. 'Of course. Of course, I'll let you find her. Goes without saying.'

Sean thanked him and excused himself from the room.

He wanted to tell her personally. He wanted to explain that going back to Manchester once he found Friel wasn't his idea. But her prick husband was still with her, and Sean knew that, if he presented himself at the car and asked to speak to Lorrie, Colin would kick up a fuss.

When he stepped out through the front door, he was surprised to see that her car was gone.

Half an hour later, when they were all finished at the house, Sean rang her.

'It's me,' he said. 'Can you talk?'

'I'm at a hotel with Colin. He's down in the bar getting pissed.'

'I didn't think that you'd leave without speaking to me first.' He was hurt and it showed in his voice.

'He punched the PC guarding the front door. I had to get him out of there before he did anything more stupid.' She was still reeling from the shock of Colin's actions. As if things weren't bad enough, he had to go and assault that young lad who was only doing his job.

'Are you all right?' Sean said, breaking into her thoughts. 'Do you want me to come and get you?'

'No, that's not a good idea. I'm okay.' She wasn't, but Sean didn't need to know that. 'I'll stay here tonight and go back home in the morning.'

'Scully and Connor turned up at the house.'

'I know. I saw them just as I left.' Her voice lost every shred of emotion. 'I guess you found it?'

'Yes, we found it.'

'What did Scully say?'

'They've given the case to Simon.' He heard her sigh. 'I'm sorry,' he said. 'I'm so sorry, Lorrie.'

'It's okay.'

'Friel is still missing.'

There was a long silence and Sean had to check his phone to confirm that they were still connected.

'I can't believe any of this,' Lorrie finally said.

'Me neither.'

'But, it's all true, isn't it?'

It was Sean's turn to sigh. 'It looks that way.'

'Will you keep me informed?'

'I wish I could.' He closed his eyes and dragged in a ragged breath. 'Scully is sending me back to Manchester.' He waited. Lorrie said nothing. 'I don't want to go. I won't go. I'll find Friel and I'll take some leave from work. I'll resign if I have to.' Lorrie still said nothing. 'Lorrie? Are you still there, Lorrie?'

'I'm still here,' she replied. 'I can't think about this now. I have to go.' With that, Sean heard her disconnect the call.

COLIN SAT RIGID AND angry. He had arrived back in the room just as Lorrie had ended the phone call. He knew who had been on the other end of the line. It had been the bastard Kelly and he was livid.

'I can't not speak to him, Colin.' Lorrie was exhausted, wrung-out, and desperate to keep her husband from going off on one. If he lost his rag, and if she had to contend with one of his infamous tantrums, it would be the end of her.

He knew that he had to get some level of control over his anger. He needed her to see a better side of him.

'I don't mean to be such am arsehole,' he said. 'I can't help being jealous.'

'We need him, Colin,' she said. 'No one knows that he's Ollie's father and we can use that.'

'Use it for what?'

'To keep him on the case and to keep us in the loop with what's going on.'

'It doesn't take a rocket scientist to work out what's going on. We don't need Kelly for that.'

'I need to know the moment they find Ollie. He'll need me.'

Colin contemplated his next words carefully. He didn't look at her as he spoke them.

'You think your son killed all of those people. You've been playing the cop all along and allowing Ollie's room and our home to be turned upside down. You're doing nothing to protect him and you're doing nothing to safeguard his best interests. Why the Hell do you believe that he would need you, or even want you?'

'Please, Colin. It's not like that.' Even as Lorrie spoke the words, she knew she was doing exactly what Colin accused her of. It sobered her and she suddenly realised what Ollie's motive was. She had made her son hate her. All of his young life, she had shown him that she was a police officer first and foremost and his mother second. Even now – even when he needed her the most – she was putting him second to the job of catching a killer.

# DAY SEVEN: NIGHT

No bodies were found at the burned-out warehouse. The fire crew had secured the site and finished up.

Friel was found dumped at the side of a quiet road. She was dead and her body had been posed in a grotesque parody of lewdness.

Ollie was still missing, and the biggest man-hunt ever known to the United Kingdom was rolled out at seven minutes passed ten.

There wasn't a single police officer left untouched by the events. To say that there was a sense of stunned disbelief was an understatement. That an eighteen year old boy could be responsible for such unadulterated horror was unbelievable, but for that boy to be Lorrie's son was so far out of the stratosphere of credibility that, initially, no one gave it any credence. It took Simon, laying out all the evidence to a packed incident room, before the realisation dawned on every face that Superintendent Lorrie Sullivan's son was the Reaper.

Sean listened to Simon and watched as the DI attempted to get everyone on point. He fought a losing battle because every member of the team was too stunned to fully comprehend the true dreadfulness of the situation.

One of their own had been murdered. DS Friel may have joined them from Manchester temporarily, but she was still one of them. The senior investigating officer was the mother of the murderer. The murderer was a serial killer. The press were in a frenzy and the public were out for blood. And no one had a clue where the killer was.

The one fear that Simon failed to share with anyone was that the killing might not be over. He'd decided to keep that little nugget to himself for the time being. Neither Scully nor Connor had cottoned on to the fact that the parking tickets were still in the machines and, according to Ricky, likely to remain potent for several more days. He wanted time to think. He wanted to ring Lorrie and get her advice, but he knew that was impossible. He didn't want to be the one that shut down every car park across the country. He didn't know if that was even possible.

'You okay, Simon?' Sean placed a hand on the DIs shoulder. 'You look as if you're going to be sick.'

Simon shrugged Sean's hand off and found an empty chair to sit in. 'I'm okay,' he said.

'Is there anything I can do to help you?'

Simon grimaced. 'I wish there was.'

'You've given everyone a job to do and that's good. They need to be busy right now.'

'I'm sorry about DS Friel.'

'She might not be the last, Simon.' Sean's eyes were sharp with calculated knowing. 'You think the same, don't you?'

Simon sighed and nodded. 'I don't know what to do about it.'

'It's not up to you to know. You simply have to push it up the chain of command. Let Scully and Connor worry about it.'

The relief Simon felt was palpable. Sean was right – it wasn't his responsibility to make a decision about the ticket machines.

'They'll have to close the car parks and change the tickets,' Sean said.

'I don't think it's quite as simple as that. They'll have to find another supplier.'

'As I said – let Scully and Connor worry about that. Your job is to find Ollie.' Sean dragged a chair over and sat down beside Simon. 'Are you on top of it?'

Simon shrugged. 'Maybe.'

'You do know that you'll have to bring Lorrie and her husband in for questioning? They might know something about where he might hide.'

Occasionally, Simon longed for a job where no one depended on him. At times he did not thrive on the responsibility of being a senior police officer. He believed that this was one such time.

'I can't question her, Sean. How can I question her?'

'I can do it for you,' he offered. 'You can take Colin and I can take Lorrie.'

'I thought you were heading back to Manchester?'

'That was Scully's plan for me, but what he doesn't know won't hurt him.'

'I don't know, Sean. I don't want to fuck it all up.'

Sean regarded him with sympathetic eyes. 'You won't fuck anything up,' he said. 'Lorrie taught you well.'

'She did.'

'We'll bring them both in tomorrow morning. Let Lorrie have the night. She needs to rest.'

LORRIE LAY ON THE BED in the hotel room and watched as Colin fussed about making drinks. She didn't want a drink. She feared she would choke on it. Her mind was racing, and her head throbbed. She wanted to be left alone to think, but Colin was determined to stick to her like glue.

For the sake of peace, Lorrie took a swallow of brandy and forced her throat to close over the burn of the alcohol. She permitted Colin to sit beside her on the bed and allowed him to brush the hair off her forehead. He was being kind. He was being thoughtful, so why did she think it was all an act? Why couldn't she accept that her husband was worried about her and worried about Ollie? What was it in his demeanour that set her teeth on edge and caused her to doubt his sincerity?

'We'll get away somewhere as soon as this is all over,' he said. 'Abroad, perhaps. It's been years since we had a holiday.'

A holiday? Was he fucking kidding? Instead of voicing her thoughts, Lorrie simply nodded.

'Afterwards, you'll find something else to do. You don't need the London Met. You don't need the police force. I can help you find something.'

'What do you mean, Colin?' Lorrie raised herself up on one elbow. 'I'm not leaving the force.'

'What? Of course, you are. Don't be silly. They won't want you... not after this.'

Was he right, she wondered? Did she care? She thought about it and concluded that, no, she didn't care. She sank back once more against the pillows. She didn't care about the force. She didn't care about anything.

# DAY EIGHT: MORNING

DS Sonia Lovell wanted to go to DI Grant and say something to him. She couldn't quite work out what it was she actually wanted to say – she just wanted to say something. She thought that they had a close working relationship. She knew that she loved him, and she knew that he like and respected her, but ever since the mantle of senior investigating officer had landed on his shoulders, he hardly looked in her direction. It had only been a matter of hours since Superintendent Sullivan went on administrative leave – had been less than a day since Simon was tasked with taking over from her - and Sonia was already worried that he wasn't coping.

Simon needed her. She was his sidekick, his sounding board. She was the one who was always at his elbow – steering and pushing him on. He was brilliant and perceptive and a great detective, but he needed her to complete him. He needed her to light the match to his ideas and to make him think outside the box. Simon thought in straight lines. To him, everything was black and white and that was okay most of the time because Simon always made it okay. She couldn't fault his good sense, or his reason, or his razor-sharp intuition, but - as opposed to his straight lines - she preferred her lines wobbly and, to his black and white, she preferred shades of grey. Their differences made them an invincible team.

So, she needed a reason to talk to him. The Superintendent and her husband were coming in to be questioned soon and Sonia could see that Simon was anxious about it. Sean Kelly was going to interview the Superintendent and Sonia thought that was best. Simon wouldn't be able to do that interview.

Interviewing the husband would be easy in comparison. It should be a walk in the park for Simon, so she was at a loss as to why he was dreading it.

There was no way she was going to sit back and watch Simon struggle. She was going to make him listen to her. Simon would not be allowed to fail – not on her watch.

She forced herself to move, and it was only at the moment of crossing the threshold to the office that Simon had temporarily inherited from Sullivan, that she'd worked out what it was she needed to say to him.

'Can I have a word, Guv?' Sonia stepped into the office and closed the door. 'It will only take a minute.'

'Sorry, Sonia,' he replied. 'I don't have a minute.'

'Make me a minute, then, sir. It's important.'

Simon looked directly at her and nodded. 'Okay.' His voice was wary. 'What is it?'

Sonia cleared her throat and squared her shoulders. 'Actually, sir, it's about you.'

'Me?' he gave a nervous laugh. For one horrified moment he thought she was going to profess her love for him.

Sonia saw the anxiety in his eyes and her stomach dropped. She could see that he knew how she felt about him. She closed her eyes and prayed to God for the strength to overcome her acute embarrassment. She wondered how long he'd known about her feelings for him. She wondered if it meant the destruction of what relationship they'd manage to forge over the years.

Simon felt a wave of pity for her. Too late, he'd realised she had no intentions of confiding her feelings to him. She obviously wanted to talk to him about something else.

He decided to play the fool and let her off the hook.

'Come, on Lovell. Spit it out. Have you come to tell me you're about to run off with one of those goons from SO15? Well, I'm telling you straight, my girl, you can do much better.'

Sonia felt a moment's sorrow. She knew exactly what he was doing, and it greatly saddened her.

She forced a smile onto her face. 'No, sir – not that,' she said. 'I wouldn't touch any of those lot with a ten foot pole.'

'What, then?'

'Well, sir, I've come to tell you that you need me in there with the husband. You need me to be in on the interview with you.'

'I do?' Simon was genuinely confused. 'It's a straightforward interview. He's not under caution. He isn't suspected of anything. Why do you think I need you?'

'Because you don't like him for personal reasons and the thought of interviewing him is making you anxious.'

'What?' He stood up abruptly from behind the desk and walked to the window. 'I hardly know the man. I neither like nor dislike him.'

'That's rubbish, and you know it.' Sonia lapsed into the usual frank manner she had with him. 'You've mentioned him to me a few times over the years. Just little snippets of information but those little snippets painted a picture of a man you can't stand because of the way he treats the Superintendent. Oh...' she flapped a hand at him. 'I know the Super thinks we don't know just how much of a dick she's married to, but you know, and I know. Now you're worried that you might be tempted to punch him in the face. You're worried about being in a room with him. I want to be there to make sure that you don't do anything stupid.'

'That's... that's rather perceptive of you.' There was no fooling Lovell. 'It's true – I can't stand him - but I would never punch him, and you know it. When have you ever seen me lose my temper?' He smiled. 'What's really going on?'

Her eyes widened. 'I'm sure I don't know what you mean, sir.'

'Pull the other one, Lovell. I've worked with you for too long not to know when you're worried about something other than me squaring up to the likes of Colin Sullivan. Why do you really want in on the interview?'

She decided to come clean. Honesty was really the best policy – it always had been between them. 'You're no good without me,' she began. 'We're partners and pretty damned good partners at that. I'm less than brilliant without you and vice versa. I'm worried that you now think you have to do everything on your own. I'm worried, now you're wearing the Super's hat, that you think you've got something to prove.'

It would have been so easy to get angry at her. She was well out of order, and he would have been within his rights to send her from the office with a flea in her ear, but that wasn't Simon's style. He was a man with very little ego and a very thick skin. It had been true, what he'd pointed out to her – that she'd never seen him lose his temper – and, so, he couldn't be angry with her.

Lovell was right. It was important to remember that he had a partner.

'Okay,' he said.

'Okay, sir?' That had been easier than she'd thought. 'Okay, what, sir?'

'You're in on the interview and there's no need to 'sir' me all the time. Guv is fine.'

Sonia smiled and nodded. 'Okay, Guv.' She made to turn and then quickly turned back when he spoke once more.

'And, Lovell?'

'Yes, Guv?'

'You'll be in on everything else as well. I won't shut you out again.'

Relieved, Sonia left the office and went in search of a cup of strong coffee. She had a feeling it was going to be a long day. On the way to the kitchen, she caught sight of the Superintendent and her husband arriving and she was shocked at how exhausted and ill the Super looked. DI Kelly would have to handle her with kid gloves, lest she be shattered into a million pieces, and she hoped that Sean was sensitive enough to realise that.

'SIT DOWN, LORRIE,' Sean said, making a concerted effort not to lift her gently from the floor and place her in the chair himself. They weren't alone – a young, uniformed officer was in the room with them - and he had to be careful.

Lorrie lowered herself into the chair and dropped her eyes. She didn't want to look at him. If she looked at him, she feared she would collapse. She was so close to a complete meltdown that the softness she would see in his face would be her undoing.

Sean spoke to her bowed head. 'I don't have a lot of questions for you, but you understand why I need to ask them?'

She nodded. 'I understand.'

Sean felt like crying. Her voice – usually so vibrant and commanding – was a mere squeak. The sight and the sound of her was breaking his heart.

He spoke gently to her, saying, 'We haven't found him, Lorrie. Ollie... we haven't any idea where he might be.'

Lorrie began to shake. It started as a slight tremble in her hands and then her whole body was shivering. She had very little willpower left in her but, the little she had, she used to command her body to be still.

Sean went on, 'Have you any idea where he might be?'

'No.'

If he expected more than a curt, single syllable response, he made no show of it.

'With friends? People from university perhaps?'

'I don't know.'

Sean had an uneasy feeling that Lorrie was on the verge of something catastrophic. She looked like death and her demeanour was all wrong. She should be sitting straight with fire in her eyes, demanding they find Ollie, and not sitting hunched over like an old woman barely able to string a sentence together.

'Is there anything I can get you?' he asked kindly. 'A glass of water? A coffee?'

'No. Nothing.'

Sean flicked a glance at the officer standing at the door and then his eyes returned to Lorrie. He made a decision. He turned fully to the uniformed officer and told him to leave the room. He would speak to her alone.

When he was alone with her, he wasted no time in rushing around the table and picking her up and folding her into his arms.

'Oh, Lorrie. Oh, my darling,' he whispered into her hair. 'What can I do? What can I do?'

Lorrie hung like a rag doll from his arms. She neither returned his embrace nor made any attempt to respond to him.

Sean was more frightened than he had ever been in his life. He had to get through to her. He had to reach her somehow. She was obviously in deep shock. She wasn't in any state to answer the questions he was required to ask of her, so he decided to change the subject.

An idea came to him. 'Tell me about his bedroom,' he said. 'Describe it to me.'

His words affected her. She jerked in his arms and pulled herself back.

'What?'

Sean placed her gently back into the chair and hunkered down next to her. 'His bedroom... describe it to me.'

'It's just a bedroom, Sean. What do you want me to say?'

'Who chose the colour of the walls?'

'Ollie.'

'He likes white?'

She nodded. 'Ever since he was a little boy. He always wanted white.'

'There are no pictures on the walls.'

'No.' She shook her head, confused. 'I used to hang posters from the movies he liked, but he took them down.'

'Why did he take them down?'

'He said he knew that they were pretend. It was the same with photographs. He got upset if I put any in his room.'

'They weren't the real thing, so that upset him?'

'Yes, I think that he couldn't bear anything that wasn't real.'

'Why did he want white walls and white curtains and white lamps?'

Lorrie didn't realise that she was smiling. 'He loves white. It's clean and pure and clinical. When he was a little boy, he said God made white because it was a good colour.'

'Ollie believes in God?' Sean was surprised.

'He did. I don't know what he believes now. We don't talk about things like that. Anyway, he's a scientist. Do scientists believe in God?'

'I don't know, Lorrie, but I think Ollie believes in what's good.'

She looked at him for the first time. 'How can he?'

Sean swallowed down the truth and said, 'Because I don't believe that he's the Reaper. I don't believe that a boy who was raised by you and who surrounds himself with white walls is capable of such awful crimes.'

Lorrie gulped painfully. For the briefest of moments, hope bloomed in her chest. She began to cry silently. There was no sobbing and no other evidence of her keen emotion except for the tears that literally gushed from her eyes. She believed Sean when she couldn't find it within herself to believe Colin when he said the very same thing. Sean didn't even know Ollie. He was aware of all the evidence stacked against her son, and yet he didn't believe he was the killer.

She shook her head. It was no good. It didn't matter what Sean, or Colin for that matter, believed. She knew the truth. 'I know he did it,' she said. 'It all adds up. You know what you found in the house. I know it was the Reaper costume. It had to be there. Where else could it be?'

'Lorrie...'

'No.' She raised a shaky hand. 'I know you're only trying to make me feel better, but nothing will ever rid me of the dread ripping at every bit of me or rid me of the grief I feel for my son. I know that he is your son, too. I know that you're clinging onto anything that will prove he's innocent. But, he's not innocent, Sean.'

He had got her attention. He had reached her, but at what cost? He felt shitty for tricking her. He loved her so very much and he literally ached for her, but he had required her to snap out of her mood. He needed her talking and he needed her focussed. He had no doubts that Ollie was guilty. The evidence was too great.

His eyes misted. He said, 'We have to find him, my darling. Will you help me?'

She looked into his face and her heart lurched in her chest. Next to her son, she loved this person most. She needed him more than ever, but she also knew that she had lost him just as much as she had lost Ollie. They would never be together now. She knew that for a fact.

'Lorrie, will you help me find him?'

She shook her head. 'I don't know where he is. Don't you think I want you to find him? I've been wracking my brains, but I just don't know.'

'I know you want us to find him. I know how worried you are about him.'

'I am worried. I'm worried sick.' The violent shaking overtook her once more. 'God knows what he's going to do now.'

'Okay, then let's work our way through every conceivable place he might go. He hasn't disappeared off the face of the earth. He's got to be somewhere. Are you up for that? Are you up for working with me?'

She nodded. 'Of course. I'll do anything to find him.'

NINETY MINUTES LATER, Sean left Lorrie and – armed with thoughts he had plucked from her brain – he made his way to Ricky Burton. Lorrie had no clue as to Ollie's whereabouts, but, despite the disintegration of her senses, she still had a mind like a steel trap. The more they had talked, the more Lorrie morphed back into copper mode, and she had given him an instruction – speak to the pathologist and find out what clues Friel's body had as to where she'd been kept prior to her death. Find out where Ollie had kept her and, perhaps, they'd find out where Ollie was hiding.

Sean wanted to ask Simon to join him at Ricky's lab, but he was busy interviewing Colin, so Sean went alone.

# DAY EIGHT: AFTERNOON

'You've had me here all morning. It's gone lunch time and I'm not staying any longer.' Colin had spent the morning being cantankerous, obstructive and not in the least inclined to help the police with their enquiries. He scowled as he said, 'Lorrie will think that I've been arrested.'

'Lorrie knows that you've not been arrested,' Simon returned. 'She probably also knows that you're being an arse and that's why this is taking so long.'

Colin sat forward in his chair and placed his elbows on the table. His expression spoke volumes. 'You're not getting me to believe that Ollie killed all those people, so you're wasting your time with me.'

'We only want to know what he was up to at the warehouse,' DS Lovell put in, 'and, to find out if you have any idea where he is. You could've been out of here hours ago if you'd been straight with us.'

Finally, Colin relaxed back in the chair and surveyed the two police officers through lowered lids. He chewed on his bottom lip, motioned with his head and said, 'Ask your bloody questions. I want to get back to my wife.'

Simon sat up straight. 'Thank you, Mister Sullivan. I'm pleased that you've seen sense.'

'Just get on with it.' Colin folded his arms defensively across his chest. 'I want to take my wife to lunch, and, at this rate, we'll be lucky to make dinner.'

Simon did not immediately begin questioning him. He had already asked him every question in one form or another over the preceding hours, only to be either stonewalled or rebuked. It was his turn to make him wait.

The seconds ticked past and, just as Colin was about to stand, Simon asked, 'How easy would it be to tamper with the parking tickets boxed in the warehouse?'

'Easy enough, I suppose. I didn't have someone guarding them. They're parking tickets, for fuck's sake.'

'Was Ollie alone in the warehouse very often?'

Colin shrugged.

'How often would you say he'd been alone?'

'I have no idea.'

Simon nodded as if he understood. 'I can see that you didn't have much of an oversight. Ollie must have ran rings around you.'

Colin looked away and his face reddened.

'Would you say that Ollie pretty much pulled the wool over your eyes, Colin?'

'No, I wouldn't say that. I knew he was up to something, but it had nothing to do with him tampering with the boxes.'

'How can you be so sure? Someone spiked them with poison. Why not Ollie?'

'Look,' Colin spat back. 'You have no proof that the tickets were tampered with in my warehouse. It could've happened anywhere.'

'Convenient that the warehouse burned down,' Lovell interjected. 'Do you think Ollie did that?'

'No, I don't.' He was back with his elbows on the table. 'He isn't a murderer, and he isn't an arsonist. Ask me something that makes some sense and let's be done with this.'

'Okay.' Simon relaxed back. 'Where is he?'

Colin shook his head vigorously. 'I don't know. Ask me another.'

'Does Lorrie know where he is?'

'Nope.'

'You're sure about that? Does your wife confide in you, Mister Sullivan?'

'She's my wife.' A mulish look crossed his face. 'Of course she confides in me.'

'You know that we found a costume hidden in the house?'

'Lots of kids have Halloween costumes. Finding one means nought.'

'Hidden behind the bath panel? Really, Mister Sullivan?'

'I've only got your word for that.' He shifted uncomfortably. 'Who's to say you didn't plant it?'

'Did we plant the poison as well?' This was Lovell. 'We found that with the costume.'

'Yeah, right.' Colin closed his eyes and tipped his head back. 'Framing an eighteen year old boy is beyond contempt. You should be ashamed of yourselves.'

Simon let that pass. He said, 'Let's talk about the work Ollie did for you.'

'What about it? He did odds and sods.'

'Did he pack the boxes for dispatch?'

'Sometimes, but there was always someone with him when the tickets went in the boxes. It wasn't a one man job.'

'Who would've been with him?'

'Different people. Depends who was on shift.'

'We'll get a list of employees from you later. What about the distribution centre? Did Ollie work in there?'

'Once or twice. He preferred the warehouse.'

'All the boxed tickets went through the distribution building before being loaded onto the delivery vans?'

'That's right. The orders and delivery addresses were managed from distribution. It's quite an operation. I deliver all across the country and have a few customers in France and Germany.' The pride was resonant in his voice, and then it dropped dejectedly. 'I don't know how I'm going to claw my way back from all of this.'

Lovell asked, 'You said that you thought Ollie was up to something. What did you mean by that?'

He shrugged. 'I had words with him about going through my computer.'

'Oh? What had he been looking for?'

Colin's eyes shifted. 'Customer information.'

'We'll need to look at your computer.'

'What if I don't want to give it to you? It has all my stuff on it.'

'We won't keep it long.'

'Why don't you cut my heart out whilst you're at it? My business is going down the toilet and you want to pick over the bones?'

A look passed between Simon and Lovell and, simultaneously, they both stood.

'We're finished with you, for now, Mister Sullivan. If you wait here, I'll go and find Lorrie. You might still be in time for lunch.'

With that, they left him alone in the room.

Colin stared after them. He sat stock still and went through in his mind all of his responses to their questions. He wondered if he'd done any damage to Ollie and, after another few moments of thought, concluded that he had not. He only hoped that Lorrie had been as careful, but he doubted it. She had convinced herself that the boy was guilty and, although in some perverse way that gave him a sick sense of satisfaction, he wished she would be more of a mother and less of a police officer. It grieved and angered him in equal measure that his wife remained a true-blue copper even when her son needed her protection the most. Just what would it take to knock her off her self-built pedestal? If her son being accused of such heinous crimes wouldn't do it, what would?

SEAN WATCHED AS RICKY meticulously examined Friel's body. He used a large magnifying glass, extended on a long metal arm, to go over her skin inch by inch. He used forceps to pluck hair and debris and other particulates from the skin's surface and from every orifice, and he used a tiny vacuum to inhale and store dust and dirt from around her, under her and from her hair as well as between her fingers and toes.

Satisfied, he prepared the body for the post-mortem.

Ricky didn't mind Sean being there. Police officers weren't always in attendance at the forensic post-mortems, but Ricky had always been of the opinion that they should have a presence. Quite apart from the chain of custody, they tended to ask intelligent questions and Ricky believed that witnessing the procedure enhanced their insight into the crime.

When Sean looked at the body, he didn't see DS Friel. He didn't see her shy smile or her shrewd eyes. He didn't see the woman who always aimed to please and who went out of her way to be useful. He saw, instead, mere remains. The essence of who Friel was had gone and the body on the table wasn't her.

Sean didn't have to be a pathologist to read the story Friel's body told. The ligature marks on her wrists and her ankles told him that she had been bound so tightly that her skin had peeled back on itself to expose the raw flesh below. Her shoulders looked as if they had been wrenched from their sockets and most of her slim body was covered in scuffs and scratches and multi-coloured abrasions. Then, there were the tell-tale signs of the poison that had ended her – the swollen tongue, the grotesque leeching of blood and pus from her nose. Friel had suffered, and suffered greatly – Sean was left in no doubt about that.

Had Ollie really inflicted such horror on the pleasant, vital Friel? Had Ollie destroyed her? Had his son, the Reaper, wiped her from existence in a manner that beggared belief? How fucking cruel would that be – that it was his flesh and blood who had inflicted such monstrous injury?

One thing nagged at Sean's brain. She had been posed at the side of the road and, no matter which way he looked at it, Sean couldn't quite get his head around the sexual nature of that pose. All of the other victims had been anonymous and, although Friel had died from poison exactly as the others, she had been held prisoner, abused and then dumped. He could see Ollie – the clever, introverted scientist – killing the others, but something didn't sit right with him regarding Friel. Why the sexual connotation? Was there more to Ollie than they all thought? He made a mental note to look into Ollie's sexual history. Perhaps there was a disgruntled girlfriend or a girl he'd come on too strong with? Perhaps he'd hurt someone? Perhaps he liked sex games?

He shook his head to clear away the thoughts and concentrated intently on the pathologist's expert dissection of his friend. He would suffer through every knife stroke, through every moment of the procedure. It was the least he could do for her.

When it was over – when everything had been examined, weighed and measured – Ricky and Sean stood over the body, and both shared an emphatic sadness. She had been one of their own and the manner of her demise left them equally shattered.

'I've managed to get quite a few bits and pieces from her body and her clothing that might give us a clue as to where he kept her,' Ricky said after a long moment. 'It'll take a bit of time, but I'm hopeful.'

'Thanks, Ricky. If I'm not around, let Simon know.'

'You going somewhere?'

'Manchester,' he said. 'Just for twenty four hours. I want to tell Friel's parents personally. I'll be coming straight back.'

'You'll still be on the case, then? A little bird told me that Scully sent you packing.'

'I think the Assistant Commissioner might go to bat for me. I'm hoping so, anyway.'

'Well, good luck in Manchester. Nasty business... giving the death notice.'

Sean stared into his face and gave him a watery smile. 'Always is, my friend. Always is.'

LUNCH WITH COLIN WAS an unmitigated disaster. Lorrie wasn't hungry and the topic of conversation at the table eradicated what little appetite she might have had. Colin just wouldn't let it go. At first – when he had expressed the opinion that Ollie was as innocent as a lamb – she had been grateful. Someone needed to believe in her boy, and she was quietly pleased that it was Colin. After years of running the boy down and appearing to begrudge him every kind word, she was humbled by the fact that her husband was firmly behind him, but his prattling on about how she, as Ollie's mother, had an obligation to protect him, was grating on her already shredded nerves.

Yes, she wanted to protect her son. Yes, she would continue to love and support him no matter what he did. But, no – she would not wear blinkers and she would not put aside the evidence in favour of a mis-guided belief in his innocence. Ollie was obviously sick in the head. He needed to be found and put somewhere where he could be helped. She wasn't a fool – she knew that he would probably be placed in a high security hospital such as Broadmoor – but at least he would be safe.

'You're not listening to me,' Colin said, interrupting her thoughts. 'We need to talk about this, Lorrie. You can't just accept everything that's happening to our family.'

'I'm sorry,' she sighed. 'I don't want to talk about it. I understand your feelings – really, I do – but I just want to let the police do their jobs and not go over and over every detail of how you think they're screwing up.'

It was on the tip of his tongue to tell her that she needed to get her head out of her arse and start behaving properly. He didn't know if she imagined that, by turning against her son and placing herself squarely on the side of the police, that it would somehow save her career. He wanted to accuse her of just that, but he wisely held back. He was fast learning that he could get what he wanted from her through honey rather than through vinegar.

'Can't you at least try and eat something? I swear I can see the weight dropping off you already.'

To please him, Lorrie took a mouthful of food. He had ordered for her – her favourite, duck with plum sauce – but the food stuck in her throat. She choked the mouthful back and placed her fork back on the table.

'I just want to sleep,' she said. 'Can we go home?'

Colin readily agreed. He had somewhere he needed to be and, having Lorrie tucked up in bed – dosed with a sedative he had handy – would fit in with his plans nicely.

Showing the deepest regard for her wellbeing, he helped her to her feet and on with her coat before leading her from the restaurant. He had come to the conclusion that, if he couldn't persuade her to publicly defend her son and distance herself from the investigation, he would do the next best thing. He would keep her cocooned in her bedroom at home, safely away from her police colleagues and safely away from that bastard, Kelly.

# DAY EIGHT: EVENING

Amid the public spectacle of outcry and the righteous clamour for blood, DI Grant attempted to get the press on-side. He was as honest as he could be with the reporters and was not backwards at coming forwards in sharing with them his absolute desperation for their co-operation. Scully and Connor – with the agenda of self-preservation first and foremost – had insisted that Simon be the one to lead the press conference. Luckily for all concerned, Simon's straight talking, humility and lack of angst at the intruding of a hyped-up media, endeared him to the press and to the public.

Editors lined up to help him find Ollie. They refrained from demonising the boy and they, for the first time since the murders began, took a more civic-minded approach and urged their readers to co-operate with the police.

The Assistant Commissioner was pleased with the DI's stance and was impressed by his logic. She gave credit where it was due – knowing that Simon Grant was the product of Lorrie Sullivan's mentorship – and wished there was something she could do to help the woman she had, herself, mentored years before. She hadn't spoken to her, as yet, but she meant to remedy that very soon. First, she had to instruct Scully to keep Sean Kelly on the team. She knew he wouldn't like being told. She knew he would rail against her, but she didn't give a damn. Kelly had lost a colleague and he had begged her to intervene on his behalf with Scully. Regardless of how much trouble Scully could stir up, she was determined to allow Kelly to be instrumental in bringing the killer of his colleague to justice.

JUST AS SIMON WAS FINISHING up with the news conference, Sean was on his way back to Manchester. He had been on the road less than an hour when his bladder insisted he stop at a service station. Irritated with himself for not going to the little boy's room before he had set off, he pulled off the motorway, parked and made a dash for the toilets.

He grabbed a coffee before he headed back to his car and caught sight of a familiar face out of the corner of his eye. He recognised him immediately, then a second familiar figure appeared in his periphery.

The sight of the two men together sent a surge of adrenalin spiking through Sean's bloodstream. Without the least hesitation, he rushed to his car and – instead of continuing on his way to Manchester - he pointed his car back in the direction of London.

LORRIE HAD SLEPT SOUNDLY for four hours and, after a quick visit to the toilet, she had climbed back into bed and immediately went back to sleep. She slept through her mobile phone ringing and slept through the urgent knocking on her front door. Her brain and her body had completely surrendered to the protection that sleep offered her and nothing – no ringing phone and no amount of knocking – could penetrate the dark, safe place that sleep took her to. She was completely oblivious to everything. An earthquake would not have dragged her back to consciousness.

SEAN HAD RETURNED TO the house and was on the verge of breaking down Lorrie's front door when Colin pulled up in his car.

'What are you doing here, Kelly?' he demanded. 'Lorrie's resting and you're the last person she needs to see.'

'With fists clenched at his sides, Sean bit back a retort. There was no way he was getting into anything with Colin. 'I need to talk to her,' he said genially. 'We're still looking for Ollie and I think she can help.'

'Well, that's too bad,' Colin said. 'Unless you have a warrant to enter my home, then I suggest that you piss off.'

Sean pulled himself up straight. At six foot two, he towered over the smaller man, and he knew he could quite easily knock him into the middle of next week without even breaking a sweat - and he was sorely tempted to do just that - but his better judgement prevailed, and he merely nodded and walked away.

Colin watched him go and knew that it wasn't the last time he would see him. The man was just not going to give up. He wanted his wife, and Colin was adamant that Kelly wasn't going to have her. All this with Ollie was his chance to finally get Lorrie all to himself and there was no way he was going to stand back and allow the likes of Sean Kelly to put the proverbial cat amongst the pigeons.

Upstairs, Colin looked in on his wife. She was unsettled and on the verge of waking so he went back downstairs to the kitchen to make her a cup of coffee. He laced it with a liberal dose of the sedative he had used on her earlier and returned to her bedroom.

SEAN THOUGHT CAREFULLY about his next move. He could confide in Simon – he really should confide in him – but something made him hold back. He couldn't go to him with a half-cocked hypothesis and expect him to follow what, at that moment, was no more than a vague idea of the truth. Circumstantial evidence was no match for the hard evidence already accumulated. No, he had to think things through more carefully and come up with some hard proof before he approached anyone. With that in mind, Sean parked his car in a quiet street not far from Lorrie's house and put his brain in gear.

# DAY EIGHT: NIGHT

Ollie was sighted all across London and sightings even came in from Edinburgh, Birmingham and Belfast. All told, within hours of the press conference, forty eight individuals had phoned in to claim that they had seen him.

Sonia, alongside Powell and Baxter, did what they could to weed out the downright cranks from those who genuinely thought they'd seen him. It was an almost impossible task to determine what a genuine lead was and what wasn't and so, they had to painstakingly follow up on the majority of the calls just in case they missed the one that turned out to be the clincher. Uniformed officers, across a multitude of forces, were sent on dozens of wild goose chases and, as yet there was no worthwhile news.

All hopes were being pinned on Ricky and his forensic team coming up with the goods. The trace amounts of evidence found on Friel was being tested. Microscopic analysis, chromatography and mass spectrometry were techniques being used to analyse the hair, skin, soil and fibres found in the crevices, under the nails, in the hair, on the shoes and in the clothes of DS Friel. Everyone was trying to be patient, but every time Simon's mobile phone rang, they all stopped what they were doing to check if it was the call from Ricky.

Simon was most hopeful about the soil samples. Next to finger-prints and DNA, the analysis of soil was, scientifically, astonishing - in that, exact locations could be determined based on the unique identification markers found in the soil properties. Unfortunately, they wouldn't have a soil sample to compare their samples with - until they started searching places they thought Friel had been kept - however Simon hoped that Ricky would be able to use information from the UK Soil Observatory to, at least, give them somewhere to start looking.

Ricky's first hit was welcome, but not helpful. Some of the soil was clearly from the road where she was dumped, but what was help-ful was the fact that other trace evidence – sediment and the soil that had developed on that sediment - was clearly from someplace else. All they had to do was discover where it had come from.

As well as the forensic examination of the trace from Friel, the Reaper costume found in Ollie's bathroom, was also being examined, mainly for DNA. The poison found in Ollie's bedroom had already been confirmed as a match for that used on the parking tickets, but it was disappointing that the vials held no fingerprints. Colin's com-puter was being forensically gutted and every one of Colin's employ-ees were already sitting in interview rooms. With all of that, and the running down of the leads from the phone-ins, the team was stretched to maximum capacity. Not for the first time, Simon re-alised just how much they needed Lorrie.

SEAN WAITED IN HIS car on the road and hoped that Colin wouldn't spot him. He waited until all the lights went out in Lorrie's house and then five minutes later, he was rewarded by Colin pulling out of the drive. Leaving his headlights switched off, he followed him.

Lorrie heard the front door close and Colin's car start up on the drive. She tried to force her eyes open, but it was as if they were glued shut. She was so tired that it was impossible to summon the strength to move. Her body felt so heavy that she imagined she was inside the mattress. She struggled, but she simply couldn't find enough energy to fight her way out of the bed.

Time passed and she slowly felt the absolute exhaustion ease a little.

She could open her eyes and keep them open for long seconds at a time and she found that, if she concentrated really hard, she could move her fingers.

More time passed and she was, at last, able to drag herself into a seated position on the edge of the bed.

She immediately reached out and, after a few attempts, succeeded in switching on the bedside lamp. She cast her eyes along the bedside table in search of her phone. She dropped her gaze to the floor and panned across the carpet. No phone. She turned and her eyes searched the bed and then the bedside table at the far side. Still, no phone.

She would have to make her way downstairs to use the house phone, but she decided to give herself a few minutes rest first. Just the mere effort of sitting up had drained her of the little reserves she had and, falling back once more against the pillows, she succumbed to sleep once more.

'BRICK DUST, CLAY AND soil,' Ricky trumpeted across the room. 'London brick, residual clay and hard strata soil. How's that for news?'

All eyes were on him. They wanted more.

'No round of applause? Now, I am disappointed.' He walked directly to Simon, his fat little legs almost skipping. 'Getting these three components will help narrow the search down, but I'm still waiting on feedback from my chum at the observatory. Shouldn't be too long now.'

Sonia approached carrying a sheaf of papers. She addressed Simon. 'None of the sightings panned out,' she said, 'but the calls are still coming in.'

'I'm organising a shift change on the phones and sending some people home. Everyone is dead on their feet.'

'I know how they feel,' Ricky said, yawning. 'I'm going to find a quiet corner and have a nap. My phone will wake me when my pal calls me with information.' He flapped a hand in farewell and waddled off.

'You should try and get some rest, too,' Lovell said to Simon. 'I'll come and get you when there's something new to report.'

He shook his head. 'I daren't close my eyes, Sonia.'

'Afraid you wouldn't be able to rouse yourself? I know where there's a big bucket. Filled with cold water, it would soon get you up.' She smiled, but no amusement carried to her eyes. She too, was exhausted.

SEAN WAS FORCED TO turn his headlights on. Thankfully the traffic was heavy enough to cover him. Colin took him all the way to Edgware Road and then headed towards Canal Close where he meandered in and out of some derelict buildings before pulling up in front of a disused warehouse. Sean had to stay way back so as not to be seen but he had enough of a view to see him unlock the door and go in.

IT WAS JUST BEFORE midnight and the telephones were blessedly silent. Colin's employees had all been questioned and were on their way home to their beds. The team were taking a much needed break and the atmosphere was, temporarily, relaxed.

Over coffee, Simon thanked everyone for their hard work and promised that drinks would be on him as soon as they found Ollie.

Their moment of peace was interrupted by the appearance of Scully and Connor.

'Do they go everywhere together?' Lovell whispered to Simon. 'We never see one without the other these days.'

Simon stood as the terrible twosome approached.

'I don't think there's time to sit around drinking coffee, DI Grant,' Scully said. 'Your people should be working.'

Every member of the team took the hint, put down their coffee cups and made to move back to their desks.

Simon stopped them in their tracks. 'Sit back down, you lot,' he ordered. 'Finish your coffee and don't move until I come back.' To Scully and Connor, he said, 'Join me in the office. My team need a bit of peace to unwind and have a breather.' With that, he turned on his heel and marched from the incident room. Scully and Connor hesitated a moment before following him.

'I see you learned your bad manners at the tit of your Superintendent,' Scully sneered. 'She should have warned you that I don't appreciate being shown up in front of subordinates.'

Simon had witnessed the subtle and not so subtle ways Lorrie had undermined Scully and he had beheld her getting the better of him on almost every occasion. Simon did not quite have her strength of character nor her guts, but he would be damned if his knackered workforce was going to be harassed by the likes of him.

Before he could respond, Connor piped in.

'Let's not get carried away, sir,' he said to his boss. 'The girls and boys have been working round the clock. Best to give them a little slack.'

Scully cut his eyes at Connor and bit back a slap-down. 'Fine,' he said. 'We won't let it be said that I don't understand the pressure you are all under.' He looked Simon square in the face. 'As for you, Grant, watch your step. You have a chance here. Now that you're out from under Sullivan's petticoats we may see you make something of yourself.'

'Did you want something, sir?' Simon asked, ignoring his words.

'Want something?' Scully suddenly roared – all pretence at civility gone. 'Of course, I bloody well want something. I want you to tell me that you've caught that little scrote. I want you to tell me that I can inform the Assistant Commissioner, so that she can tell the Home Secretary, that it's all over.... that the case is closed, and we can get ready for the trial of the century. That's what I want, Detective Inspector.'

Simon said nothing.

'Well?'

'Well, what, sir?'

Scully's face was beetroot red, and he looked on the verge of a stroke. 'Have you got him? What have I to tell the AC?'

'We haven't got him, sir.' Simon smiled inwardly. He was sure Lorrie would be so proud of him. He hoped that, one day, they would be able to compare notes on how easy it was to rile the Commander.

Connor took over. He didn't want the hassle of the paperwork that would ensue if his boss dropped dead on the floor through high blood pressure and vitriol.

He asked, 'How close are you?'

Simon shrugged. 'Not close, sir, but we're hoping word back from the soil observatory will give us a lead.'

'What's this?' Scully put in. 'Soil observatory?'

'We're hoping to narrow down a location from trace evidence found on... found on DS Friel's body.'

'Friel?' Scully looked confused. 'Ah, yes... the murdered policewoman. She was from Manchester, wasn't she?'

Simon nodded. He didn't trust himself to speak. The disrespect from the senior officer was obscene.

Connor cleared his throat and placed a hand on Scully's arm. 'Perhaps we should leave them to it, sir? I'm sure we'll have news in the morning.' He nodded curtly to Simon and led his boss from the room before the idiot said something much worse and they ended up with a mutiny.

LORRIE WOKE AND WAS surprised to see that it was midnight. She felt better, stronger, and managed to get fully off the bed to stand on fairly steady legs.

It never occurred to her that she'd been drugged. She just thought that her body had completely shut down as some form of defence mechanism to protect her from the agony of Ollie. She was thankful for the extended sleep. Her mind was much clearer, and she was ready for an update on her son.

She searched the room for her mobile phone and, not finding it, she made her way across to the door. She would have to use the house phone, after all.

The door was stuck. No matter how hard she pulled, it wouldn't budge. It took her a few moments to realise that, in actual fact, the door was locked and there was no key.

SEAN HAD WAITED UNTIL nearly midnight before exiting the car and creeping up towards the building Colin had entered some time before. He was sure that Colin was still in there. His car was still out front, and Sean had not seen him leave. He was about to find out what he was up to. Whatever it was, it wasn't good – he knew that much – and he was determined to confirm his suspicions.

There was a light in one of the windows and he stealthily approached it. He hunkered down and peered up over the sill.

Colin was framed with his back to the window. Sean watched him for a few moments and tried to come up with a plan. He could simply go in and confront him or he could call Simon and put his theory to him, and they could both work out how best to proceed.

He mulled it over for a few minutes and had just decided that contacting Simon was best, when he heard a footstep behind him.

He turned and, when something heavy struck him on the side of the head, he went down.

# DAY NINE: MORNING

The team had managed a few hours' sleep but, from the yawns and the lethargic way in which they went about their duties, they were all still exhausted. Simon feared that, if they didn't find Ollie that day, they would be fit for nothing.

The soil observatory had finally come through, but the news was far from encouraging.

Simon looked at the information and found an industrial map of London on the internet and put the image up on the big screen. He spent a few minutes comparing what the observatory had provided with specific locations on the map.

'Any luck?' Sonia asked.

'There are too many,' he replied. 'We know that it's an industrial building made of London brick, but most are... the older ones, anyway. We can narrow it down from the clay and particularly from the properties in the soil, but that still leaves around twenty locations.'

'Not good.' Sonia picked up the observatory's report and studied it. 'I'm surprised they managed to get this much detail from a few bits of dirt.'

'Yes, it surprised me as well.'

'How do we do this?'

'We'll have to prioritise those buildings closest to where Friel was found.'

'That might not be helpful.'

Simon sighed. 'I know, but what choice do we have?'

'Perhaps...?' Sonia looked thoughtful. 'Perhaps if we try and identify a particular place that Ollie might have had an association with?'

'How do we do that? What could an eighteen year old boy have in common with an industrial building?'

'Through Colin, perhaps?'

Simon snapped his fingers. 'Good thinking, batgirl.' He thought a moment. 'But, I'd rather run it past Lorrie first. Let's pay her a visit.'

Just as they made to leave, Simon's phone pinged. He took it out of his pocket and looked at the screen.

'It's a message from Sean. Looks like a video.' He opened it and automatically reached a hand out to steady himself on the desk.

'Simon?' Sonia was alarmed by his sudden pallor. 'What is it, Simon?'

LORRIE HAD BEEN AWAKE all night. She had tried everything she could think of to free herself from the room but to no avail. She had put a lock on her bedroom door some months before in an attempt to keep Colin out. He had a habit of visiting her room in the middle of the night and she had lost count of the times she'd awoken to find him sitting staring at her as she'd slept. He also had a habit of entering her room and searching through her things when she was out at work and a lock on the door seemed a good idea at the time. Now... now it didn't seem such a good idea.

An hour earlier, she had tried calling out the window but, as her bedroom was at the back of the house, there were no passers-by to hear her. Her neighbours were too far away to be of any good, so, she was well and truly trapped. She had resigned herself to sitting it out until Colin returned.

She had no clue as to what her husband was up to. He had locked her in and stayed out all night and she was more than a little alarmed. She wondered if, somehow, he'd found Ollie, and was trying to help him. It was the only thing that made any sense. He knew that she believed her son needed to be apprehended and, so, she understood that he wouldn't want to involve her. She hoped that they were both safe.

SIMON'S HAND SHOOK as he stared at the small phone screen. The sound was muted. He always kept the media volume switched off as he was easily annoyed by the noise that the videos that popped up on his Facebook feed made.

'Simon, you're scaring me.' Sonia placed a hand on his arm. 'What's wrong?'

Simon cleared his throat and turned off the image on the phone. 'Get me a techie,' he said. 'I need my phone linked up to the video screen and then track down Scully and Connor... and the Assistant Commissioner. They all need to see this.'

Sonia hesitated and Simon – his face contorted with agitation – ushered her on with an exaggerated flap of his hand. 'Move,' he said. 'Get them all up out of their beds if you have to.'

COLIN RETURNED TO THE house but did not immediately go upstairs. He was dishevelled and tense. Things had taken an unexpected turn and, although he was on top of it, he couldn't help but feel anxious.

He could hear Lorrie moving about and he steeled himself for what he had to do next. He knew that she would be incandescent with rage, but he was confident that her mood would soon change.

He made himself a coffee and sat at the kitchen table. It was obvious that Lorrie realised that he was home because he could hear her calling out his name. He ignored her. There was time enough to confront her.

Lorrie heard Colin return and she had waited patiently for him to come upstairs. As the minutes ticked by, and there was no sound of him on the stairs, she began to call out to him. Her voice got steadily louder until she was virtually screaming. She'd kill him, she thought furiously. She didn't care what he'd been up to – she'd kill him.

When she finally heard the key turn in the lock, she was ready for him.

'THIS BETTER BE GOOD,' Scully said to Simon. 'Do you know how little sleep I got last night?'

'Probably more than me,' Simon returned. His colour had returned to normal, however his eyes remained haunted.

'What's going on?' Assistant Commissioner, Annie Gordon, asked as she strode into the major incident room. 'I got an urgent call.'

She was immediately followed by Connor who, unlike the others, accepted that he was required to be there without questioning the why of it. One look at DI Grant's face had told him that, whatever it was, it was serious.

'Would you all care to take a seat?' Simon asked. 'In front of the big screen, if you don't mind.' He ushered the members of his team to do likewise.

Annie Gordon raised a quizzical brow, but took a seat nevertheless. Scully blustered a little, but he too, acquiesced. Connor remained standing.

'I got a video from DI Kelly's phone earlier,' Simon began. 'It was sent it to me on my mobile.'

'Kelly sent you the video?' Scully asked. 'From Manchester?'

'No.' Simon shook his head. 'I don't think he made it to Manchester, and he didn't send it.' He gestured to Lovell who used the remote to bring the image to life on the screen.

'What the fuck?' Scully reared to his feet.

Annie Gordon inhaled sharply and closed her eyes in distress.

Simon sank into a chair and listened, for the first time, to the video he had watched earlier. It turned out to be much worse than he'd imagined.

THE BEDROOM DOOR SWUNG open, and Lorrie sprang toward it from the middle of the room. Her claws were out, and it took all of Colin's strength to pin her arms to her side and push her back.

'Cut it out,' he said, wrestling her down onto the bed. 'Calm down, for fuck's sake.'

'You bastard,' she screamed. 'You locked me in. How could you lock me in?'

'I was worried about you.'

Lorrie bucked beneath him. The smell of sweat from his unwashed body was overpowering and she was desperate to get him off her.

'Will you give it a rest, Lorrie? You're going to hurt yourself.' Colin eased back a little. 'Calm down and let me explain.'

Lorrie was in no mood to listen to his lies. She knew exactly what he'd been up to, and she had no hesitation in informing him that she had sussed him out.

'You found him didn't you? Where is he? You tell me, right now, where he is.'

Her words shocked him and caused him to relax his hold on her for a brief second. Lorrie took full advantage. She gave one final buck, and she was free.

Instead of jumping up from the bed and running for the door, Lorrie stood her ground and rounded on him. 'I've had it with you,' she spat. 'You may think you're clever, but it will be worse for Ollie in the long run. You've got a screw loose, Colin, and I want nothing more to do with you.' She made for the door.

Colin was on her in an instant. He yanked her back and into his arms. Lorrie struggled. Colin held on tight.

'Will you listen to me,' he said breathlessly. She had the strength of a lion and was as slippery as an eel and it took every bit of strength to hold onto her. 'I'll take you to him if you'll just calm down.'

She heard him, but she didn't believe him. 'You're a fucking liar,' she said. 'You won't take me anywhere near him.' As she spoke, she ceased struggling. He had too tight a hold on her and she needed to change her strategy. Fighting him would get her nowhere, so she relaxed and went limp in his arms.

Colin was not to be fooled. He tightened his hold still further and kicked closed the door.

They were both panting with the exertion, and both took the opportunity to simply stand there and recuperate.

Finally, Colin loosed her and stood with his back pressed firmly against the closed door.

'Where is he?' Lorrie asked. 'How did you find him?'

Colin laughed. 'I'm not going to tell you that.'

'But, you'll take me to him? That would be stupid and you're not stupid, Colin.'

'What else am I going to do?' he cut his eyes at her. 'I need you to trust me.'

SIMON KNEW THAT, AS soon as the video ended, he would be removed as senior investigating officer. He didn't mind – in fact he was relieved. Things had developed into an absolute nightmare and someone with a great deal more experience would now need to take over.

Sean was on the video. He was bound and gagged and tied to a chair. His face told the story of a severe beating and he looked as if he was hanging onto life by the skin of his teeth.

The Reaper was also on the video – obviously wearing a second costume – and he wasted no time in rubbing their noses in the fact that he had outsmarted them.

'A second costume,' Simon noted. 'We only searched for purchases of one costume. That was a mistake.'

They listened in silence as the Reaper spouted mouthful after mouthful of contemptuous vitriol. It was obvious that he meant to kill Sean and, indeed, made it perfectly clear that he would take great pleasure in extinguishing his life with as much pain as possible.

Sean remained unconscious throughout the duration of the three minute video. He was clearly breathing - and that was a relief to everyone watching – but it was equally clear that he was in pretty bad shape.

Once again, a video of the Reaper left everyone speechless. What was there to say? An eighteen year old boy had murdered over thirty people, escaped capture and succeeded in overpowering and imprisoning a big, strong, experienced police officer. He was obviously smarter than they were, more resourceful than them and he was going to get away with murdering another one of their own.

The AC was the first to speak. 'I want that fucker caught and manacled to a chair before the day is out.' She looked directly at Chief Superintendent Connor and added, 'I want Sean Kelly found alive and I want you to make sure it happens. You're now in charge, so get your finger out and get me that little shit in chains and get me Kelly.'

# DAY NINE: AFTERNOON

It was freezing in the room. A faint wintry sun struggled through the dirt and grime on the windows to cast faint shadows and there was enough light for Sean to understand a little of where he was.

Large, mildewed boxes were stacked to his right and, to his left – within his limited periphery – he saw an old table and a couple of rickety chairs. He couldn't see behind him as his bindings were tight enough to hold him rigid, and all he could see in front of him was a set of double doors.

The chair, to which he was bound, creaked when he shifted his weight, but it seemed sturdy, and he decided against tipping over on-to his side on the floor in the hope that it would break. That, he told himself, only worked in movies.

He remembered being hit in the head and then recalled waking when being pummelled mercilessly by a pair of angry fists. Everything else that had happened to him was a blur.

They wouldn't be looking for him. They thought that he was in Manchester. He wondered if he would ever see Lorrie again.

SIMON OPENED THE OFFICE door and gestured for Connor to enter ahead of him.

Connor said, 'I still want you to run point on this. Operationally, you're still in charge.'

Simon frowned. 'The Assistant Commissioner...'

'Can mind her own bloody business.'

'Sir?' Simon was perplexed. He had trouble fathoming the Chief Super's meaning.

'Look, DI Grant...' Connor sat behind the desk and motioned for Simon to take the seat on the other side. 'Do you know how long it's been since I led an operation? No? Well, I'll tell you – fifteen years. I'm a paper-pusher, my boy, and I make no apologies for that. What I'm not is a fool. There's no way on God's green earth that I'm going to lead on this manhunt. I'd only cock it up and Kelly's life is on the line. I will, however, take the credit when you apprehend the Reaper and save Kelly.'

For a moment Simon didn't know what to say. He was at a loss for words. Finally, he found his tongue. He said, 'What if I cock it up, sir? I mean – I'm not sure if I can pull it off.'

Connor thought a moment and then said, 'I think you'll do all right. How long have you worked with Sullivan?'

'Four years.'

'Four years, eh? Long enough, I'd say.'

'Sir?'

'To have her magic rub off on you.'

'I didn't think you liked her.'

'Like her?' Connor laughed. 'Who says that I like her? Truth be told – I can't stand the mardy bitch. I do respect her, though. Bloody good copper.' He drew his brows. 'I'll castrate you if you ever tell her I said that.'

'I don't think she'd believe me.'

'No? No, I guess not.' He stood up. 'Just carry on doing what you've been doing. I'll touch base with you later for an update.' He walked to the door and added, 'You do know that we've not got much time? Kelly will be a gonner pretty soon – if he's not dead already – and I don't have to tell you what a shit storm that would cause. The AC has a soft spot for Kelly. I wouldn't give a bent pound for our careers if we let that happen.'

SONIA THREW HER PEN across the desk and picked up the folder of maps she had been studying and flung it the length of the room. None of her colleagues batted an eyelid. Her frustration was their frustration.

Baxter dodged the flying folder and handed her a mug of coffee. 'No luck?'

Scowling, shaking her head, exasperated, she said, 'Yes, all bad. I can't narrow the locations down and I'm about ready to scream.'

'I thought the DI was going to speak to the Super'?'

Lovell took a swallow of coffee. 'That was before the AC handed everything over to Connor.'

'And, I guess, Connor won't want to involve Sullivan?'

'Not unless Hell froze over first.' She savoured a second mouthful of coffee and sighed. 'Thank God for caffeine.'

'Why don't you call the Super'?' Baxter plopped himself down next to her. 'Better to ask forgiveness, than permission.'

'I like my job, Baxter.'

'Your job is safe enough. The DI would back you, no matter what.'

She studied the mug in her hands and then turned her eyes to her mobile phone sitting on the desk. Simon might thank her for taking the initiative and there was no reason for Scully or Connor to find out that she'd spoken to the Superintendent. She picked the phone up. Sullivan's number was in her list of contacts and, before she could change her mind, she rang her.

The phone went to voicemail and Sonia hastily ended the call without leaving a message.

'Shit,' she swore. 'I should have left a message... asked her to call me back.'

'Ring the number again,' Baxter suggested.

Simon approached them. 'Ring what number again?' he asked.

Surprised, Sonia jumped to her feet. 'Guv?'

'Were you ringing Superintendent Sullivan, by any chance?' Simon was well aware of her habit of knowing the right thing to do. In most circumstances, her intuition was spot-on. He didn't wait for her confirmation. 'You didn't get through to her?'

'No, Guv. Went straight to voicemail.'

'Try again and leave a message if she doesn't answer. Tell her we're popping round.'

THE AFTERNOON RUSH-hour traffic delayed their progress. Colin kneaded the steering wheel impatiently, whilst Lorrie dozed in the seat beside him. He thought about what the afternoon would bring and was surprised to find that he felt a sense of regret. To dispel the growing awareness of self-doubt, he recalled to memory all the reasons he had taken the actions that he had. Bolstered with a refreshed feeling of self-justification, he made the remainder of the journey satisfied that he had been right to do what he did and that he was without blame for what he was about to do.

SIMON AND SONIA PULLED onto Lorrie's drive and were immediately gratified to find that her car was parked in front of the garage. It looked as if she was home.

She might not want to help us,' she said. 'Ollie is her son, after all.'

'She'll help us,' Simon returned. 'She knows what's right.'

They both climbed from the car and approached the front door. Simon rang the bell and they waited.

'Doesn't look as if she's home,' Simon said. He rang the bell again. 'Unless she's asleep.'

'Should I try her phone again?' Sonia asked.

Simon shook his head. 'You've tried umpteen times already. Just give it a minute.' He rang the bell for a third time.

'I'll go around the back.'

Simon watched her make her way to the side of the house and disappear towards the back. He stepped back from the door and gazed up at the bedroom windows. It was a grand house, and the windows were in keeping with the period.

He looked for movement behind the curtains and, seeing none, made a final attempt on the bell.

Sonia returned and shook her head. 'All locked up and no one in sight.'

'I guess we're out of luck.'

'What, now?' Sonia's anxiety was evident. 'Shall we try and track down her husband?'

'It's worth a try, I suppose. Let's head back and I'll track a phone number down for him.'

A KEY RATTLED IN THE lock and Sean braced himself. He had a feeling that more pain was imminent. He was expecting Colin and was shocked and frightened to see Lorrie enter.

Colin followed – a hand on Lorrie's back.

It took Lorrie a moment to fully comprehend what was in front of her. A beaten, bloodied man, gagged and tied to a chair, faced her and when her eyes suddenly recognised him, she blundered forward only to be yanked back by Colin.

Colin was taking no chances. He tasered her and she flopped, twitching, to the floor. Sean screamed beneath the gag and fought ferociously to free himself.

To Sean, Colin said, 'Don't worry about her. Worry about yourself. I have plans for you.' With that, he dragged Lorrie by an arm over to one of the chairs to Sean's left and unceremoniously hauled her up and flung her into it. He wasted no time in securing her and then turned his attention back to a still struggling Sean.

'My friend will be here directly,' he said, 'and then, the fun can begin. Be patient – he won't be long.

# DAY NINE: EVENING

'What is it with these Sullivans?' Chief Superintendent Connor shook his head in disbelief. 'We can't find the murderous toe-rag of a son and now mum and dad are on the missing list?'

'I'm not suggesting that they're all together, sir,' Simon put in. 'It's just that we need either the Super or her husband to have a look at the twenty locations we have in mind for where Friel was kept prisoner to see if any of them are familiar and that Ollie might know of.'

'And, you've wasted the whole day looking for mum and dad?'

Simon moved from one foot to the other and looked everywhere but at Connor. 'I've had tactical support working through the list of twenty, sir. Searches are going on as we speak, but there's not enough people on the ground to get around them very quickly. Most of them are huge, disused buildings and they take a lot of looking 'round.'

'Then, get more men on the ground, Grant. Pull them from traffic. Get the community officers involved.'

'Yes, sir.'

Connor's eyes, flinty hard and fiercely pissed-off, stared at Simon until the DI was forced to look back at him. 'You need to grow a pair, detective inspector. You won't get anywhere in this job without a bit of cheek. So what if you rub someone up the wrong way because

273

you've nicked their manpower? So what if someone complains to the AC that you've acted outside of your rank? Do you honestly believe Annie Gordon is going to give a flying fuck that you've robbed traffic division?' He shook his head. 'Lorrie Sullivan may not have an actual pair of balls, Grant, but she sure as Hell always acted like she had. Take a leaf from her book.'

'Yes, sir.'

'Stop fucking well yes siring me. It's not doing you any favours.'

No, sir.'

Connor sighed in exasperation and checked his watch. 'It's just gone six. If you get your skates on, you can recommission the night shift from traffic. Grab them and use them to get all of those locations searched before tomorrow morning.'

'Will do.'

Connor smiled for the first time. 'You're learning lad, now – tell me – should we be worried about Lorrie and her husband? Any chance the boy snatched them?'

The thought hadn't entered Simon's mind, but – now it bounced around his brain like an intercept missile. Shit, he thought – how could he have missed that possibility?

Simon knew that he dared not piss the Chief Super' off any further, so he kept his faux pas to himself. He said, 'I'm going to get that possibility looked into, sir.'

Connor's smile widened. 'I bet you are, lad. I bet you are.'

LORRIE AND SEAN COULD only communicate with their eyes. Neither of them were in a position to speak because of the filthy rags gagging them, but their eyes spoke volumes.

Each was terrified for the other. Each pair of eyes mirrored that same gut-curdling agony of terror, and each pair of eyes remained riveted on the other. Both Lorrie and Sean thought that this was the last time they would see one another and neither of them could bear not spending every second drinking in the sight of the person they loved.

That Lorrie was shocked beyond all imagining, went without saying. She had genuinely thought that Colin had found Ollie and was keeping him safe so, when she was faced with what he had done to Sean – and what he was now doing to her - she had automatically believed that it was a jealousy thing. When Colin's friend arrived, she suddenly realised it was nothing of the sort.

Colin had opened the door and the friend had walked through. She had recognised him immediately – as did Sean – and things then got a whole lot worse for both of them.

SCULLY CORNERED CONNOR. Once again, Scully had to swallow what the Assistant Commissioner had dictated, but there was nothing in the rule book to state that he had to like it. Connor groaned inwardly when he saw his boss approach and forced a deferential expression onto his face. Scully liked and appreciated his subordinates to brown-nose and arse lick, and Connor wasn't averse to giving the fat little prick what he craved.

'Are you looking for me, sir?' Connor asked politely.

'Who else would I be looking for?' Scully bit back. 'What's this I hear about Sullivan being AWOL?'

'We're looking into it. Might be nothing.'

'Why am I always the last to know these things? The AC ignores me and fucks with my business and now you keep me in the dark?'

'I can assure you, that's not intentional on my part. I've only just found out myself.'

Slightly mollified, Scully scowled and changed the subject. 'Kelly's probably dead by now. I expect his body will be dumped just like the other one.'

The insensitivity of Scully's words sent the blood rushing to Connor's face. 'DS Friel,' he grated – all pretence at civility gone. 'The other one – her name was Friel.'

'I know that,' Scully returned sharply.

'And, we're working under the assumption that DI Kelly is still alive,' Connor added.

'That means that you'll be dividing resources. The search for the Reaper should take priority. Kelly's dead, I say, and there's no point wasting manpower on looking for a dead body.'

Connor could not let that comment go unchallenged, however, he held his temper. He knew exactly how to stick it to his boss, and said, 'The press and the public would go ape-shit if they found out that we weren't actively looking for Kelly. They're sick of the dead bodies piling up and just imagine how good it would be for public relations if we brought Kelly back alive.'

'Yes, well....' Scully was, for the first time ever, stuck for words.

Connor decided to let him off the hook. Scully was a prize plonker, and didn't exactly engender respect, but he was to be pitied rather than condemned. Anyway, they played golf together regularly and Scully had even invited him and his wife around for drinks. Normally, Connor tolerated him and even went out of his way to protect him against the backlash his thoughtless words provoked. So, he said, 'You're probably right, sir... about Kelly being dead. I just think it's in all our best interests to keep the search a priority.'

Scully nodded agreement – magnanimous now that Connor was agreeing with him about Kelly being dead. According to his way of thinking, he not only deserved to be obeyed, he expected it. He had a simple belief – subordinates were there to be told what to think and what to do and, if they played the game, then they would be rewarded. With Connor, it was golf and drinks at his house, and also the privilege of being allowed to ride on his coattails. It was obvious that he had tried to break ranks with him – all that about the press and the public – but Scully would let it go. He needed Connor – and people like him – to ease his way up the greasy pole. Connor, like the other senior officers under his command – with the exception of the bitch, Sullivan – knew how to toe the line. They all knew what side their bread was buttered and, although they might, like Connor just did, try it on, they always came quickly back to heel.

COLIN WAS LAUGHING. The shock in Lorrie's eyes at seeing the man at his side was hilarious. He tried to speak, but the laughter completely overtook him. He allowed himself the pleasure of total surrender to his fit of giggles.

Sean thought... this man is stark staring mad.

Lorrie thought... it wasn't Ollie. My God, it wasn't Ollie.

The man at his side looked on with wry amusement. He, too, was delighted at the look in the two prisoner's eyes. He was the last person they had expected to be involved and that was, in part, down to how good an actor he was.

Professor Napier – the Bear – towered over them. Lorrie felt her heart lurch in her chest as the final pieces of the puzzle fell into place. A deep sadness overtook her. Ollie wasn't the Reaper, after all. She had believed the very worst of her son, and he had been innocent all along. The truth was devastating to her, not least because it meant that she had betrayed her son and probably put his life in danger. She felt a crushing sense of shame.

She looked across at Sean. His eyes were fixed intently on her face, and she saw him nod in recognition of the truth. She could see that he ached for her. He knew how shattered she was. The sudden recognition of the reality of the situation had immediately destroyed her and he was powerless to do anything about it.

Colin stopped laughing and wiped a hand across his eyes to wipe away the tears of merriment. He could finally speak. He said, 'Thank you for that. I needed a good laugh. I guess you've both sussed it all out now. I'm the Reaper, as if you didn't know, and my pal, here? Well, he's the brains of the operation.'

Lorrie closed her eyes in distress. Sean merely stared straight ahead. He had no intention of reacting any further to the sight of Napier or to Colin's words.

Suddenly, Lorrie felt her hair being ripped from her scalp as her head was jerked back.

'Open your eyes,' Colin roared. He kept his fist in her hair and continued to pull. 'Don't disrespect me. Keep them open or I'll gouge them out with my fucking fingers.'

Sean began to struggle. The sight of her being hurt was too much to bear.

He would get out of his bindings if it killed him, and he'd beat the fucker to death with his bare hands. But, it was no use. His struggles only succeeded in further tightening the rope.

Colin loosed Lorrie's hair. A few strands stuck to his fingers and he brushed them off. Lorrie groaned but kept her eyes firmly open.

'Settle down, now,' Colin said, unexpectedly amicable. 'I've a few things to say. I think it's only fair that I fill you in on everything.'

He nodded to Napier who smiled, turned and left the building.

'He's going to check on Ollie,' Colin said in explanation. 'I've got him tucked away somewhere quite safe and, Lorrie?' he grinned at her. 'If you behave yourself, I might consider allowing him to live.'

Lorrie nodded eagerly. She would do whatever the bastard wanted.

'Good girl. I hope you're still as eager to please when you find out what it entails.' He turned to Sean and said, 'I'm afraid you have to die, Kelly. I was going to kill you anyway, but I really don't mind that I have to do it earlier than I had planned.'

Sean ignored him. He had moved his eyes and he now kept them firmly fixed on Lorrie. He hoped that she read in them that he wasn't afraid. He hoped that she would see the great love he felt for her and be comforted and fortified.

'But,' Colin went on, 'I promised to fill you in on things.' He turned once more to Lorrie. 'You remember all those parent things that you could never attend? The evenings when Ollie wanted you to go and see his work and meet the professors? You remember those times?'

Lorrie shook her head.

'No, of course you don't. You were always too busy working to be bothered about your son. I went instead. I met Professor Napier at one of those events. We hit it off straight away. We had one thing in common – Professor Napier and I – we both thought that Ollie was rather too big for his boots. Don't get me wrong...' He began to pace up and down. 'I sometimes loved the boy. Admittedly, more so when he was younger... before he learned to have a smart mouth. I didn't quite love the teenager so much, but I still trekked to those events.'

Lorrie forgot herself and closed her eyes. She wanted nothing but blackness. Luckily for her, Colin was mid-way through a turn in his pacing, and his back was to her.

'Napier is a greedy bastard. Gambling is his downfall, and he owes thousands. It was easy to bribe him. He really doesn't have any morals, that man. Clever, though – I'll give him that. He made the poison, and I did the rest." He pondered a moment. 'Although I like the sound of my own voice, I think I'd quite like some audience participation.' He removed the gag from Lorrie and then from Sean. 'Feel free to ask questions.'

Sean spat a globule of blood onto the floor at his feet and then struggled through a bruised and battered mouth to say, 'Don't hurt her, Colin. Let her go. Do what you want with me.'

'Now, now, Sean... I'll put that gag back on if you persist in saying stupid things to me. Lorrie is my business. What I do with her is nothing to do with you.' He turned to Lorrie. 'What do you say, darling? Are you anything to do with Sean?'

'No.' The air tasted sweeter without the gag, and she gulped it in. Her wits were returning somewhat, and she knew enough to try and keep Colin calm. 'Sean is nothing to me.'

'Okay, then... where was I? Oh, yes – I remember. It was far easier than I dreamt. I was worried that the poison would wear off the tickets before they could be used, but Napier gave the poison a shelf-life long enough to at least get a few people. How many are there? Thirty?'

'Thirty-three with DS Friel,' Sean replied.

'Thirty-three? Imagine that. It caught far more than I imagined. The aeroplane was the best. I only wish the pilot had used the car park. An air crash to start the ball rolling would've been magnificent.'

'Why, Colin?' Lorrie asked. 'I don't understand any of this.'

'I'm coming to that,' he returned, impatiently. 'Let me tell it in my own way.'

'Okay. Sorry.'

Colin continued. He was warming up nicely and he couldn't wait to get to the best bit, but first, he said, 'I always planned on Ollie getting the blame. Someone had to take the fall and it just had to be him. I must say, though, I was very surprised that you were so quick to point the finger at him, Lorrie.' He then looked directly at Sean. 'And, what about you? He is your son, after all. Did you find it easy to accuse him too?' He shook his head. 'Poor Ollie. Imagine having parents like you pair.'

'You were very clever,' Sean said.

'Why, thank you for that, Sean. Praise, indeed.'

'Did you kill Friel or was it Napier?'

'Napier, of course. I wanted to do it but the warehouse burning down scuppered that plan. I think Napier enjoyed it a little too much.'

'Did you burn it down?'

Colin's features tightened. 'That wasn't me. Ollie worked out what I was up to and torched the place. I caught him in the act and found your mate snooping about at the same time. Needless to say, I had to act.'

'Friel wouldn't have gone quietly.'

'Blunt force to the head made her quiet enough. Ollie was a bit more problematic.' He continued pacing. 'I got him though, and he's now licking his wounds and shitting himself.'

'Is he okay?' Lorrie's voice trembled with fear for her son. 'How badly did you hurt him?'

'Not nearly enough after what he did. Everything was destroyed in that fire. No more poison, except for my own personal supply right here.' He patted his jacket pocket.

'You still haven't told us, why.' Lorrie still couldn't wrap her head around the unfolding events.

'For you, my darling wife. I did it for you... and us.' He smiled and licked his lips like a cat that nabbed the cream. 'I had to do something quite drastic to get you out of that fucking job. What better than a serial killer for a son? You'd need me, then. You could be a proper wife to me.'

'You're insane,' Lorrie said, shocked.

She gathered up every ounce of strength she could muster and threw herself forward in the chair.

Colin, taken unawares, jumped back like something scalded.

'You're mad,' she screamed. 'You did all of this... killed all those people... because you're mental in the head. I hate you. I fucking hate you.'

She was silenced by a punch from Colin's fist. Unconscious, her head flopped to the side and blood dripped onto the floor.

Sean was throwing obscenities at him, and Colin considered using the Taser to shut him up. He thought better of it. He much preferred Kelly awake and alert. All the better to suffer.

# DAY NINE: NIGHT

'I've found another three locations that fit the profile,' Sonia told Simon.

'How many have been searched so far?'

'Only eight. It's slow going. Even with the increase in boots on the ground, they're struggling. The buildings are all huge industrial units. The next four or five should be quicker, though.'

'Oh?' Simon perked up at that.

'The next ones on the list are all in use. Hard to imagine Ollie hiding in a busy building.'

'No. That wouldn't work for him. He kept Friel prisoner some-where off the radar - an abandoned building. Now that he's got Sean... well, I'm sure of it.'

'Should we just concentrate on the empty ones – leave the work-ing ones 'til last?'

'Makes sense. That would be a better use of time.'

'I'll get on it.' Sonia walked away and immediately made a call on her mobile.

Simon clenched his fists in an effort to control his agitation. He wanted to be out there, searching with the others, but he was a chief and not an Indian, so he had to wait until he got word that the loca-tion had been identified. Only then could he leave.

He kept Sonia with him. She calmed him and kept him on point. She wasn't one to sit twiddling her thumbs, so she had kept herself busy going over the information and identifying other possible sites. She had also acted as the main communication officer and kept Simon updated on the progress of the search.

He was grateful when Connor had taken himself home. The man had a habit of hovering and Simon couldn't function properly with him looming over his shoulder. The AC had popped in earlier in the evening, but Simon didn't mind her being there. She asked sensible questions and didn't try to interfere. She popped off again with the promise of more support should he need it.

Now, with Sonia off refocussing the troops and Connor out of his hair, Simon took the time to go over everything in his mind. The one thing he could not reconcile was Lorrie being missing. She was nobody's fool and, even though she was in a bit of a state, she wouldn't be tricked into being taken by Ollie. That Colin was missing as well only added to the conundrum.

Sean should have been in Manchester. Simon had watched him leave. What could possibly have happened between leaving New Scotland Yard and showing up on the Reaper's video?

COLIN WATCHED LORRIE battling it out with herself. He had told her that his motivation for the murders was simply to ruin her career and have her at home with him where she belonged.

It couldn't all be a surprise to her. She must have realised how much he hated her career and hated that she was not a proper wife to him. She must know that everything was her fault. He wasn't a born killer – she had made him into one. She'd said that he was mental, well – if that was true – then that was just one more thing she'd done to him. Now, she'd turned him into a wife-beater. Was there no end to the harm she would cause him?

He watched her expression change as everything began to make sense to her. She wasn't a fool, and Colin banked on the fact that she would come to her senses and realise she had no choice. Her eyes told him that she had, at last, fully comprehended the cunning of his plan and that she was trapped.

With the exception of her committing the murders herself, having her son be the notorious Reaper was the one sure fire way of finishing her as a police officer. If his plan had unfolded as it should, and if the bastard Kelly hadn't buggered it all up, she would have turned to him for comfort and their marriage would have strengthened under the horrendous fall-out of Ollie's notoriety. Sean would be out of the picture because Colin had always planned to kill him.

The fact that everything had gone tits up, and Colin was now outed as the Reaper, didn't change his plans. Lorrie would still be at his side – meeker and more malleable – and Sean Kelly would be six feet under the ground. To be other than the dutiful wife would mean the death of her son.

'You won't get away with it,' she finally said. All her working life, Lorrie had believed in the power of justice. She believed that right would ultimately conquer wrong, and it went against the grain for her to believe that an innocent boy would be held accountable, and the guilty party get off scot-free. Oh, she wasn't naïve when it came to the realities of life. She knew that it could take years for the authorities to finally realise the truth, but she had faith that they eventually would.

'I'll get away with it all right,' Colin returned. 'You'll convince them that Ollie is, indeed, the Reaper. They already believe it, so it won't be too hard to rubber stamp it. You'll be the grieving mother and I'll play the wonderful part of the supportive husband. Of course, they'll only too readily accept your resignation. Who would want a serial killer's mother on the force?'

'I won't do it.' Lorrie looked defiantly into his eyes. 'You'll have to kill me.'

He laughed. She really was funny. 'No, my dear – I'll kill Ollie. Your co-operation is the only thing keeping him alive.'

'They'll never stop looking for him. They'll find him and the truth will come out.'

'They won't find him. I think they'll scale down the search once they realise there are no more deaths. The pressure will be off, and he'll soon fade into the background. Some new horror will take over the headlines and resources will be shifted to solve the latest monstrous crime.'

'You think you've got it all figured out, don't you? Well, what if I tell you to go ahead – kill Ollie and then kill me?'

'I'd say that you were lying. You may be a lousy mother, but you don't want your son dead.'

All the while, Sean sat and listened in mounting horror at the plan Colin laid out. Unlike Lorrie, he saw the merit in it. He saw that Colin had all the cards and he realised that Lorrie had no choice. He wondered what Colin had in store for him, but he thought he could guess. Colin would kill him.

'I'm going to leave you both alone for a time,' Colin said. 'I have things to do, places to be. I'm going to leave the gags off. No one will hear you if you scream and shout. This building is sound-proofed.' He hunkered down at Lorrie's knees. 'You won't remember this warehouse, Lorrie. It was my first... long before your time. I kept it... sentimental reasons.'

He reached up and wiped a drop of blood from the corner of her mouth with the ball of his thumb. 'I won't apologise for hitting you. You deserved it. I'll hit you again if you do or say anything to upset me. I'm done being the one who has to always turn the other cheek.'

He stood up. 'Time for the finale.'

He reached into his pocket and removed a vial of poison. 'Yes, I'll leave the gags off. Don't say that I'm not good to you. Another, in my position, would be cruel. I want to be kind at the end.'

'No!' Lorrie screamed, her body bucking against the restraints. She saw the blur of his fist moments before it connected with her jaw. She slumped in the chair and only just managed to hang onto consciousness.

'I warned you, my dear. I'll beat you until you're in a coma and you'll miss all the sweet goodbyes with Kelly. Behave, now.'

Sean could do nothing. He knew what was coming and there was nothing he could do to stop it.

Lorrie mumbled incoherently, still trying desperately to stave off the inevitable. She tried to convince herself that none of it was happening, but Colin's wicked giggle brought the reality of the situation home. Sean was going to die. Colin was going to murder him in cold blood, and he was going to make her watch.

'I think you know by now,' Colin said through his insane giggling, 'that it takes about fifteen or twenty minutes to work. Plenty of time to say goodbye.'

He removed a handkerchief from his trouser pocket and carefully applied a few drops of the poison. His giggling had abruptly ceased. He had to concentrate so as not to spill any on his hands.

Sean jerked his head from side to side in an effort to avoid the approaching handkerchief. Colin stopped in mid-air and he stepped back. 'Tell you what, Sean,' he said. 'If you won't co-operate, then I'll give it to Lorrie instead.' He turned towards his wife.

'No!' Sean called out. 'I'll co-operate. Just get it over with.'

Lorrie, by this time, was sobbing uncontrollably.

Colin smiled, satisfied that Sean would sit still long enough to receive the fatal dose. He approached him once more and gently smeared the liquid poison on his broken and bleeding lips.

'You might not have as much as fifteen minutes,' he said, stepping back. 'Those cuts on your lips and in your mouth from the jolly good beating I gave you should hasten things along.'

'Jesus... Jesus... Please, Jesus,' Lorrie cried.

Sean attempted to console her. 'It's all right, Lorrie. All that matters is you and Ollie. Don't give the bastard the satisfaction of seeing you destroyed.'

'I can't... I can't...' She lapsed into a further bout of sobbing.

'I'll be off, now.' Colin replaced the vial back in his pocket and threw the handkerchief on the floor. 'I'll see you later, Lorrie. Try not to miss me.' He walked away and stepped through the door. The key rattled in the lock, and he was gone.

'Sean. Oh, my God, Sean. What can I do? We've got to get out of here.' She tugged frantically at the ropes around her wrists.

Sean felt the first tingle of death in his mouth. It wouldn't matter if they managed to escape – he was dead anyway. He knew that he needed to say something to Lorrie. He knew he needed to find the words that would enable her to go on, but no words came.

'Sean... Sean, try and get free. Don't just sit there.' Her voice rose until it reached a crescendo of hysteria. She repeated his name over and over again until she was wracked with sobs.

Through her noisy tears, she heard him say her name. She looked at him and, seeing his pain, seeing his life begin to ebb, caused an excruciation of hurt in her chest. She wanted to tear her eyes away. She wanted to stop her ears. Seeing him and hearing him die was unbearable.

'Listen to me, Lorrie,' he said, his voice slurred. 'It's important.' His tongue had begun to swell, and the excessive salivation made it difficult for him to get the words out. He persevered. He had noticed something, and it was important that he make her hear him.

Lorrie's terror-fuddled brain would not concentrate on what Sean was trying to say. She was wholly focussed on trying to say or do something that would help him. She was, however, at a loss. She tried to lean forward in the chair to be as close to him as possible and could only whisper, 'Oh, Jesus help him. Please, Jesus, please Jesus...'

Beneath the pain, beneath the fear of his imminent death, Sean was growing impatient. 'Be quiet... listen,' he rasped.

He tried to spit to clear his mouth a little, but his lips were numb. He made a second attempt and blood sprayed his knees.

'Don't exert yourself, Sean. Don't try to talk.'

Sean ignored her. He said, 'He's tied your hands to the arms of the chair at the front. He made a mistake, Lorrie. He should have secured you behind like he did to me. Can you see how he's tied your wrist over the plaster cast?'

Lorrie couldn't register what he was saying. She looked at him dumbly.

Sean mustered what strength he had left and screamed at her. He screamed at her to listen. He saw her eyes clear and witnessed her brain rebooting.

'You have to break the cast, Lorrie. If you break the cast, then the rope will slip over your wrist.'

'Break the cast?' Her eyes dropped to her arm. She saw immediately what he meant. Colin had inadvertently secured the rope holding her arm to the chair over the plaster cast. But, how on earth could she break it? She lifted her eyes once more and they sent Sean the mute question.

Sean had already considered it. 'Throw yourself on the floor. Tip yourself over. You can try and break the cast on the concrete floor.'

His voice, low and resonating with desperate petition, somehow brought her senses fully back.

'I don't think that'll work,' she said. 'I won't be able to free it enough to get leverage to smash it on the floor.'

Sean thought about it. She was right. 'You have to get on your knees and then work your way over to those boxes.' He gestured with his head. 'I can see something jagged sticking out from behind them. I think that it's metal. Use it to cut through the rope.'

She knew that he was clutching at straws. There was no possibility of her travelling that distance tied to a chair.

'I don't have much time,' he said.

His voice had dropped, and Lorrie had to strain to hear him.

'I don't want to die knowing you're not safe.' His breath caught in his throat, and he wanted urgently to cough. He wanted to clutch at his throat – to open it up and allow a little more air in – but his hands were secured behind his back and there was no easement to his suffering.

He choked more words out. 'Do... what...I told you, Lorrie... Try, please. You have to get away.'

It was almost over. Lorrie felt it. She fought back the primal urge to scream. She didn't want Sean dying with the sound of her hysterical distress ringing in his ears, so she swallowed back the impulse. She lowered her head. She was being a coward. It was much too difficult to look at him. She didn't have the courage to watch him die.

'Lorrie?'

She raised her eyes. He seemed to shrink in front of her.

'I... love you... Lorrie.'

His words brought her courage hurtling back. 'I love you, Sean.' Her eyes were now firm, steady, and she determined not to even blink until it was finished. She had to bear witness. She had to watch until the bitter end so that she could behold the evil that Colin had perpetrated. She would stand for Sean. She would be his voice from beyond the grave. If it ever came to court, if Colin was ever caught, she would describe the agony of his death and demand justice.

She had to do one more thing. She had to give Sean hope. 'I'll do it, my darling. I'll get on my knees, and I'll get over to cut the rope. Colin won't have me, I promise. I'll find Ollie and we'll both be safe.'

It was as if an electrical charge existed between them. The very air seemed to resonate. No more words were necessary. Their love existed to the very end of his life and then beyond.

He died miserably, but not alone.

A solitary tear escaped. 'Goodbye, my darling,' she sighed.

COLIN HAD AVOIDED ANSWERING his mobile phone for most of the day, but he was feeling confident and more than a little pleased with himself, so he risked returning the call from DI Grant.

'Thank goodness,' Simon said. 'I've been trying you and Lorrie for hours.'

'Why, what's up?' Colin knew full well what was up. Lorrie's little lapdog was worried about her. 'Lorrie didn't mention any missed calls from you. Is everything all right?'

'We're still trying to find Ollie. He's taken Sean Kelly.'

With a huge grin on his face, Colin said, 'Oh my God. I hope he's okay?'

'We don't know. We don't think so. Where's Lorrie?'

'Asleep. I brought her to a hotel to get away from the house. She's shattered, poor thing.'

'I wanted to ask her if she'd thought over where Ollie might be.'

'I'm sure she's done nothing but think. Frankly, it's all getting too much for her. If she found out about Sean, it would tip her over the edge. Best that we don't disturb her with that news just yet.'

If you think that's best,' Simon said, deflated. 'Perhaps you can help?'

'If I can. What do you need?'

'We've got information that points to a location.'

'Oh?' Colin's heart stopped for a second. 'You know where Ollie is?'

'No. That's just it – we can't identify exactly what location. We have a list a mile long.'

'I see.' Colin let out a relieved breath. 'How can I help?'

'Can you take a look at our list? It's a bit shorter now that we've searched about a dozen buildings, but there's still a dozen more on there and we're running out of time to find Sean before he ends up as the latest victim.'

'How would looking at your list be of any help?'

Simon sighed. 'It's a shot in the dark. We're hoping one of the locations might be familiar to you. Perhaps somewhere Ollie would know about?'

'Well,' Colin acted unsure. 'I can look, I suppose.'

'Great. What hotel are you staying at? I can bring the list to you.'

'No. No. I'll come to you. I don't want Lorrie disturbed.'

SHE HAD MADE HIM A promise and she meant to keep it. She had no idea how long it would be before Colin returned so she wasted no time.

She tensed her muscles and tried to tip the chair. It rocked on its legs and then settled back firmly onto the floor. She tried again and, suddenly, it was over. She landed with a thud on her side and all the air was knocked painfully from her body. Now what, she wondered?

Her legs were secured by the ankles to the legs of the chair, and she wasn't sure if there was enough play in the ropes to allow her to bend her knees. She just about managed to drop her chin sufficiently to enable her to look the length of her legs and she immediately smiled. It was going to be much easier than she had thought. She was surprised that Sean hadn't noticed what had just made her grin.

She flicked her gaze over to him. 'I'm going to do it, Sean,' she said. 'I'm going to get out of here.'

She wasn't sure why Colin had made so many mistakes. Perhaps he didn't think those mistakes would matter? Perhaps he simply underestimated her?

Colin's first mistake was securing her hands to the front rather than the back. His second mistake was in tying the rope around the plaster cast. His third mistake was the most serious.

The ropes securing her ankles to the bottom of the chair legs were a little loose but, what made Colin's mistake one of epic proportion, was the fact that the chair legs weren't joined by a rung. That meant – and she could barely believe her luck – the ropes weren't actually secured to the chair. If she managed to find a way to manoeuvre both ropes down the inch or so to her heels and then manoeuvre them over her heels to the bottom of the wooden legs, then the ropes would slip off.

She thought about it. What had seemed simple enough, now confounded her. She couldn't think of a way to move the ropes.

Sean would help her. Her feet were less than a metre from where Sean sat. If she wiggled her hip and dug in her heels, she was sure that she would achieve enough momentum to cover the distance between them. She would then place herself parallel to his feet and use the side of his boot to work the ropes downwards and over the bottom of the chair leg.

It was easier said than done. By the time she succeeded in covering the short distance, her hip was throbbing, and she was sure both her heels were blistered. But, she did it.

She took a moment to lean in and touch her lips to his cheek. He already felt cold. She closed her eyes and placed her forehead on his shoulder.

'I'm so sorry, my darling. Please forgive me.' She kissed him once more and then set about freeing herself.

It took an inordinate amount of time to free the first leg but, in doing so, she found that she could then move more easily. She used her free foot to assist her in bumping the chair around in a circle so that the second rope was against Sean's foot.

It was quicker the second time and, once that leg was free, she struggled onto her knees and then onto her feet.

She staggered and almost crashed to the floor. She felt faint. Dragging in a deep breath, she steadied herself and turned so that she was facing Sean.

'Thank you,' she said. She bent at the waist and placed her cheek against the cool skin of his face. She held it there for long minutes before swallowing down a sob and standing as erect as the chair still attached to her upper body allowed.

Now, to free her hands. Walking with the chair attached to her body was problematic and twice she fell crashing to her knees. She finally reached the stacked boxes and was relieved to see a twisted, jagged piece of a broken metal shelf. It was sharp and it had the capacity to slice through skin and rip open a vein but, luckily, she made the right decision and used it on the rope on top of the cast. It was so sharp that it took less than a minute. Her fingers were numb with cold, but they worked sufficiently to untie the second hand.

She was free. Relief flooded through her. Before she made to leave, she stood for a moment and thanked God then turned and told Sean that she would be back for him.

She went to the door. It was locked. She recalled the sound of the key in the lock when Colin had left. She didn't bat an eyelid. Instead, she picked up the chair that had held her prisoner and hurled it through a window.

# DAY TEN

I t had snowed in the night, but the low winter sun had already instigated a thaw. Colin arrived back at the disused warehouse a mere five minutes after Lorrie had escaped. He immediately noticed the broken window, the abandoned chair and the footsteps in the snow. He rushed to unlock the door and stepped into his worst nightmare.

He had no clue as to how long she had been gone but, as her footsteps were quite fresh and untouched by the thaw, he guessed it had been a brief amount of time. He believed he could catch up with her before she had a chance to raise the alarm. He had a car, and she was on foot. She had no chance.

'THAT WAS A WASTE OF time.' Simon threw his list of locations onto his desk. 'He left us waiting all night then waltzes in here this morning just to give us the run-around.'

Sonia grimaced. 'I don't know what Lorrie ever saw in him.'

'Perhaps you should ask me.'

Simon and Sonia's heads swung around on their shoulders. Neither could believe that it was Lorrie standing framed in the doorway. She was filthy, bruised and battered.

Simon reached her just in time to catch her before she fainted clean to the floor.

LORRIE INSISTED ON going with them to recover Sean's body.

'I'll go to the hospital later,' she said.

Simon didn't know how to refuse her.

Ricky Burton and his team went ahead to process the scene and Lorrie, Simon and Sonia planned to follow once Lorrie had a hot drink inside of her.

'We still have to find Ollie,' Lorrie said, shivering with equal parts cold and shock. 'Napier is with him, and I'm scared about what he and Colin will do now. They don't need my boy anymore.'

'We'll find him, don't worry,' Sonia said. She had listened with Simon to Lorrie's fantastic story and, if it had been anyone other than Lorrie telling it, she wouldn't have believed it.

Simon said, 'The AC has been on the phone. She's called in every favour she can and there are more boots on the ground searching than we even need.' He smiled reassuringly. 'Your husband and his sidekick won't escape, and Ollie will be found safe and sound.'

Lorrie wasn't convinced. Colin had turned out to be a wily fucker and he was more than a little deranged; that combination didn't bode well for her son.

'I've been such a fool,' she said. 'There I was, telling that profiler that I know what a psychopath was and I had one right under my nose and didn't see it. Sean is dead because I couldn't see it.'

'Enough of that,' Simon retorted. 'Colin had us all fooled.'

Lorrie shook her head. 'I can't believe I thought my son was the Reaper. I was absolutely convinced. I only hope he can forgive me.'

'Time enough for recriminations after we get those two bastards.'

Sonia agreed. 'That's all we need to focus on at the moment.'

'Let's go and get Sean. Let's get him out of that place.'

Simon and Sonia nodded and got to their feet. They both helped Lorrie to stand, and they left the building together.

When they got to the warehouse, Lorrie found that she couldn't go in. To see Sean again, cold and dead, would be her undoing. Lorrie had learned a great deal about herself. She had learned that she was stronger than she had previously given herself credit for, but she also learned that she was weaker in some respects. She could be brave when it mattered, but pathetic when it came to seeing a loved one annihilated. So, she paced slowly up and down on shaky legs whilst Ricky and Simon and the team rescued the dead Sean.

When Simon eventually emerged and walked towards her, his face was like a death mask. At first, Lorrie thought it was the shock of seeing Sean, but she soon realised that it was more than that.

'What is it?' She stretched out a hand to him. 'Tell me.'

Simon couldn't tell her. He shook his head and his mouth opened and closed like a drowning fish.

'Tell me,' Lorrie insisted.

Sonia approached. 'There's another body,' she said. 'Hidden at the far end of the warehouse.'

'A body?' She knew. All the air left her body. 'Ollie?'

Sonia nodded.

Lorrie fainted for the second time in her life.

.

# EPILOGUE

'You have to come back, Lorrie. It's been six months.' Annie Gordon sat in Lorrie's kitchen and tried, for the hundredth time, to persuade her to go back to work.

Her Superintendent was a mere shadow of her former self, but the AC was determined to get her back on her feet and back on the job. It was the only thing she could think of to save her.

She eyed her from behind her glasses and felt the usual sadness overwhelm her. Lorrie had come through the ordeal of losing her son, losing Sean and being, forever, labelled as the wife of the Reaper, with the weight of guilt still lying heavy on her thin shoulders. Nothing anyone said to her penetrated the wall she had erected around herself, and the AC feared for her sanity.

The fact that Colin was still at large didn't help matters. Until he was apprehended there could be no closure, but who was to say that they would ever catch up with him? Lorrie had to learn to live with things the way they were and pick herself up off the floor.

Annie tried again. She said, 'Do you want to be his final victim? Do you want to give him exactly what he wanted all along – to give up your job, your career?' She shook her head. 'I never thought I would see the day when you let that bastard win.'

Lorrie made no reply. What could she say? The AC was right – so what?

'Napier goes to trial in a couple of weeks.'

'I know. I have to give evidence.' Even Lorrie's voice was different. There was no life in it. 'I hear he's had a hard time on remand.'

'Well, you can imagine how much he's hated. He's lucky to have survived long enough to go to court.'

Lorrie couldn't have cared less. As far as she was concerned, Colin was the one she needed to see in court.

'Will you think about it? Will you consider coming back?'

'How can I move on to other cases when he's still out there? All my time is used up in looking for him. I don't have a single minute to spare for the job.'

'You're killing yourself with this. It's not healthy.'

'I don't care.' Lorrie's voice was sharper than she had intended. 'I'm sorry,' she apologised. 'But, it's all I can think about right now.'

'It won't bring them back, you know.'

'I know.' Lorrie sighed and closed her eyes in distress. 'It's just something I have to do. He can't get away with it. We got Napier... Colin lied - of course he wasn't away checking on Ollie. Ollie was dead. How could I not have known that his body was only a few feet away from me and Sean?'

'It's terrible. I know just how terrible it is, Lorrie. You lost your son and your son's father...'

'Colin was not Ollie's father.'

Annie gave her a rueful smile. 'I was talking about Sean.'

'What?' Lorrie's eyes widened in shock. 'You knew?'

'Of course, I knew. I've always known.'

'How? I never told a single soul.'

She shrugged. 'Let's just say, I'm perceptive. Sean and I go back a long way. There isn't anything I didn't come to know about him.'

'Then, surely you understand?'

'About your soul-destroying quest to find your husband? Yes, I understand, but I don't think it's going to give you anything but more grief. You must realise that we'll never stop looking for him - I'll make sure of that – and we'll find him one of these days. Come back to work. Give it a few months and see how it goes.'

Lorrie wavered. She knew that her search for Colin would benefit from her being within fingertip distance of the special resources and information the Met had to offer.

Annie knew what she was thinking, and she played on it. 'I'll turn a blind eye to any snooping you might do on our databases. I'll allow you the time you'd need to keep up with the search. I can't do more than that. What do you say?'

'I'll think about it.'

'Well, whilst you think about it... have you seen the news about the Member of Parliament found murdered in his bed?'

'I don't watch the news these days. Why – what's so special about this MP?'

'It's not that he's all that special. It's the way his body was posed.'

'Oh?' Lorrie perked up.

'His face was grotesquely painted, and he was dressed as a clown.'

'So?' Lorrie had quickly lost interest. The only murderer she was interested in was Colin.

'What the press doesn't know yet is that we've found another body.'

Once again, Lorry's interest was piqued. 'A clown again?'

Annie nodded. 'And, another MP.'

'Who's got the case?'

'You, if you want it.'

Ah, how clever. Annie Gordon knew exactly how to play her. For a moment, Lorrie felt anger stir in her belly, but it soon dissipated. The AC knew her even better than she knew herself.

Lorrie wasn't quite ready to smile. Her great loss was still much too raw, but she felt her mood lighten just the tiniest bit. She wasn't quite dead inside, after all.

'You want it?' Annie raised an eyebrow and held her breath.

The seconds ticked by, and Lorrie remained silent.

'DI Grant is on the case.'

Still, Lorrie remained silent.

Annie asked again – 'You want it, Lorrie?'

At last - 'I want it,' she said.

IF YOU ENJOYED READING Maelstrom of White, why not pick up a copy of the second book in the Superintendent, Lorrie Sullivan series?

# A Murder of Clowns

## by

## Angela Hossack

Superintendent, Lorrie Sullivan, returns to lead the investigation into the brutal murders of a growing number of MPs. Still reeling from the loss of her son and the man she has loved all of her adult life, she struggles to come to terms with the fact that her husband – the serial killer known as the Reaper – is still at large.

As the number of MPs found dead, and posed as grotesque clowns, rises by the day, her immediate superiors once again question her abilities, and she has to fight tooth and nail to keep her position.

The truth behind the clown murders slowly emerges and the repercussions of that truth will have far-reaching consequences for the whole government unless Lorrie can be silenced. Against all the odds, Lorrie Sullivan battles the establishment, takes on the government, and fights for the truth to be heard.

Other books by the author
The Superintendent Lorrie Sullivan series:
*A Murder of Clowns*
*A Flock of Innocents*
*A Bouquet of Brides*
*A Rhapsody of Rage*
*A Brace of Fiends*
*A Bloodbath of Bones*
The Detectives Friar and Tuck series:
*Case Number One - The Missing*
*Case Number two – The Forsaken*
*Tomorrow – an apocalyptic dystopian thriller*
The Beyond the Bloodline trilogy:
*The Empty Throne*
*The Rise of the Witch*
*Kulku*

Printed in Great Britain
by Amazon

28985067R00175